TANGO

HUNT BROTHERS SEARCH & RESCUE
BOOK 4

JESSICA ASHLEY

HUNT BROTHERS CHRONOLOGICAL READING ORDER

While the Hunt Brothers are written in a way that you *can* read in any order, I do recommend you read in this order to avoid any possible spoilers.

Happy reading!

1. Bravo
2. Echo
3. Romeo
4. Tango
5. Delta
6. Lima
7. A Hunt Brother Valentine's Day *(Website exclusive available in 2026)*
8. A Hunt Brother St. Patrick's Day *(Website exclusive available in 2026)*

TANGO

By Jessica Ashley

Copyright © 2025. All rights reserved.

Scripture used in this novel comes from HOLY BIBLE, New Living Translation®, NLT®.
Used by permission. All rights reserved worldwide.

Edited by HEA Author Services
Proofread by Love Kissed Books, LLC
Proofread by Dawn Y.

BLURB

Trust is fragile, love is risky, and faith is their only hope in a game where a single betrayal could cost everything.

Tucker "Tango" Hunt is a tech genius with a reputation for solving the toughest cases. When he's hired by a security firm to track down an employee threatening to leak sensitive documents, he expects a quick mission—until he finds Alice.

Alice has always been driven by a desire to make the world a better place, but when the choices she's made lead to a dangerous betrayal, she's forced to run. The good she once believed in is now entangled with dark secrets—and the cost is more than she ever imagined.

Tucker is determined to bring Alice to justice just as he was hired to do, but when he finds her in a remote town, everything changes. Her strength and vulnerability stir something deep within him—something he can't ignore.

The more time he spends with her, the more he questions the mission he was sent on.

In a race against time, Tucker and Alice must uncover the truth—while battling the growing love between them. But with enemies closing in, can their faith and love survive the deadly game they're caught in?

NOTE FROM THE AUTHOR

Darkness is the absence of light.

Evil is the absence of God.

This realization hit me far later than I care to admit. I used to be so angry about everything my brothers and I went through. Why couldn't we have a dad who *wanted* to be there? Why did we have to move around so much? Why couldn't we have a *normal* life like our friends did? It still makes me ache to think about how lost that little girl felt all those years ago.

How silenced she felt by situations that were entirely out of her control.

While I may never know the answers to those questions this side of heaven, I do see the bright side from my pain. I see now, that if I hadn't gone through everything I did, then I wouldn't be standing here with a testimony as to how God saved me.

How He brought me through the fire when it should have *devoured* me.

I wouldn't be the person that I am without what I went through. I know that doesn't make it any easier when you're trapped in the flames, but I can promise you that there is a bright side. There is a light at the end of the tunnel, you just have to REACH FOR HIM.

There are so many times when my poor decisions led to terrible consequences—but to be honest—those consequences should have been a lot worse. I still struggle to really understand how I am standing here today, alive and blessed with a wonderful life that I know I don't deserve.

Except, God.

He didn't let me fall. Even though I turned away from Him when I should have been running into His waiting arms. Even when I was so ashamed, I pushed Him away when I should have been surrendering to Him.

No matter how bad things got, He was *always* there.

It just took me a while to see it.

And now that I do, I look for Him in everything.

"When you go through deep waters, I will be with you. When you go through rivers of difficulty, you will not drown. When you walk through the fire of oppression, you will not be burned up; the flames will not consume you." (Isaiah 43:2)

There are moments when we are so overcome with fear and obstacles, it becomes hard to turn our eyes to the One who is with us all the time. Trials, tribulations, all of those come to every one of us in varying degrees.

The enemy will distract with every tool he can to keep us engulfed in such turmoil that we struggle to find our way back to the light. But you need to remember that if there wasn't something special inside of you, the enemy wouldn't be trying so hard to destroy you.

As that spiritual warfare wages on, you have to put on the armor of God and let Him fight for you. Read your Bible, engulf yourself in scripture, surround yourself with God's light. Because He is all that we need.

Jesus has already won. He defeated death when He rose from the grave. And He did it for you and me. For the salvation of all who turn to Him.

We were never promised peace in this life. But if we put our faith in Jesus Christ, our Savior, then we are promised peace when He returns.

It's not easy to change your life.

To walk away from vices that have become a comfort and embrace Him instead, but it is so worth it when you do.

No matter what you are going through, He won't let you drown.

Pray through the pain.

Pray through the joy.

Pray through *all* of it.

-Jessica

To the hard-fought Hallelujah.
Psalm 27

CHAPTER 1
ALICE

With tears in my eyes and my back pressed up against a server tower, I remain as still as I possibly can. The warmth at my back is nothing compared to the fire in my veins. How did this go so wrong? How did we end up here? This shouldn't be happening. *God, why is this happening?*

The flash drive in my hand feels like it's made of lead as I quietly slip it into the pocket of my jeans. It's all I have left. The only proof I have that my best friend was murdered in cold blood. All because he'd stumbled onto a hole in Web Safe's security. He was just doing his job, and now— He paid for it with his life.

I try to keep my breathing steady, but with the adrenaline pulsing through my system, it's nearly impossible. I can hear muttering somewhere behind me, likely the security team planning their next move. Why they haven't just come in here already, I can't be sure. It's not like I'm much of a fighter. Not compared to their training. The gun in my hand isn't even mine. Ramiro brought it with him. Almost as though he was prepared for a fight.

With a deep breath, I slide down the server tower then set the weapon beside me. My arm might as well be covered with acid with all the pain shooting through my nervous system. I reach over and gently tug the sleeve of my shirt to the side to check the bullet hole. It's deep, but not deadly—I don't think. Blood saturates my fingertips when I pull them away.

For the span of a few heartbeats, I close my eyes. I will not die here. His death will not be in vain.

But how am I supposed to survive? It's not like I can shoot my way out. My mom's words echo through my mind—*when things get overwhelming, take them one step at a time.*

One step at a time.

I can do that.

First step—stop the bleeding. Using my good arm, I slip the bandanna off my hair. I put one corner between my teeth, then wrap it around my arm, and tie it. I choke on a whimper as fresh pain shoots through my arm. *Step one, check.*

Now, step two—get out of here alive so I can take the information I have to the authorities. With my injured arm wrapped, I retrieve my weapon again then stand and glance to my right. Ramiro's body is lying unmoving in a pool of blood. His eyes are closed, and if it weren't for the blood saturating the gray T-shirt he'd worn the last time we did trivia night, I might have thought he was merely sleeping.

The bloodstained truth is staring me in the face though: He's gone. My best friend is dead, and there's nothing I can do about it if I join him.

Grief constricts my throat, making it nearly impossible to breathe.

It all happened so fast.

Zero to a million in less than three heartbeats.

"I know you're in here, Alice!" Darren Wade, a member of the security team, calls out. He's taunting me—something he's enjoyed doing since I started work here and turned him down. Though, until now, a gun was never involved. Guess I made the right choice there—sadistic psychopath and all. "There's no way out. Give up, and I promise to give you a chance to fight back."

I take a deep, steadying breath. This is hardly the first fight I've been in, but it's definitely for the highest stakes.

Even more than life-or-death.

Because the secrets they're trying to steal could burn the world to the ground. And now I'm the only outsider who knows about it.

"Come on, Alice, you're a lost cause." *He's close.*

I scan the area in front of me. The sole door is behind me, which would mean having to engage directly with him.

Given I only have two bullets left while he has at least nine, thanks to the double-stack magazine in his .45, it's suicide to try and shoot my way out. Especially since I give it about two minutes before the rest of his team descends on this room like wolves.

Okay, Alice. Think. Think. One step at a time.

The far wall is made entirely of heavily tinted glass that I don't believe is bulletproof. Now, I could be wrong, but if I am, then I'm dead anyway. There's no chance I'm getting out of this alive unless I'm granted a miracle.

God, please give me a miracle.

I'm two stories up, but the front of the building has a canopy over the entrance, and if I can jump out at the right angle, then I might be able to hit it to break my fall.

Maybe.

I glance over at Ramiro again, and anger replaces my grief.

They gunned him down, and all he'd been doing was trying to find the truth.

They won't do the same to me.

Lord, be with me. Guide my steps, and let me survive this. Please, Lord. I don't want to die. In Jesus' name. Amen. Tears stream down my cheeks, but I face the wall across from me and take a deep breath.

A sense of calm washes over me. Understanding that, even if I die here today, it's not the end. So with my heart hammering against my ribs and my entire body aching, I raise my weapon—and start running.

Bullets whiz past me the moment I'm no longer shielded by the tower, but I do my best to shove fear aside and keep running rather than pausing to seek refuge behind another tower.

One foot after the other, I run. And as soon as I'm close enough—*bang, bang.*

The glass cracks, but it doesn't completely shatter. *Here goes nothing.* I raise my uninjured arm to cover my face then slam into the glass. Shards slice my arms and cheek, but it gives beneath the force of my body, and I plummet.

All the way down.

CHAPTER 2
TUCKER

Hot and exhausted, I remove my baseball cap and withdraw my red bandanna from the back pocket of my jeans. After wiping up the lake of sweat that's formed on my forehead, I stick the bandanna back into my pocket and replace my baseball cap.

Despite the fact that it's only eight in the morning, it's already nearly a hundred degrees out here in the hot summer heat. *Thank you, Texas.* Still, even though it feels as though I'm standing on the surface of the sun, there's nowhere else I'd rather be.

After making a secure loop with one end of a broken barbed wire strand, I attach the fence stretcher and crank it down. I tighten it until I can slip the new wire through the loop of the one I made, then let the fence stretcher hold it while I use pliers to fully join the two pieces.

As soon as it's secure, I undo the stretcher and step

back to survey my work. "Good work, huh, Tango?" I glance back at my dog, who has been watching happily from the shade cast by the utility vehicle we'd driven out here first thing this morning.

He tilts his head to the side, ears perked. "That's what I think too, bud," I reply, then retrieve my tools and stick them in the bed of the vehicle. After taking a swig of my water, I hop into the driver's seat.

"*Hier*, Tango," I order, using the German command my dog and my brothers' dogs are all trained with. It's a lot easier to ensure the dog will do his job when the average person probably won't know the commands.

Less confusion for the dog, more security for us.

He hops into the UTV, so I fire up the engine then start driving the fence line, looking for any other holes. Unfortunately, broken fences are just a part of life on a ranch. As is predawn mornings and—occasionally—late nights.

I don't mind either of those, though, because this place is my home. Happiness in a world filled with chaos and—unfortunately—darkness.

Ahead, I offer a wave to two of our ranch hands—Leon, who's been here since I was a kid, and Keith, who just started working here last month. They're both on horseback, riding through the pastures, checking on the cattle. We've had some predator issues lately—bobcats and coyotes—and have already lost three heifers. They're out counting to make sure last night didn't claim any more.

I crest the top of a hill and stop for just a moment, taking in the breathtaking view of the cabin-style four-bedroom ranch house I built on my parents' land about seven years ago. Before then, I'd been living in a rental house I shared with my brother Riley and my twin, Dylan. Five out of six of us own houses here on the property, and Lani—my younger sister—has property prepped for her whenever she's ready.

All with my parents' house at the center of our ranch, just as they're the heart of our family.

With a smile on my face, I head down the hill, beyond ready for a fresh cup of coffee and one of the muffins my mom dropped off yesterday. I can practically taste the blue-berries already. But as I get closer and see who's waiting on my porch, my hope of a quiet morning vanishes.

Time to work.

After parking my UTV in front of my garage, I climb out and call Tango to follow. "Well, this is a surprise," I say as I climb the steps and greet my oldest brother, Bradyn, as well as Frank Loyotta, the owner of Find Me, an organiza-tion run by veterans. Their mission is to track down and stop human traffickers while rescuing as many victims as they can. We've helped them out quite a few times, just as he's used his resources to help us out when things get, for lack of a better word, dicey.

"I'm sorry to drop in on you like this, Tucker," Frank says, holding out his hand. I shake it then move past them to open the door. His expression is a lot less joyful than it usually is, and I note the dark circles beneath his eyes.

"Not a problem, Frank. Come on in." The blast of AC is beyond welcoming. Tango immediately runs to his water bowl and drinks happily as I take a bottle of tea from my fridge. "Would either of you like anything?"

"No, thank you," Frank replies.

Bradyn shakes his head.

"Okay, what can I do for you?" I ask.

Bradyn crosses his arms. His expression is somber at best, and my unease grows. Not much puts that look on my brother's face.

"What is it?" I ask again.

"I need help," Frank says. "My nephew is missing." His voice is strained, as though each and every word is a fight to get out. Because I know that sometimes the hardest parts of these conversations are getting through the beginning, I don't ask any details—yet.

Frank removes an aged cowboy hat and runs a hand through his short, graying hair. "Ramiro is a good kid. He had some trouble here and there, but he's been getting through it." Tears brim in his eyes. "He works for Web Safe as a threat analysis expert."

"The cybersecurity company?" I ask, mentally running through everything I know about the Los Angeles-based business. It was started up fifteen years ago and quickly gained a reputation for its intense security measures.

Mainly because they hired a team of hackers to try and break into the system.

They all failed.

I didn't, of course. But I wasn't after prize money. I just did it to see if I could. And since I was able to, I anonymously submitted my findings. After waiting a month for them to fix it, I broke in again just to see if I still could.

"Yes. He's been there for the past five years and is darn good at his job." He closes his eyes for a moment then takes a deep breath. "I'm sorry."

"Don't be. Come and have a seat." I gesture toward my dining room table, so he and Bradyn take seats. After grabbing the notepad I keep on my counter for random thoughts, I sit as well. "Tell me what you need from me."

"The last contact my sister had with him was three days ago. He said he was going to a trivia night at a local library with a friend of his. When he didn't show up for their planned dinner the next night, she tried to call him. Went to his place, all of that, and—nothing. It's like he vanished."

"The friend?"

He clears his throat. "Alice Sterling. She also works for Web Safe, though she's in a different department."

"What department is that?"

"According to my sister, Ramiro used to joke that it was his job to break stuff and hers to fix it."

"Got it."

"My sister tried calling her too, but she's not answering.

I even called her folks, but they said they haven't heard from her either and had filed a missing person's report with the local police."

"So we have two missing security experts and no clues," I summarize, making a note on my notepad.

"You can see why I came here."

"Any chance they just ran off together?" I hate asking it because, chances are, Frank has already investigated that angle, but it's part of my job. I need all the facts before I can properly come to a conclusion.

"They weren't romantic, as far as I could tell. And according to my sister, he took nothing with him. His suitcase is still in his closet, all his clothes—his car is even in the parking lot of his apartment building since the library is within walking distance."

"It's unlikely they ran off then," Bradyn comments.

"Did you talk to Web Safe?" I ask.

He nods. "They were my first call, but all they said was the two of them hadn't shown up for work or called in. They said they have no idea why, either. That both of them were good workers and Alice Sterling had never missed a day. They wouldn't give me any other information."

"Even if they knew something, it's unlikely they would get involved without a warrant explicitly ordering them to," I say, considering just how big of a panic it would cause if the clients discovered two high-level employees simply didn't show up for work. Banks, billion-dollar companies…the list goes on and on. There's even been talk about the government using them on a contract basis for certain situations.

"I'm flying out there tomorrow morning to be with my sister and see what I can find, but you guys are the best at finding something from nothing, and I really need help here."

"I'll take the case," I tell Frank. Since my brothers and I all operate on a rotation, and Riley just got back from mission, I'm up next.

"Thank you."

"No need to thank me, Frank. You know we'll always support you in any way we can. You said you're flying out tomorrow morning?" He nods. "Send me the flight information. I'd like to grab a ticket and join you—if that's okay."

"Of course. It's on one of our company's private planes, so there's no need for a ticket. I'll get your name on the flight log. Plane is wheels up at 0700. Same airport as always."

"I'll be there."

He nods. "Thanks again. I-I'm really hoping for some good news here, guys, but I have this sinking feeling in my gut that something horrible happened. My sister's barely spoken since she called me. She's worried sick. In my line of work, I've seen some horrific things." He shakes his head sadly. "But I never thought I'd experience this so close to home."

Bradyn clasps a hand on his shoulder. "We'll find answers," he assures Frank. "Do you know if Ramiro had any other friends who worked for the company?"

"A few he talked about, but none he was as close to as Alice."

"Can you get me those names? Places he liked to go? The name or address of the library he went to? Anything might help."

He nods. "I'll call my sister and see if I can get her to email all of that over."

"Great. Give me a few hours, and I should have something to report back."

"Thank you." Frank takes a deep breath. He's one of the best men I know, completely dedicated to saving the innocent, and to see him suffering absolutely crushes me, even though I know all too well that good men suffer.

Some die far too soon.

Others face realities worse than death. *No, that stays buried.* I shove the memory down and force my attention back on Frank.

"No need to thank us," Bradyn replies as he stands. Frank does the same.

"I'll let you know as soon as I have something." I shake his hand again.

"I appreciate that," he replies sadly. "I'm headed back

to Dallas right now to pack, but I'll see you in the morning."

"Sounds good."

Frank offers me a tight nod.

"I'll walk you out." Bradyn opens the front door and follows Frank out, but I know that he'll be back in as soon as the man is in his truck. He'll want to talk details and give me his own private opinions—the same as I want to do. There are just some things you can't say in front of a client. And right now, Frank is a client.

I glance down the hall toward my bedroom where my shower is waiting. But even as badly as I want to rinse the dirt and sweat from my skin, the shower can wait. This missing persons case cannot.

Resigned to this change of plans, I head into the kitchen, wash the dirt and sweat from my hands, then get the coffeepot started. Tango is already passed out on his bed, and I can't help but grin. For a dog who can be so intense he's literally terrified criminals into peeing his pants, he's also a giant goof.

Leaving the coffeepot to do its thing, I take my notepad and head down the hall toward my office. After pushing inside, I hit the light then press the power button on my computer. It hums to life, and the trio of monitors on my desk come on a second later.

As the computer does its thing and wakes up, I glance up at the wall of screens across from my desk. The center one is a projection screen I use for mission briefs. Surrounding it, there are nearly a dozen smaller monitors I use to track security here at the ranch.

While the property is too large to cover every inch of it, we make sure we have cameras on the exterior of everyone's homes—just in case. There have been times when they've come in handy, especially lately.

As soon as my computer is on its login screen, I sit down and log in then open up a program I'm not technically supposed to have access to. Starting with our original missing person, I type "Ramiro Caine" into the search bar and hit enter. As it scrapes all known databases and social media accounts for information on Frank's nephew, I pull up Web Safe's site.

"Here." Bradyn offers me a cup of coffee as he steps into my office.

I jump in my seat, shocked that I'm no longer alone. "Thanks, brother. Didn't even hear you come back in," I say, accepting the coffee.

"That's because you never hear anything once you're behind a screen," he replies with a grin.

He's got me there. My twin, Dylan, jokes that my brain is part computer, and whenever I sit down in front of one, it's as though I'm 'plugging in.' Chaos could be erupting around me, and I'd never even know.

The hot coffee slips down my throat, and I nearly groan in delight. There's not much quite like that first sip of caffeine. Since I avoid it for the first ninety minutes of every day—striving for normal cortisol levels and all that—this is my first taste.

"You have a chance to look into this case at all yet?" I ask Bradyn.

"Not yet. Frank called about fifteen minutes before you got in and asked me to meet him here. I didn't find out until I arrived that he was here for personal reasons."

Ramiro's information hits, pulling up a driver's license photograph of a man in his late twenties, dark hair, brown eyes—as well as a series of minor traffic violations. Overall, his record is clean.

Leaving that window readily available, I open another one and type in Alice Sterling's name. Since she was close to Ramiro (a girlfriend, maybe?), it's possible she's either with him or knows what happened to him and is hiding. If I can track her down, I might be able to find the truth a whole lot faster than waiting around while trying to scan thousands of cameras all over LA, hoping to catch Ramiro on one the night of his disappearance.

"What are your initial thoughts?" I ask Bradyn, turning my chair so I can see him.

Bradyn sets his coffee down on my desk and crosses his arms. I know from experience that he's processing all available information and running through different scenarios before responding.

"I don't know that I believe they ran off together. Something about that theory just doesn't sit right."

"I don't see why he wouldn't have at least packed a suitcase if they'd left voluntarily."

"Exactly."

"Unless they left in a hurry." I consider. "Two people, relatively high up in a cybersecurity company that protects information requiring top-tier clearance levels to even breathe on, disappear without a trace, and the company is quiet about it," I say then decide to ask the hard question. "Do you think it's possible that they were involved in something illegal?"

Bradyn considers, his expression hardening. Neither one of us would ever want to deliver that news to Frank. It would destroy him. "I hope not. But no matter what the outcome is—or who it will hurt—we find the truth."

CHAPTER 3
ALICE

With a groan, I pour another round of rubbing alcohol into the refusing-to-heal bullet hole in my arm. Unfortunately, with every day that passes, the injury just gets angrier. Even now, I can smell the infection that's taking root.

Since I can't go to a doctor or risk the police getting involved, it's back-alley medical care for me at the moment. I can't even go back home because Web Safe has my apartment being watched. That, or there are two walls of muscle in black suits who just happened to move into a black SUV in the parking lot the day after Ramiro was killed.

Seriously, could they be any less discreet? They might as well have had a bumper sticker on the back that says, "Alice, stay away."

"Okay, that should do it." I gently apply a fresh

bandage to my arm then hop off the bathroom counter and store my supplies in my backpack. Armed with a worn Bible, my laptop, a gun with no bullets, and now some medical supplies, I step out of the bus station bathroom, ensuring the baseball cap is low over my face.

I'm dressed in baggy clothes I bought from a second-hand store after I barely escaped my apartment with what little I could carry, so my hope is no one will recognize me. Especially since I tucked my black hair beneath the baseball cap.

I need to be invisible. It's the only chance I have.

After handing my ticket to the bus driver, I move down the aisle and take a seat in an old pungent-smelling striped bench at the back of the bus. My arm aches, but it doesn't hurt nearly as badly as my heart does.

I lost my best friend.

My home.

And all of my belongings in a matter of hours.

All because of someone's greed.

I'll find the truth, Ramiro. And I'll fix everything. The weight of my grief is crushing, but I refuse to live in that pain. To find the truth, I need my head clear. The time for crying will come after, when I'm standing at Ramiro's gravesite.

I keep my head down as a man sits next to me. The bus is relatively full, so it's not unusual, though there is at least one seat toward the front that's empty.

My heart rate quickens.

He leans in. "I have a gun aimed directly at your gut, Miss Sterling. Scream or do anything except what I explicitly tell you to do, and I'll shoot first and ask questions later. Got it?"

"Yes," I reply softly. My pulse is deafening, and I turn my head to look at him. Silver eyes are narrowed on my face, and his hair—a bright gold—is cut short on the sides but longer on the top. He looks like a clean-cut businessman, but I'm guessing he's never carried a briefcase in his life.

No, this man is a killer.

Hired to finish what Darren couldn't.

Lord, help me.

"I wonder what your plan was," he says softly as he uses the hand not currently holding the gun in his pocket to shove a handful of peanuts into his mouth.

"Run. Isn't it obvious? Or are you all muscle and no brains?"

He jams the barrel of the gun into my side. "Did you forget I'm armed? Irritate me, and I won't deliver you in quite as good of shape as I promised."

"Deliver me to who?"

He grins, but the smile is dripping venom. "You'll see, cupcake. Just enjoy the ride. You'll be getting off at the next stop."

I swallow hard. *Lord, help me*, I repeat again because I

know I won't survive without Him. The bus begins moving, and the drive to the next stop takes less than ten minutes. All the while, I'm urging someone—anyone— around me to notice what's taking place. Would they even step in to save me if they knew? Most people in the world today would rather record an abduction than step in to stop one.

What a sad reality we live in.

"Get up," he orders. "Bring the bag, but make any sudden movements and—"

"You'll make me regret it, yeah. I have a decent enough memory, thanks."

"Good." He urges me forward as we climb out of the bench seat. Doing what I can to keep my gaze focused on anything but the people around me, I keep walking forward —putting one foot in front of the other.

My mom always told me that, if someone grabbed me in a parking lot and told me to get into the vehicle, it would be better to fight there and get shot than end up in a car alone with them.

It's a life tip I haven't had to use until now, but I know that, if I get off this bus with him, then I'll likely never see the light of day again. The problem is, if I bring too much attention to myself, the police will get involved, which means their contacts will let Web Safe know exactly where I am.

So my only choice is to either let him take me off of

this bus and try to get away as quick as possible, or throw a fit right here and call his bluff on shooting me in a bus full of people.

I pass a woman cradling her baby, and that last option becomes a moot point. I won't risk these people getting hurt…not even to save my own life. Outside of the bus, there will be fewer chances of innocents getting hurt. So, with my heart in my throat, I carefully move down the stairs and onto the relatively sparse sidewalk.

"Good girl. We've established that you can follow directions. Stand here, I'm making a call." He reaches into his pocket, so I take the only chance I have. I swing out with the bag and slam it into his face.

He yells, but I've already started running. My black boots hammer the pavement as I sprint down the street and disappear into an alleyway. The man follows—right on my heels. He fires a single shot—it barely misses me. And then, I reach a chain-link fence. Without stopping, I jump up and grip it, trying to climb my way to safety like they do in the movies, but he grips my leg and rips me down.

With a heavy thud and what is probably now a concussion, I hit the pavement so hard it dazes me. Before I can even fully process what's happening, he's on me, one hand around my throat.

"I told you I was going to make it difficult if you didn't listen, didn't I?" he growls, looking even more menacing now that blood from the hit he took to his nose is dripping down into his mouth and staining his teeth.

His hand tightens around my throat. I fight against him, thrashing my body as much as his hold will allow, all while trying to find something—anything—to use as a weapon. And then, I see it—a chunk of old brick just out of reach.

I reach out for it, my fingertips barely brushing the surface as spots invade my vision.

I'm going to pass out—and then there's no telling what will happen to me. I could wake up halfway around the world—or not wake up at all.

Come on. Please, not like this.

My hand closes around the brick, and I swing. It slams into the side of his head with such force that he topples to the side and goes still. Gasping for breath as I suck so much oxygen into my lungs that it makes me even more light-headed, I jump to my feet, prepped for another fight. But it only takes me seconds to realize with stomach-churning certainty that it won't come.

A piece of old rebar is protruding from his chest. He stares down at it in disbelief then looks up at me as though I did it on purpose. I rush forward, bile burning in my throat. "I'm sorry. I'm so sorry, I didn't mean to. Just hang on, I'll get help." Since the only thing I do know is that I shouldn't pull him off the bar, I reach into his pocket for the cell phone he'd had only minutes ago.

He says something, but it comes out as gibberish. Blood trails from the corner of his mouth.

"9-1-1, what's your emergency?" the operator answers almost instantly.

"There's a man. He was impaled on rebar. I think he's dying." My words are frantic, my tone just as panicked. "You have to send someone."

"Okay, honey, calm down. What's your name?"

"I—uh—there isn't time. It's an alley near the second stop of the three o'clock bus that runs out of the South Station. Please, he's barely breathing."

"Okay, I'll send someone. But I need to know your name."

I start to give it to her; then I realize that, if I do that, I'm giving Web Safe another reason to paint a bull's-eye on my back. So, I hang up the phone. "They're sending someone," I tell him, but as soon as I've hung up the phone, I know it's too late.

His eyes are frozen open.

His breathing, no more.

No. No. Tears burn in my eyes as the realization hits home: I killed a man.

How did this happen?

God, what do I do?

Sirens wail in the distance, so I quickly wipe the phone off then leave it on the ground beside him as I grab my bag and rush from the alleyway, ensuring my baseball cap is pulled back down low over my face.

This time, to also hide my tears.

I SHOULDN'T HAVE COME HOME.

I know it as soon as I unlock the back door using an old hide-a-key, but I had nowhere else to go. Ever since I was thirteen and Jemma and Fred Sterling adopted me, they've chased away every nightmare and helped me through the years of trauma I suffered while being a kid in the system. They can help me here too, right? They have to help me. Because I'm so lost. So afraid.

"Who's there?" my dad calls out as the light over the stairs comes on. "I can hear you, and you should know I'm armed!"

I stop in my tracks—standing in the hallway that leads from the kitchen into the living room. He comes down the stairs, and the light shines on my face.

"Ali?"

No longer an adult of nearly thirty, I'm once again a child as I crumble at the sound of my nickname. "Daddy."

He rushes forward and wraps his arms around me as I collapse to the ground. "It's Alice!" he calls out. "She's hurt!"

"Don't call the police. You can't trust the police."

"Don't call anyone!" he yells as my mom rushes down the steps.

"What happened?" She reaches me right as my dad is pulling me to my feet.

"I killed someone. I didn't mean to. He attacked me, and I killed him." I shake my head. It doesn't matter that I'm twenty-nine years old; right now, I'm a thirteen-year-old girl, and there's a monster in my closet in need of slaying.

"Shh, baby, come sit down." My dad guides me into a kitchen chair while my mom turns on the light overhead. It's so bright I have to shield my eyes.

"I'm putting coffee on," my mom says. "Grab the first aid kit, Fred. And a towel. She's soaking wet."

Am I? I hadn't even noticed.

He brushes the hair out of my eyes and tucks it behind my ear, then rushes out of the room to get the first aid kit they keep beneath the bathroom counter. Seconds later, he's returning. "Take off the sweatshirt," he tells me.

I unzip the front and use my good arm to push it off. He wraps a towel around me, though he leaves my injured arm uncovered.

"Who did this to you?" he demands as he slowly removes the bandage over my injured arm.

I don't even know how much is safe to tell them.

"I'm in trouble."

"Tell us what happened," my mom urges. In the background, the coffeepot hums as it prepares the coffee. My mom pulls a chair over and slides her glasses onto her nose. She leans in closer to get a better look.

Given she's a nurse—and a great one at that—she'll be able to help with my physical issues. And, well, my dad's a therapist, so if I ever get past this, I imagine he can help me with my internal demons just like he did when I was a kid.

That's if I survive and don't end up in prison.

"Ramiro is dead." It's the first time I've spoken those words aloud.

"Did he do this to you?" my dad demands, fury etched in every line of his expression. "Is he the one you killed?"

I shake my head. "No. They killed him and tried to kill me, too, but I got away. Then a man found me on the bus and told me he was going to take me somewhere. I fought back, and he—he's dead. I hit him, and he fell back into a piece of rebar."

"Is he the one who killed Ramiro?"

I shake my head again. "I can't tell you everything. The more I tell you, the more at risk you are." And then, it hits me that I *really* shouldn't have come here. I try to get up. "I have to go."

"No, you don't. There are all kinds of glass shards in this injury. I need my tweezers from the bathroom," she tells my dad. "The good ones."

"On it. You stay put, Ali. We'll keep you safe, okay?"

But they can't. Not when killers are looking for me.

"I'm sorry I came here. I didn't know where else to—" A knock sounds on the door, and I stiffen.

It's nearly ten at night. No reason anyone should be knocking.

My eyes go wide. Did I just sign my parents' death warrant? "I have to go. Now." I shove the towel off of me and start to get up, grabbing my sweater as I do, but my mom shakes her head.

"Come with me."

My dad goes down the stairs and pauses by the front door. He and my mom exchange a look before she drags me through the kitchen and toward the basement door at the back.

"Mom, you don't understand, if I'm here—you're in danger."

"I do understand, and I don't care. You are my daughter. Do you hear me?" She pauses at the bottom of the basement steps. "I've loved you as my own since we first saw you, and I will love you as my own until the day I die." She quickly lifts a door in the floor. "Now get inside so I can cover the entrance with a rug, okay? You stay down there until your father or I come get you." She gently squeezes my good arm. "We will iron this out, okay? Everything is going to be fine, darling. You'll see."

I nod because, even if I leave now, I know it's unlikely they'll leave my parents alone. At least, if I'm here, I stand a chance at helping. Maybe.

Without argument, I descend into what we've always called the cellar. It's a crawl space beneath the basement where an old repair was made to some piping a while back. Instead of fully filling it in, they just cemented it up and turned it into a weird little bonus room.

I barely fit.

Keeping my breathing as steady as I can while stuck in what's basically a concrete coffin, I listen for any sound that something bad is happening upstairs.

God, please protect them. Please keep them safe.

CHAPTER 4
TUCKER

It's nearly eleven at night, but I can't shake this feeling that I need to at least drive by the Sterlings' home. Why I should be doing anything at this hour but sleeping, I've no clue. But I learned a long time ago not to ignore feelings like this. So, here I am, turning onto their suburban street.

I come to a stop and glance over at the passenger seat. Tango is sitting up, staring at me, his head cocked to the side. "Yeah, I know. I'm tired too, bud, but it doesn't hurt just to lo—" A shrill scream catches my attention through my rolled-down window. Quickly, I fire off a text to Dylan, asking him to contact Alaric Simmons, a detective with the LAPD. He's on my short list of people to trust because he's the former partner of a man who works with my cousin, Silas, at their private security firm in Maine.

Given the sensitive nature of the case I'm dealing with,

my goal is to keep people out of it—not invite more. But with lives on the line, I really don't have much choice.

As soon as the message sends, I withdraw my weapon, shove the door open, and climb out. "*Hier,* Tango." *Here.* He leaps out at the command, already in work mode.

Moving slowly, I creep toward the house, sticking to the shadows as much as I can.

Another scream.

I round the back of the house. It's just faint enough that, unless someone is out on the street, no one is going to hear it. Step by step, I head around back to find a way in.

A window shatters to my right. I spin and aim my weapon. Tango lets loose a warning growl. And then, I see a pair of eyes so pale they might as well be crystal, staring up at me through a sliver of window no larger than six inches.

My breath catches, and the world stills.

Alice Sterling.

"Who are you?" she demands, ripping me back into the moment.

"Tucker Hunt. A friend of—"

"You're a Hunt brother."

I'm not often speechless, but—another scream. "Please stop!" a woman yells, her voice muted by the walls separating us.

"You have to get in there. Please. They're going to kill

them." Tears in her eyes, Alice tries to climb out through the broken glass.

"You're not going to fit through there. Not without seriously hurting yourself. Can I go in through the back door? Do you know where they are in the house? How many there are?"

"I think I heard two voices aside from my parents. But my mom blocked the basement door, so I can't get out. There's a hide-a-key under a turtle in the flower bed near the back door."

"On it." I leave her, Tango on my heels, and rush up to the porch. The turtle is right where she said it would be, so I retrieve the key and slide it into the lock. Slowly, I inch the door open. I need to know where they are in the house before I go in, gun blazing. Otherwise, the Sterlings could get caught in the crossfire.

The back door leads into the kitchen. There's another door directly to the right, but it's been blocked by a drink cart wedged beneath the handle. *The basement.* Because I sense she'll climb out of that tiny window and tear herself up if I don't, I cross over to the door first and slowly slide the cart away, then flip the lock on the top of the door to let her out.

Alice stares at me, her eyes wide, when I pull it open.

I press my finger to my lips, and she nods in understanding.

Her face is scraped, her lip bloody, and there are bruises

around her slender throat, but I ignore those for the moment to focus on what's more pressing.

"We don't know where she is," a man says. He's breathless, and I can hear the pain in his voice. *That would be Fred Sterling.*

The kitchen leads to a hallway near a set of stairs. "What's over there?" I whisper, keeping my voice barely audible.

"Living room," she mouths back.

I nod then gesture for her to stay behind me. Tango moves into place between my legs as we head toward the danger. Ears perked, he's ready for my command.

A hand cracks against flesh, and a woman whimpers.

"Don't touch her!" Fred bellows.

The adrenaline in my veins kicks up a notch.

"Then tell us where to find—"

Glass shatters, and I turn to look behind me. Alice is wide-eyed, her face pale, and beneath her boots is what used to be a picture frame that must've been on the wall. *Well, element of surprise is over.*

"Go see what that is," a man orders.

I press back against the wall, getting as close as I can, and move Tango out from between my legs so he can stand directly at my side. As soon as I hear the boot steps grow closer, I order, "*Fass,* Tango!" My dog launches himself at the man right as the man raises his weapon.

Fear ices through my veins, but Tango is faster. His

powerful jaws lock on the man's arm, and the weapon clatters to the ground. I rush forward, using my bodyweight and the advantage of surprise, to hit the man and slam him to the ground.

He falls, and Tango adjusts his hold. I raise my weapon again. "I'd stay like that, or he's going to tear your arm off."

The man glares up at me. "I'm not scared of no do—Ow!" he yells as Tango bites down harder when he tries to move.

"Hurt my dog, and that bite wound will be the least of your problems." I glance back at Alice. "Watch him. If he moves, yell."

She nods, so I move fully into the living room. Fred is seated in a floral chair while his wife, Jemma, is on the couch. A second man in a black suit stands next to her, one hand on her throat, the other holding a gun to her head.

"Put it down, or I'll kill her."

"There doesn't need to be any more bloodshed tonight," I tell him. "The police are going to be here any second, and if you kill her, there's no walking away from this. As it stands now, you're looking at breaking and entering and assault, but no murder charge—yet."

"You don't hold the cards here," the man says. "I don't know who you think you are, but I assure you, you have no idea who you're dealing with."

And because I'm not one to take chances on this ending

badly, I take a breath and adjust my aim. "You okay, Mrs. Sterling?"

She nods.

"Question. What do ducks yell when someone throws something at them?"

Jemma's expression momentarily shifts from fear to confusion, and the bruiser holding her narrows his gaze at me.

"Duck!" I fire. Jemma lunges forward as the bullet hits the shoulder of the man, opposite to where she'd been sitting. His furious yell is only momentary before I'm rushing forward and slamming him onto the ground, then withdrawing another zip tie and securing both arms behind his back.

As soon as he's no longer an issue and the Sterlings are embracing each other, I move back into the hallway where Tango is being the good boy he is and keeping his hold on the first attacker.

"*Aus*," I order. *Let go.* Tango releases him, so I flip him over onto his back and yank both arms—including his injured one—behind his back so I can secure them as well. He mutters under his breath, but I pay it no mind.

They *always* mutter. As soon as he's secure, I grip his shoulder and drag him into the living room, flipping him over so he's lying next to the other one.

Behind me, Alice joins her parents, all of them shaken and bruised.

I kneel. "Who are you?" They don't answer. "Got it. No worries." I withdraw my cell phone and snap two pictures before sending them off to a friend I trust out in Maine. He's on call tonight, so an ID shouldn't take more than a few minutes. "Now, who sent you here?"

"Do you really think we answer to you?"

"I think you'll answer to the LAPD when they get here."

"You called the cops?"

I glance over at Alice. "Home invasion typically calls for the police." She pales, so I get up and cross the living room. "Who did this to you?" I ask, tone low as I take a closer look at her injuries. With the current risk subdued, I look her over, noting the cuts and scrapes on her face, the bruises around her throat, and her bandaged arm. "Was it them?" I gesture toward the two unwanted guests.

"No. It wasn't them."

"Then who?" When she doesn't answer, I turn back toward the two men. "Who sent you?"

"Someone who will own you before this is all over," one of the men sneers.

My phone dings, so I withdraw it and check the message. *Thank you, Elijah.* "Nice. So, we have a Harry Olean and a Kris Marsh." Both men glare back at me. "I told you I was going to find out. Wow, nice records. Lot of time between both of you. Armed robbery. Assault. I don't see any murder charges here though. Given how many times you've been caught, I'd say you're nothing but the muscle they send in when they want someone to be scared. Muscle they'd likely be all too happy about throwing under the bus, given the circumstances." I look from one man to the other, taking special notice of the way they side-eye each other. "Tell me, does it feel good to pick on people half your size? Make you feel like big men?" Neither of them answers. "Now, the question is, who's going to crack first?"

"Listen, if you called the cops, I have to go." Once again, Alice distracts me.

One of the men grins. "She's the real killer."

"I'm not a killer."

"Then what happened to our boy Josh?" he asks. "Because I'm fairly certain you left him with an extra hole than he had when you found him."

Alice pales and takes a step back.

It infuriates me that they're intimidating her even now that they're zip-tied on the ground. "Tell me what's going on, Miss Sterling. I can't help you unless you do."

"He would have killed me. It was self-defense."

"Sure it was," one of the men says. "Just like that Ramiro kid was self-defense."

Ramiro. "Ramiro Caine is dead?" I ask.

Alice's face turns beet red, and she clenches her hands into fists. "I didn't kill him!" She sprints toward them, and

I have to wrap both arms around her waist to keep her from leaping onto the men.

Outside, sirens sound. *It looks like Simmons got the call.*

Alice pales further.

"You need to tell me what's going on," I demand as I release her.

She's quiet as she looks out the window. Slowly, she turns back to me and closes her eyes. After a beat, she opens them again, and even with everything going on around me, I'm captivated by their crystal depths. "Fine. But you have to promise to keep my parents safe."

"I will."

"Then give me a second. I need to get something from my room to show you."

An inkling of unease trails up my spine. *She's going to run.* I can feel it in my bones. "And what makes you think I'm stupid enough to fall for that?"

She doesn't even try to deny it. "I don't think you're stupid. You'll find me again. If you're as good as they say you are. But if you don't let me go, they're going to toss me in a cell where Web Safe will send more people like this to take me out. The truth will never come out unless you trust me now."

I stare at her, trying to discern whether she's telling the truth or not.

She's beaten. Bloody. And the two bruisers here certainly helped her case by coming after her parents.

"Alice, you can't run. You're injured," her mom says. Jemma's lip is split, her eye blackening, but otherwise, she looks okay.

Her husband, Fred, took a few hits but still stands with his arm around his wife. "Ali, let the police help."

"Dad, they can't help. Not until I have proof."

"Proof of what?" Jemma presses.

Alice shakes her head but steps forward. "I love you both so much. I thank God every day that He blessed me with the two of you." She smiles at them, and they hold on to her for a moment before releasing her.

"I will find you," I tell her. "I give it forty-eight hours max."

Alice smiles softly, though it doesn't quite reach her pale eyes. "I guess I'll see you then, Mr. Hunt."

"THIS IS QUITE a mess you've got here," Detective Simmons comments as he watches Olean and Marsh get hauled out to cruisers in front of the Sterlings' house. Both Jemma and Fred are currently talking to the police now, giving their statements, including how their daughter showed up and then took off again.

"You're telling me." The two of us stand in silence for a moment. "What do you know about Web Safe?"

"The cyber company? The LAPD contracts with them, but that's about all I've got. Why?"

"Alice Sterling—the daughter? She works for them. She and her friend Ramiro Caine fell off the grid two days ago; then this happens."

Alaric arches a brow. "What are you thinking?"

"Just that it seems fishy. Olean said something too, he asked if Ramiro was self-defense too."

"Self-defense? You think she killed him?"

I shake my head. "I know she didn't. But she did say that she killed someone else in self-defense. Someone they referred to as Josh—"

"Aah, well, that answers that one. Joshua Pollinger. We've collared him a few times on theft and assault. Found him impaled on a piece of rebar in an alleyway after a woman called 9-1-1 to report it. She refused to give a name, but I'd bet my paycheck it was Alice Sterling." He runs his hands over his face.

"Then that definitely fits with self-defense. Cold-blooded murderers don't tend to call 9-1-1."

"You'd be surprised," he replies. "But I listened to the recording, and she was frantic when she called. Terrified."

And if Web Safe is somehow involved, they have their hands in the LAPD cookie jar. Which is likely why Alice didn't want me to call the police.

"She had bruises around her throat and was pretty banged up."

"Which also fits the self-defense angle."

I nod.

"Man, I have no idea what you walked into here, but it's a mess."

"Can you do me a favor?"

"Sure thing, what?"

"Hold off on putting out an APB on Alice Sterling if you can. Give me a twenty-four-hour head start."

Alaric hesitates for just a moment then nods. "I can give you that."

"Great, thanks."

"Just let me know when you find her, okay? Keep me in the loop, and I'll do the same."

I hold out my hand to shake his. "Agreed."

My cell rings, so I withdraw it from my pocket and answer when I see Bradyn's name on the caller ID. "News travels fast even across state lines, I take it?"

"Elijah called. Said he tried you but you didn't answer."

"I was briefing Alaric."

"What happened?"

"Two bruisers were working over Alice Sterling's parents when I got to her house. I managed to put a stop to it."

"Any sign of Alice?" he questions.

I hold up a finger to Alaric then step out of earshot.

"She was here when I got here. Bruised, scared—I'm not entirely sure what's going on, but whatever it is—it's big."

"Where is she now?"

"In the wind—for now."

"She got away?"

"I let her go."

Bradyn is silent for a moment. "Any particular reason why?"

"She was adamant that Web Safe is behind this. That she'll be arrested and tossed in a cell, where they'll send someone after her just like they did her parents."

"Do you believe her?"

"She believes it," I tell him. "I'll find her again, and then I'll decide what to believe." I take a moment, trying to decide how best to word this next part. "There's more."

"What is it?"

I hesitate, hating what I'm about to say. "I believe that Ramiro Caine is dead."

CHAPTER 5
TUCKER

"You just *let her go*?" Frank demands as he paces my living room. He's frustrated and rightfully so. He wants answers, and the only one who can give them to us ran off into the night, leaving us with even more questions.

Frank packed up his sister and brought her to Dallas so she wouldn't be alone. Then he flew back a few hours after I returned to the ranch with Alice's parents in tow. He's been here for the last ten minutes while I briefed him on everything that took place back in California.

Alice's parents are currently settling down in one of our ranch hand cabins where they'll be safe while we figure this out. Meanwhile, I've got to try and track down their daughter…again.

I haven't told him about my suspicions about his nephew just yet because I'd really like to know the truth before I break his heart. It's the same kindness I wish had been given to my family back when the government told me that my twin brother was dead.

"I'll find her again," I tell him as I withdraw a bottle of water from the fridge. My cell rings, so I reach into my pocket and withdraw it, noting Alaric Simmons' name on the screen.

"Hunt," I answer.

"I keep saying this, but it deserves repeating." He sighs. "I don't know what you've got yourself into, but it's bad," he says, tone aggravated.

"What do you mean?"

"FBI just showed up and pulled your guys out of my interrogation room."

"Seriously? Did you get anything out of them?"

"Nope. Neither one would talk. I did what I could to stall, but they're gone."

Frustration tugs at me, worse than usual, given how absolutely exhausted I am. An all-nighter and two different time zones twice in twenty-four hours will do that to a guy. But I can at least say that I held up my end of the bargain. Alice's parents are safe. "Do you have the names of the agents?"

"Already emailed them over to you, along with the surveillance footage. See what you can pull from it. They wouldn't give me any information. Just flashed a badge, showed me a letter from someone I can't argue with, then took the guys into custody."

I run a hand over my face. "Any idea where they're going?"

"Not a single clue. But I'd watch your back, Tucker. Whatever this is—it's big. And Web Safe might just be at the center of it."

"Thanks, Alaric. I appreciate the help."

"Anytime." He ends the call.

I turn to Frank. "Guys we apprehended have been pulled out by FBI agents."

"Names of the agents?" Frank asks, going from frustrated to business mode. It's a coping mechanism, something I and each of my brothers do too. Distance ourselves from the emotion of it, and focus on the actions we need to take.

After opening up my email, I copy the names of the agents and send them to Frank via text. His phone dings.

"I'll find out what I can about them." He fires off a message then raises his gaze to me. "Do you really think you can find her again?"

"I know I can. Besides, we have her parents at the ranch. And after what I saw last night, she's not letting them get far for long. I'd be willing to bet she'll make her way here sooner rather than later."

Frank nods. "Any news on Ramiro?"

I sigh. While I don't want to outright tell him, I also don't want to keep secrets. "I don't know yet."

"But you have suspicions." Frank crosses his arms. "Tell me, Tucker."

I hesitate. Do I tell him? Do I break his heart before I know it's true?

"Tucker."

This isn't *anyone*—it's Frank. So I take a deep breath and prepare to deliver a knee-dropping blow. "Something those bruisers said to Alice last night makes me believe that Ramiro is—" I trail off.

"Dead," he finishes, expression hard. "I had a feeling—" He shakes his head. "Ramiro wouldn't have just no-showed his mom. That's just not him. No matter what was going on in his life, he was there." He lifts his gaze to me. "You think he's dead, don't you?"

"Yes."

"What did they say?"

"A man attacked Alice outside of a bus stop. She defended herself, and he died after falling backward onto a piece of rebar. When the men brought it up and she told them it was self-defense, they asked her if the Ramiro kid was self-defense too."

Frank's expression goes from distraught to downright furious in less than a heartbeat. "She killed him? And you *let her go?*"

"No. She didn't kill him, Frank. My gut says that

there's more to this than meets the eye, and it's too soon for us to start drawing conclusions. They could have just as easily been taunting her, and she could very well not know whether Ramiro is alive or dead." Though my instinct is that he is dead and that Alice Sterling is *not* the murderer.

I know killers, far better than I wish I did, and Alice is no killer.

Those men last night? *They* were killers. Which means whoever hired them is more than likely the same one behind Ramiro's death.

My phone dings, and I check my texts.

Dad: Fred and Jemma just got here for coffee.

Me: Great. Thanks.

I shove my cell back into my pocket. "If you think you can keep your head, Alice's parents are awake. They're staying in one of the ranch hand cabins and just showed up at my parents' for coffee. They've been through a lot though, and I want to make sure we don't push too hard right away, no matter how badly we want answers."

"I can keep my head," he replies. "I just need something to tell Darlene." Frank pinches the bridge of his nose. "And it can't be that her son is dead. Not until we know for sure."

I clasp a hand on his shoulder and squeeze gently, hoping it will offer him even the slightest comfort. "Then let's go see if we can find some answers. *Hier*, Tango," I say as I release Frank and pat my hand against my thigh. Tango jumps up from his bed, tail wagging, and heads for the door. I grab the bottle of water I've been nursing for the last few hours, pull open the door, and step out into the near-stifling August afternoon.

Frank gets into his truck while I opt for my utility vehicle to make the short drive to my parents' ranch house, all while mentally combing through every moment of last night—from witnessing the most beautiful pair of haunted eyes I've ever seen staring up at me to watching her disappear into the night with only a backpack before the police arrived.

Is she alive now?

Has Web Safe found her again?

Alice Sterling haunted what little sleep I tried to get once I settled her parents into the cabin. After it became clear I wasn't going to get any rest, I gave up on sleep and spent the rest of the hours before dawn researching everything there is to know about her.

After her parents died when she was young and her grandparents refused to take her in, she was put into the system. Which is where she was—in and out of foster homes—until the Sterlings took her in at thirteen.

She graduated high school at the top of her class and was even voted valedictorian, despite her rocky start. Then she excelled during her first four years of college before obtaining a degree in cybersecurity. After that, she landed her job at Web Safe, where she quickly gained a reputation for being the best at determining where there's a hole and plugging it.

I'll be honest, I half fell in love with her just from the credentials in her file. Of course, it's not actual love—just fascination—which is what I had to remind myself nearly every time she popped into my head last night.

It did get me thinking though—what if she found a hole someone didn't want found? Did she bring her friend into it for help? Is that why Ramiro was killed? Why she believes Web Safe is after her?

I park my UTV in front of my parents' house then climb out and head up the porch steps, Tango right behind me. Frank remains in his truck, his phone pressed up to his ear. When I pause in front of his truck to wait for him, he offers me a wave, letting me know I should head on inside. Which is probably a good thing. It'll give me time to talk to the Sterlings without him present.

The moment I push open the door, the scent of my mother's homemade apple pie hits me square in the chest. I breathe it in, a smile spreading across my face. It doesn't matter how stressed I am or what I'm facing, that smell will always ground me.

"I smell something delicious," I call out as I step into the kitchen. Tango happily trots alongside me, though the moment he sees my mom, he abandons me to do circles at her feet.

She smiles at me. "Apple pie, baby. Hey there, sweet boy." She pats Tango on the head.

After kissing her cheek, I take a seat at the dining room table where Fred and Jemma are both sitting, cups of coffee in their hands. Fred's face is battered and bruised, the cut over his lip having crusted over.

Jemma's cheekbone is bruised, her eye black, and her own split lip crusted over. My hand clenches into a fist in my lap even as I know the danger has passed—for now.

The fact that they'd put their hands on her at all… What if it were my mother who—*nope. Bury that one.* "How are you both feeling?" I ask, hoping to steer my thoughts in a different, less dark direction.

"Sore," Fred admits. "And worried about Alice. Has there been any word from her?"

I shake my head. "I'll find her though."

"You have to find her before they do," Jemma insists. "They're going to kill her." Her eyes fill, and Fred wraps an arm around her shoulders.

"Not if I have anything to say about it." I offer what I hope is a reassuring smile, which then turns to a very real, grateful smile when my mom sets a mug of coffee down in front of me. "Thanks, Mom."

"Anytime, honey." She ruffles my dark hair just like she did when I was young before heading back over toward the stove.

"Can you tell me what happened last night?" I sit up

just enough to retrieve the small notepad tucked into my back pocket then pull a pen from my front pocket. After flipping to a blank page, I look up at them expectantly.

They exchange glances.

"If you don't tell me the truth, my likelihood of success is much lower than it could be. I need you to be completely honest with me. Even if it looks bad."

Fred nods. "We heard someone come in the back door and thought it was an intruder, so I came down the steps and found Alice standing in the hall, looking terrified and hurt. I was furious. My baby girl—someone hurt her."

"She'd been shot," Jemma says. "That's the injury on her arm. I didn't get a chance to see what it needed or pull out the glass shards embedded in the injury."

"So she'll need medical attention." I make a note on my notepad. "Go on."

"We asked her what happened, and she told us that she killed someone. Alice is the most gentle person I've ever known."

"Was she always?" I question.

Jemma's gaze narrows on me, and I can see the anger at my perceived insinuation. "Alice ran away from nearly every foster home she was in because *they* made her feel unwelcome. She was lonely, troubled, and maybe a little angry, but she was never violent."

"I didn't mean to offend, but if I have a clear picture of

who I'm looking for, it makes it that much easier to find them."

"She was always an openhearted person. And only got more so once she found her faith."

"She's religious?"

Jemma nods. "She follows God. Actually, she's the one who got us to step further into our faith." She sniffles and grips Fred's hand with hers. "We never missed a Sunday after she moved in with us."

They speak about her with so much love; you'd never know she was adopted. Much in the same way our parents talk about Lani. She's family—blood or not—and the time apart was merely a prologue to a wonderful story once she became part of it.

"What happened after she told you she killed someone?" I ask. "That had to shock you. How did she act about it?"

"Of course we were shocked. But we never—even for a minute—thought she did it on purpose," Jemma says.

Fred continues, "She wouldn't let us call the police. Said it would put her in more danger. Then she told us that —" The front door opens, and Frank walks in.

Here we go. This is either going to go well or horribly sideways. "Mr. and Mrs. Sterling, this is Frank Loyotta. He's Ramiro Caine's uncle."

Jemma is the first to stand. She rushes over and wraps her arms around Frank in a move that clearly surprises him.

"I am so sorry, Frank. You have to know we adored Ramiro as though he were a member of our family. He was such a good friend to Alice."

She pulls away, and I can tell that Frank is barely keeping it together. His bottom lip quivers with the weight of his pain.

"You believe he's dead too, then?" he asks.

Jemma looks back at her husband, almost as though she's trying to decide if she should answer. "Alice said they killed him before they tried to kill her too."

"Who killed him?" Frank demands.

"She didn't say. She told us that she's in trouble and that they killed Ramiro." She wraps her arms around herself, and her husband stands to pull her in. "Why did she run off? We should have stopped her."

"If you had, it's possible she'd be in a cell right now, which would make her even more of a target." I turn to Frank. "Alice seems to think someone at Web Safe is behind this."

His face reddens. "Why?"

"She said that, if she got caught, she'd get tossed in a cell where Web Safe will find her. She seemed pretty scared."

Frank considers that. "I don't have any contacts over there—aside from Ramiro—but I can ask around. See what I can find out."

"Just be careful," I tell him. "If they are behind it, and

they get the sense you're looking for information, you could become a target."

"I dare them to come after me." He growls then shakes his head. "No, I don't want to invite trouble. I'm just so— I'm so angry. He deserved better, you know?"

My mom crosses over and wraps her arm around him. "The boys will find answers," she tells him. "And they'll make sure justice is served."

He nods, tears shining in his eyes. It breaks my heart that he's the one now living a nightmare when he works so hard to do good. It's evidence that, oftentimes, bad things happen to good people, and while we may not understand why, God always has a plan.

Even when it's impossible to see.

I just hope I can bring him and his family at least a little closure once I've gotten to the bottom of things.

CHAPTER 6

ALICE

The coffee shop is bustling this morning, which isn't ideal, but it's the only shot I have at finding some answers. Right now, I'm an echo chamber for the theories I'm mulling over. *Fresh eyes.* Isn't that what they say in all the detective shows? That sometimes you need fresh eyes on the case to see it clearer?

The bell above the door rings, and a handsome man in his early thirties walks in. His dark hair is cut short, a buzz cut that's habit ever since his time in the army. He's wearing dark jeans and a tan, short-sleeved polo shirt.

Logan Tarmac's dark gaze scans the room until he sees me sitting in the back. Somehow, he recognizes me, which is a shock, given the baggy clothes and baseball hat I'm wearing. Without ordering a coffee, he comes over and takes a seat across from me, gaze concerned when he notes the bruises all over my face.

"What happened?" he demands. "Are you okay?"

"I'm fine. Physically, at least." I close my eyes and take a deep breath. "I was attacked. The other guy got it worse, but I don't want to talk about that right now."

"Okay," he says slowly.

I take a deep breath. "Thank you for meeting me."

"Of course. You know I would do anything for you, Al."

Al. I never liked that nickname, but since he's risking his life for me, I don't correct him like I've done in the past. "It's a risk talking to me, so if you want to go, I understand."

"If I didn't want to talk to you, I wouldn't be here."

Emotion burns in my throat. I knew I could count on him, and it warms my heart to know I wasn't wrong. "Do you know what they're saying I did?"

His expression answers me before he even nods. "I don't believe a word of it though." He leans in. "Is it true that Ramiro is missing? I know you two are close, so I wasn't sure if—"

"He's not missing. He's dead."

Logan's expression shifts to shock. "Dead? You're sure?"

I nod. "Darren Wade killed him in the server room."

"Darren Wade? As in, the security guard?"

"Yes."

"The server room? At Web Safe?" He leans in closer. "Are you serious?"

"Yes. He tried to kill me too, but I managed to shoot out the window and escape."

"That's two floors up," he replies.

"Yes. I know. I hit the awning over the entrance and bounced off. It broke some of the fall." *Not all of it, though. It hurt—badly—when I hit that pavement. Thank God I didn't break any bones.*

Logan leans back in his chair, taking in all I've said.

"Weren't you a little curious as to why the windows were broken?"

"They told us it was a drive-by. That two stray bullets hit the windows."

I roll my eyes. "Which is why the glass was on the *outside,* right? Unbelievable."

"We're not allowed in the server room right now, and most of the glass outside was cleaned up before we got to work." Logan crosses his arms. "What's going on, Alice?"

Full name. Six months of dating, and one relatively peaceful breakup later, and he's finally calling me by my full name. "I don't know. That's why I wanted to see you. There's no one else I can trust."

"You can always trust me." He covers my hand with his. "Even if we didn't work out, I'm still your friend."

"You are." I smile at him, feeling a bit of the weight I'm carrying lift. "I need to know if anything strange has been going on at work since I've been gone. Anyone acting weird, any new policies put in place…anything."

He withdraws his hand and leans back in the chair again. "Not particularly. We got a memo the day we showed up and the windows were broken. It said there was a drive-by and the windows would be getting replaced, but the server room was off-limits to everyone until the repair was made. They said it was too dangerous for us to go inside."

More like there was too much blood that needed to be cleaned up. "Nothing else?"

He shakes his head. "You said Darren shot Ramiro. Why would he do that?"

"I'm not sure. Ramiro said he found something big. An issue with the security of certain accounts."

"Which accounts?"

"He wouldn't tell me. He insisted I write a patch, so I did. That's what we were there that night to install. A patch that would make it impossible for anyone to gain access to the information hidden behind it. Well, difficult, anyway. So we would have time to find out where the threat was originating from."

"You said he wouldn't tell you which client accounts were affected?"

I shake my head. "He seemed scared. Almost like he was afraid to trust me."

Logan's brow furrows. "Not trusting you is a big red flag that something was going on."

Back when we'd been dating, my friendship with Ramiro was a bit of a sore subject between Logan and me. He'd always insisted that Ramiro wasn't around just to be my friend, and while I'd always known how Ramiro felt, we had an understanding. I just wasn't interested in him that way, and he never held it against me.

Logan couldn't see that, and his jealousy is a big reason we didn't work out. I wasn't willing to shove the friend I'd had for years aside, and Logan didn't trust him.

"That's what I thought too."

Logan is quiet for a moment, likely processing everything I've told him. "You believe Darren has something to do with this? I mean, the guy is a jerk—no one's questioning that—but a murderer—I just don't know that I could see him killing someone in cold blood."

"Well, I did see it. With my own eyes. I watched those bullets penetrate Ramiro's chest. I watched him fall to the ground. And I watched him fall still." Tears burn in my eyes.

"Alice." Logan reaches over and covers my hand with his again. "Have you gone to the police?"

"I can't. If Web Safe is behind this, then they'll do whatever they can to bury it."

"So now you're not trusting the police?"

"Not until I know how deep this is."

"Then why are you coming to me?"

"Because I know that, no matter what went on between us, you're an honorable man. I know you wouldn't do anything to hurt me."

His jaw clenches. "No, I wouldn't."

"Which is why I'm here. I need to know what's going on inside Web Safe. If anything feels off, or if you notice any issues with the accounts, can you tell me?"

"How do I get into contact with you?"

I withdraw a piece of paper and offer it to him. "This email address. Contact me here."

Logan studies it before offering it back to me.

"You don't want to keep it?"

He taps a finger to his temple. "Memorized. And if there is an issue, I don't want anyone to find it."

"Good thinking."

Logan falls silent then leans forward, taking both of my hands in his. "Come with me. You can stay at my place. I'll take the couch, you can have the bedroom, but you'll be safe. Let me protect you. Please, Alice. I couldn't live with myself if something happens to you."

It's sweet, but I'm not sure how to tell him he can't keep me safe—no one can. And I'm unwilling to have what nearly happened to my parents happen to Logan too. "I can't, Logan. It's not safe for you to be near me. I'm sorry."

His gaze locks on mine, but he nods and withdraws. "If

that changes, you know where to find me. I'm right here, Alice. Always."

"I know. Thank you. Please, just keep me in the loop. Anything, no matter how minor."

"I will."

With a smile, I stand. He does, too, then pulls me in for a quick hug.

"I'll see you soon, okay?" he says.

"Okay. Thanks, Logan."

He nods then turns and leaves the coffee shop. I wait a few minutes before following him out and going down the opposite side of the street, where my mom's car is parked. I'd gone back for it last night after the police left. I know I can't drive it to the place I plan on staying, but it'll get me to a bus stop without being accosted on the street again. So that's a win.

Eventually, they'll catch up to me. I just hope it's not before I've found proof and handed it off to someone who can help me. Maybe someone like Tucker Hunt.

Before my meeting with Logan, I'd done some digging into the Hunt brothers. Ramiro talked about them like they were superheroes. He'd never met them but knew of their work from his uncle Frank, who works with them from time to time.

I'd studied the backgrounds of every single one of them, but it was Tucker who truly captivated my attention.

From all that I read, every single one of them is intelligent, kind, brave, and motivated by a deep-rooted faith.

But Tucker—there's just something about him particularly. It could be how selflessly he'd thrown himself into danger at my parents' house last night, not even bothering to wait for backup before plunging into battle. Or it could have something to do with how he and his dog took down two armed murderers without so much as breaking a sweat.

Honestly though? I think it's more. It's the way his bright blue eyes stared straight through me. How he'd held onto me when I'd been so lost to my anger I'd lunged at men twice my size.

Then there's the fact that he's a total computer whiz. Likely one of the few who could challenge me. And that's not arrogance speaking, it's just fact. God blessed me with an aptitude for coding, and I've done everything I can to use those gifts to make Him proud. I've protected important information, kept the names of high-ranking police officers and federal agents hidden behind a wall. Shielded those in witness protection.

And worked hard to be a good steward of the time He's granted me on this earth.

Grief hits me out of nowhere. *Ramiro did that too.* I'd just started getting him to go to church with me right before he was killed. Even though his mother and the rest of his extended family are devout Christians, Ramiro struggled with his faith—likely because of losing his father at such a young age.

But he'd been close.

So close.

Lord, please let him have found You before— I can't even finish the prayer before tears well up in my eyes. *Please let him have found You. Amen.*

I unlock the door and climb behind the wheel of my mom's Kia, then start it up and pull away from the curb without any hesitation. As I drive, I continue to glance up in the rearview mirror, doing what I can to ensure I'm not being followed. My hope is that I'll be able to put some distance between me and Web Safe while working to find a way into the system without being detected.

If I can do that, then maybe I stand a chance at uncovering what's really going on and how deep it truly goes. After all, hackers *love* to leave their own signature on their work. I've certainly dealt with enough of them to know. Some, I'd even recognize. All I need is to get close enough. And if I can't do it from a safe distance, I'll have to find a way into Web Safe to do it from the server room I barely escaped last time.

Because, even if it kills me, I will bring Ramiro justice.

CHAPTER 7
TUCKER

"Can you give me a bit more insight into what happened last night?" I ask the Sterlings as we head outside and sit on the front porch. They'd locked up a bit once Frank arrived, but my hope is that a change of scenery will help move things along. I can't help but feel as though we're running out of time, and the last thing I want is to bring their daughter home in a body bag. "You said Alice had been shot and that she'd shown up at your house, looking for help."

"Yes. She showed up in shock. Her eyes were wide, her face pale—she was soaking wet because of the rain." Jemma takes a deep breath. "We barely had a chance to get her seated at the table before those men were banging on our door."

"Alice panicked. Said she needed to leave, but we convinced her to hide down in the basement," Fred adds.

"Did they not search the house?" I question.

"They did, but we had to have some maintenance work done under the house, and instead of backfilling it with more dirt, they created a little shaft around the joint that broke. It's a small concrete room barely big enough for her to hide in but perfectly hidden from view," he tells me.

"Who blocked the door?" When they both stare at me, I continue, "When I got there, I had to move a coffee cart that was wedged beneath the door handle, locking her inside."

They both stare at each other. "We didn't do that," Jemma says.

"Maybe they shoved it in front of the door?" Fred questions.

I doubt two bruisers would have taken the time to block the door to an empty room, but I don't say it out loud. The truth is, Alice being locked in that basement is likely the only reason she's still alive.

"Walk me through what they said to you."

Jemma and Fred exchange glances; then Fred clears his throat. "They demanded to know where Alice was. Said that she was a murderer and on the verge of committing treason."

"Treason?" I arch a brow.

"Yes. When I pressed, they wouldn't tell me why, just told me that, if I were harboring a murderer, I could get into a lot of trouble." He looks over at Jemma. "That's when they forced their way into the house."

"How long before I got there?" I know it wasn't long since Alice was just starting to try to come out of the basement—maybe minutes, if that—but I need a time stamp. Every detail counts.

"Less than five minutes," Jemma replies. "Or maybe right at five minutes." She shakes her head. "It felt like hours. But they'd had time to do a quick search of the house. When they went down into the basement, I thought it was over. But God shielded our little girl."

I think of the coffee cart wedged tightly beneath the handle. *Yes, I believe He did.*

"I can understand that." I offer her a smile then make another note on my notepad, jotting down the treason angle as well as the estimated timeline. "Once they were inside, what happened?"

"One of them hit Jemma," Fred growls, his gaze landing on his wife. "I lunged for them, and they grabbed me. Started hitting me and telling us that things were only going to get more difficult if we weren't honest. Then that picture broke, and he sent his partner toward you." He glances over at Tango, who is happily eating some kibble my mom put in a bowl for him. "I've never seen an animal move that fast. The second you gave the order, he was like a blur."

"Tango's the best," I reply, pride warming my chest.

"And the shot you took—that seemed impossible. I heard that gun go off, and I thought Jemma was—" Fred tears up. "I'm sorry."

"No need to apologize. It was a tense moment. Duck joke aside."

"Duck joke?" Frank questions.

"My way of lightening the mood while also getting Jemma out of the way," I reply.

"Thank you for saving us," Fred says. "I can't even remember if either of us thanked you. But *thank you.*"

"No need to thank me, Mr. Sterling."

"Please call me Fred."

"Fred." I offer him a friendly smile. "Now, you said they accused Alice of being a murderer. Do you believe it was because of the partner of theirs she killed in that alley? Or—" I trail off and glance at Frank, who's standing near the front door, completely silent. "Ramiro?"

"We don't know. But I do know that Alice would never hurt Ramiro. They were best friends. They started going to church together, did trivia night—"

"Ramiro started going to church?" Frank asks.

Jemma nods. "Alice had been trying to get him to join her for months, and he'd finally agreed. They'd gone two, maybe, three Sundays."

Frank's expression softens, and I can see the weight of their words settling over him like a warm blanket. His nephew was finding his way to God, and that's something Frank can take back to his sister. Hopefully, a little peace will come from knowing that—if it turns out that Ramiro Caine is truly gone.

"Alice is such a good girl. She had such a rough start, but she's a good kid," Fred says, taking his wife's hand in his. "There's not a violent bone in her body. You have to believe us."

"I believe there's more to this story," I tell them, mirroring what I told Frank. "And I intend to uncover the truth. No matter how hard it is." My hope is that they read between the lines. I don't believe Alice is a murderer, but if she is, I won't shield them from it. "Is there anywhere Alice might go to lie low? Any favorite places?"

The Sterlings look at each other for a moment.

"If you don't tell me, and Web Safe gets to her first—"

"Lake Tahoe," they say in unison.

"There's a small cabin up there on King's Beach. We took her there the month after adopting her and went back every year until she was eighteen. It's her favorite place in the world."

"Can you give me the address for the cabin?"

"I can. It's saved in my phone." He reaches into his pocket and withdraws his cell phone. After pulling up the information, he offers it to me. "Feel free to send it to yourself."

"I will, thanks."

"Mr. Hunt, Alice is a good kid. She's strong, smart, resilient—but she's not unbreakable. After losing Ramiro, and now this—we're worried."

"Tucker," I correct then fire off a text to myself before promising, "and I'll find her."

I just hope I'm not too late.

Jemma looks over at Frank. "You must know that Alice would never have hurt Ramiro."

"I'm not sure what to believe," Frank replies honestly. "Though I have to admit, I don't believe your daughter is behind it."

"We adored Ramiro," Jemma says. "He came to Alice's last birthday party, and we had the pleasure of meeting him."

"Thank you. He's a good kid," Frank says. His phone dings, so he pulls it out of his pocket and checks the message. When he looks back at me, his expression has turned furious. "Can I talk to you for a minute, Tucker?"

"Sure. Excuse us." I offer the Sterlings a smile then follow Frank down the steps and toward his truck. As he always does, Tango follows me. "What is it?"

"Those FBI agents that took custody of your two bruisers? Not FBI."

"You're sure?"

He nods. "I called my contact on the way here, and he just sent me a message saying that the names and badge numbers belong to legitimate agents, both of whom were at the field office when Detective Simmons said he was forced to hand over custody."

"You have got to be kidding me." I shake my head and place both hands on my hips. "Alaric said he even called to verify that they were agents."

"They must have somehow controlled where the call went. Is that possible?"

I nod. "Unfortunately, they could have rerouted it." I take a deep breath. "Okay. So they're out and likely know that the Sterlings are with me."

"We need to move them," Frank says. "I have some safe houses I can take them to. Places where no one will find them."

Bradyn's truck pulls up in front of my parents' house, and he climbs out of the driver's side while Elliot gets out of the passenger seat. A beat later, Riley steps out of the back, along with Bravo, Echo, and Romeo—their three service dogs.

"What is it?" Bradyn asks, his superpower clearly picking up on the issue.

"Two bruisers I apprehended in California were just taken out of an LAPD interview room by men posing as FBI agents."

"That's problematic," Elliot says.

"Guess we got here at the right time," Riley replies, rubbing his hands together in anticipation.

"We have a bigger problem. They're after Alice Sterling and likely know that I'm the one who has her parents. It'll only be a matter of time before they trace them here."

"I was just telling Tucker I can take them to a safe house," Frank offers.

"Won't matter," Elliot says. As always, his baseball cap is on backward. He crosses both arms. "They'll suspect they're here and come anyway. Better we keep them here where we can protect them."

Frank nods. "Tell me what I can do to help."

"Get with Bradyn," I tell him. "I'm heading out as soon as possible to see if I can track Alice down and get her off the map before Web Safe finds her." I glance back at the Sterlings, who are watching us intently from the porch swing.

"Take Dylan," Bradyn says. "These guys are going to know you're coming now, and it won't hurt to have backup."

"Will do."

PINE CREEK'S church is small, but the presence of God here is mighty. I can feel Him every time I walk through these doors, like a secure blanket closing around me. Before every mission, I make my way here to pray and just sit in the silence with God. It's my way of filling up my soul before the darkness I will undoubtedly see tries to drain me.

We are what we surround ourselves with—I believe that.

So here I sit, surrounding myself with so much light I can cling to it even when the darkness tries to swallow me up.

This time feels different though.

I can't place my finger on it, but Alice Sterling is weighing heavier on me than anyone else I've gone after. Is it the mystery? Or something else?

"Tucker Hunt. What a pleasure." Pastor Ford comes out of the hallway that leads to the church offices and makes his way down the aisle toward the pew I'm sitting in.

"Afternoon, Pastor," I greet.

"You doing okay?" he questions, getting straight to the point. It's something I've always admired about the man. He always knows when something's going on and won't hesitate to help in any way he can.

"I'm struggling a bit, but I'm not sure why."

He rests his arm on the back of the pew and turns to face me. "Tell me what's going on."

"I'm leaving tonight to go after a woman who's being targeted by her employer. They claim she's a murderer and about to commit treason. But I'm not sure I believe them."

"Interesting."

"She did kill a man in self-defense. He was attempting to abduct her, and she fought back. It looks as though he fell backward onto a piece of rebar, and she called 9-1-1 for help."

"I wouldn't say she'd be considered a murderer, then. If it was in self-defense. She took a life, yes, but not because she chose to."

"Exactly." I take a deep breath. "I've been on probably close to a hundred missions now. Not even counting the ones I went on when I was in the service, and this feels—" I trail off. "Heavier somehow."

"Is it the woman?"

"What?"

"Have you met her before? The woman."

"Briefly. When I rescued her parents."

"Then is it her that's staying with you? Or the mission details?"

"It's her," I admit. "She looks—haunted. But there's this light, I just—I can't explain it." I smile. "I probably sound crazy. I met her for five minutes, and I can't get her out of my head."

"Not crazy at all." He smiles softly at me. "God's plan is a mystery to us all. And if you're the one who will be bringing this woman to safety, then it makes sense that you'd feel a pull toward her."

"Her parents insist she's not violent. That everything they're saying about her is a lie."

"What do you believe?"

"Them," I reply without hesitation. "I think she's in

more trouble than even I realize though. There's this gnawing in my gut that things are about to get a whole lot worse before they get better."

"They always do," Pastor Ford replies. "After all, who can truly appreciate tranquil waters if they've never lived through a storm?"

CHAPTER 8
ALICE

The pain in my arm is substantially worse today than yesterday.

I drop the handful of medical supplies I managed to grab while in town earlier on the bathroom counter then search for the bottle of rubbing alcohol amidst the pile. Slowly, I unravel the soiled bandage and study the wound. It's on the side of my arm, and from what I can tell, the bullet didn't actually go inside.

I don't think.

Then again, this is my first gunshot wound, and I could absolutely be wrong. There's discharge oozing from part of it, and the area around the wound is red and raised. My entire body even feels flushed. I may not know much about gunshot wounds, but I know that this is infected.

Great.

It's not like I can just go to the doctor. Not when they're

mandated to report all gunshot wounds to the police. The last thing I need is additional attention. So I take a deep breath and open the bottle of alcohol.

You can do this, Alice. It's just a scrape. Mom helped you with scrapes all the time. Remember what she always said? "Easy peasy, Alice. Easy peasy." Mini pep talk completed, I lean over the sink and pour alcohol on the injury. Burning pain shoots through my arm, radiating from the wound then traveling down through my hand and up through my shoulder. It takes everything I have in me *not* to scream.

The neighbors are far enough away that they probably wouldn't hear, but there's a popular hiking trail right behind the cabin, and there's no telling who's on it. The last thing I need is some poor family of four rushing in here to rescue me from myself.

So I bite down on the inside of my cheek until the coppery tang of blood is all I can taste as I wait for the stinging to stop.

As soon as it's bearable, I retrieve the tube of antibacterial cream and squeeze it onto a piece of gauze, then press the gauze gently against the wound before tearing an ACE bandage wrap open with my teeth.

After tucking part of it under my arm, I wrap it around, covering the wound, then secure it back to itself.

As soon as it's done, I take a deep breath.

"Not so bad," I mutter to myself before sinking down

on top of the toilet to catch my breath. As soon as I'm sure I can stand without falling over from the pain, I get to my feet and head into the main room of the cabin.

It's not much, but the two-bedroom cabin is as close to home as I can safely get. It holds so many great memories, and since I can't physically be anywhere near my parents right now, this helps me still feel close to them.

I remove my laptop from my bookbag, set it on the table, and open the lid to power it on. Once I've grabbed a bottle of water from the refrigerator, I take a seat and open up a tracking software I've used a handful of times.

Normally, it's how I track down hackers who've attempted to breach our software, but this time, I change the parameters to track my dad's cell phone number. I'd lingered close enough to see them climb into Tucker Hunt's truck and drive off. Therefore, I can surmise that he took them somewhere safe. Where that somewhere is, I'm not sure yet.

Seconds tick by as the program works on locating my dad's phone. Then it pings, and a green dot shows up on a map. I take a drink of water as it closes in on the location. As soon as I have it, I open a secondary program and plug in the coordinates.

Hunt Family Ranch, Pine Creek, Texas.

So he did take them with him. Question is, did he do it to protect them like he promised? Or leverage their location to get to me?

"What else can I find on you, Tucker Hunt?" I ask aloud to my empty cabin. Then, because I'm genuinely curious, I open a third program and type his name into a database I have absolutely no right accessing.

But since there's no one to stop me and I have no intention of causing harm by what I find, I do it anyway.

"Tucker Hunt." I say his name aloud again as I type it into the search bar. Ramiro used to tease me because he said there could be no one else in the room, and I'd have a full conversation with myself. He's not wrong. Talking out loud is just something I've always done. Even when I was a kid—likely because of all the time I spent alone.

My thoughts drift back to my friend, and a fresh wave of grief washes over me. The fact that I'll never see him smile again breaks my heart. He had the greatest smile. His entire face would light up.

And while he'd always wanted more between us, he'd respected that I didn't feel the same. Our friendship was far too important to risk what likely wouldn't have worked out, given my past track record with relationships.

Look at Logan, for example. Granted, that was more *because* of how close Ramiro and I are. *Were,* I correct. *How close we were.* Tears burn in my eyes, but I blink them away, refocusing my attention on the task at hand. Learning all I can about Tucker Hunt before deciding whether or not I can trust him when I finally do find what I'm looking for.

A handful of boxes pop up, each with different information on the handsome hero who saved my family.

He spent eight years in the army, working his way up from a private all the way to a staff sergeant before leaving the military behind and returning to his family ranch. He has his own army of medals behind him and spent most of his career in the Special Forces.

There are no disciplinary actions in his file, and he was nothing but exemplary while in service.

Next, I move to the search and rescue team he and his brothers operate off their ranch. There are only a handful of articles that talk about them, though I have my suspicions that they've done a lot more than what's mentioned here. One of the many times Ramiro talked about them, he said they do most of their work in the shadows to avoid media attention.

He'd even joked about joining them or his uncle at one point, saying he'd like to do more with his life than sit behind a computer.

The knot in my chest tightens.

He would have been a great asset to any team. Lord knows he was an asset to my life.

I lean back in my chair, happy with what I've seen when combined with everything else I've learned.

Tucker Hunt is a good guy.

Okay.

After closing some windows, I open up a new one then

log into the VPN so all activity is routed through it and at least a half a dozen others. "Let's see how good you are, Mr. Hunt."

A FEW HOURS LATER, I'm still staring at an empty email inbox.

I'd expected Tucker to notice that I'd hacked his computer, but so far, either he hasn't been at his computer yet today, or he's planning his response. I didn't do much inside—a good portion of his files are completely inaccessible even to me—but I did change his wallpaper from the solid black geometric background to a handful of German shepherd puppies sitting in a meadow.

I smile just thinking about it. It's a game Ramiro and I would play, and while I'd seriously considered not playing the same game with Tucker out of respect for my friend, I know Ramiro would have gotten a kick out of me doing that to the big bad special operations soldier too.

So I did. And now I'm waiting.

Feeling a bit claustrophobic, I push to my feet and pull the tail of my ponytail through the back of a baseball cap before pulling it low over my head and stepping out onto the porch that overlooks the popular hiking trail.

Even now, there's a family happily making their way down the trail—the mom holding the hand of a cheery toddler and the dad wearing a baby in a harness on his chest.

Will I ever get the chance to have a family?

To know what it feels like to grow life in my belly and have a man look at me with complete adoration as we vow to love each other forever?

At this point? I'm honestly not so sure.

Ramiro certainly didn't get that chance.

The image of him smiling as we climbed the rock wall at our favorite gym pops into my head. He had so much more to give, and now he's lying dead in a morgue somewhere, likely waiting to be buried until they have answers.

Then again, as far as Logan and the others at Web Safe are concerned, Ramiro is just missing. Will we even be able to find his body to bury him?

Tears fill my vision before slipping down my cheeks. The pain is still so fresh. The grief so powerful. *God, help me through this. Please be with me. I don't know how to do this without him beside me.*

Will I even make it to his funeral?

Will I get the chance to tell his mother just how much he meant to me?

Behind me, my computer dings, so I wipe the tears from my cheeks then head back inside and lock the door. After grabbing a bottle of water, I take a seat and smile when I see that my computer's wallpaper has been changed to a rabbit hole tucked away beneath a tree.

Alice in Wonderland. Clever, Mr. Hunt.

I open my email then decide what I should say. The message has to be clever, but not blatant. A funny nickname pops into my head, so I roll with it.

MadCode,

Clever wallpaper. Fitting even, given the circumstances. I trust that you followed through on your end of the bargain?

-404Wonder

After choosing 404Wonder as a fun way to tease him that he still hasn't tracked me down while also keeping with the theme he set with the wallpaper change, I keep the message relatively vague, just in case someone from Web Safe is watching. While I'm confident in my belief that no one there is as good as I am—at least not anyone still breathing—it's still a risk I can't take. Besides, the techy twist nicknames on Alice in Wonderland characters is bringing me a bit of joy when everything around me is falling apart.

Whoever orchestrated Ramiro's death and the data breach we discovered has deep pockets and contacts within Web Safe itself. No one inside can be trusted. I may not be sure of much right now, but I do know that.

My hope though is that Tucker Hunt is everything I think he is and will be able to help me uncover the truth. Unless, of course, I'm killed first.

Which is an unfortunate possibility since I already

know they're clearly willing to kill to keep everything quiet. The trouble is, I don't know what they're trying to keep quiet—yet. Ramiro and I were trying to figure that out when they caught us in the server room. And I'm not entirely sure how I'm supposed to get into the building and actually access the information *without* getting myself killed.

Unfortunately, every answer I need is accessible *only* from Web Safe's internal servers. While the clients provide us with digital access to their databases, all delicate information is then shielded behind firewalls that can *only* be lowered by the computer in the server room.

I'm running a scan on the information not sensitive enough to be kept offline, but I'm not hopeful I'll find anything. Because Ramiro was *insistent* that we had to be in the server room to install the patch. Meaning whatever we're looking for is there and only there.

My inbox dings.

404Wonder,

MadCode, huh? Cute. I always did connect with the Hatter.

As for the wallpaper, I thought so too. Rabbit holes and all. I stuck by my word. Question is, will you? I guess we'll find out soon enough.

-MC

I consider his message then prep to type out my

response. But just as I'm ready to start, someone knocks on the door.

Oh no. Not now.

Heart in my throat, I retrieve the firearm I pilfered from my parents' safe when I'd gone back for their car and silently push to my feet. The blinds are closed, curtains over the front windows too, so no one can see inside. But that doesn't mean I have any advantage. If it's Web Safe, they won't wait for me to answer.

Slowly, I creep forward toward the door, my pulse hammering in my ears.

Maybe it's just a lost hiker? Someone who strayed too far from the trail?

There were times when I stayed here with my parents, when hikers thought we were a ranger station of some kind.

I stretch up on my tiptoes, momentarily hating how short I am, then peer out through the peephole.

No way.

Glancing over at my computer for a moment, I note a new email has come through.

OPEN ME.

I grin. This guy might be just what I'm looking for. Keeping my weapon in hand just in case, I unlock the door and pull it open to find an incredibly handsome Tucker Hunt standing on the other side, grinning in victory since he managed to track me down.

"Hey there, Wonder. Guess you're no longer a 404 code."

"I guess not."

A second man steps into view. *Dylan Hunt.* I recognize him from the research I did on the Hunt brothers. Tucker and Dylan are twins, though not identical. Dylan is the younger out of the two, the youngest of all five of the brothers. Their adopted sister, Lani, a doctor, is the youngest of them all.

"I see you brought travel companions," I comment when I note the two dogs sitting at their feet. Tango I recognize, thanks to the small white dot near his long nose. The other, I'm assuming, is Delta. That is, if they stuck with the phonetic-alphabet naming convention.

"May we come in?" Tucker questions.

"Do you plan to kill or abduct me?" I ask.

"Would we tell you if we were going to?" Tucker retorts. "Doesn't exactly seem like something we'd advertise."

I smile. "Fair enough. I'm going to remain armed. I'm assuming you don't mind."

"Not at all." Tucker turns to Dylan. "Do you mind?"

"Armed or not, it wouldn't matter," he says. The cold tone he uses is a direct contrast to the warmth Tucker gives off, but I still don't believe either man would hurt me. Not at this point, anyway.

"Come on in." I step aside, let them and their dogs in,

then close and lock the door behind them, all while ensuring I don't turn my back.

Then, I lean against the door as they turn to face me.

"How did you find me?"

"Your parents told us that you vacationed here as a kid," Tucker replies. "Then while you were changing my wallpaper, I was able to make it through all of your VPN's and narrow down the exact location as confirmation."

"That was only a few hours ago. If you were in Texas, then you shouldn't be here yet."

"Who said we were in Texas?" Tucker questions. "We've been here in California since late last night. The next cabin over, actually." He grins. "Like I said, your parents gave us your location. I merely verified it when you hacked my computer. Great choice on the Thai food you ordered for dinner, by the way. We had some too, and it was delicious."

"So you've been watching me." It's a bit of a hit to my pride that I didn't notice it, but I remind myself this guy has a military background, and—well—it's really not a surprise that I didn't see him coming. Isn't that what Special Forces do? Remain in the shadows until they're ready to be seen?

"Had to know what you were up to," Tucker replies. "So now that I'm here, are you planning to keep your end of the bargain or not?" He crosses his muscled arms, and my gaze momentarily drops. It's only a second—less than, even—but given the smirk on his handsome face, he noticed.

"How do I know I can trust you?"

"I guess you don't. But the fact that we didn't bring Web Safe or police crawling all over this place should be proof enough that we're not here to hurt you." It's Dylan who responds this time, and his tone is on the total opposite end of the spectrum compared to Tucker.

Whereas Tucker's tone is challenging in an amusing kind of way, Dylan's is a dare. As though he's just waiting for me to step out of line. *Intriguing.* Two twins, totally different personalities.

I've already decided to trust Tucker, so what's one more Hunt brother? "Good point. Okay, but buckle up, boys, because it's one heck of a ride."

CHAPTER 9
TUCKER

Alice Sterling is absolutely *stunning*.

The pictures of her online and that brief interaction we had at her parents' house did not do her justice, and as I stand here in front of her, I have to actively remind myself *not* to stare. Because—she's breathtaking.

She's on the shorter side, nearly a foot shorter than my six-foot-two. Her obsidian hair is long and wavy, falling all the way to her waist. I honestly have no clue how she managed to hide that underneath the baseball cap she'd been wearing when I found her in that basement. Or how I failed to notice the length of it when I'd been standing feet away from her in that living room.

Her eyes—a crystal blue—are so pale they don't seem real.

And then there's the spark in her soul. The fight that has been evident since the moment we met.

"We can take it," I tell her, clearing my throat in hopes of pulling my attention away from the dark-haired beauty and placing it firmly in the present where it belongs. I'm here to figure out whether or not I believe Alice Sterling is a murderer and a thief, or if she's just someone in the wrong place at the wrong time.

"I'm assuming you already know my background." It's a statement, not a question.

"Your parents passed away when you were young; you were adopted by the Sterlings when you were thirteen. Graduated high school as valedictorian, excelled in college, degree in cybersecurity. How am I doing so far?"

"You forgot that I prefer crunchy peanut butter to creamy and can't stand marshmallows." Her tone is annoyed, and it only amuses me further.

"I'll be sure to bookmark that for later, though the marshmallow thing is crazy." I cross my arms. "Walk us through what happened the day Ramiro died." I settle back in a chair, ready for the story. Tango sits beside me, his gaze firmly on Alice. He's likely assessing the situation just as I am, waiting for a command. Dylan remains standing, not at all unusual for him, and Delta leans against him—something the animal does whenever he senses Dylan's fight response triggering. Which, unfortunately, happens fairly frequently.

Alice remains close to the door, a quick getaway her main focus at the moment. Not that I can blame her. If she is innocent in all of this, then she'd be foolish to trust us after everything she's been through. Even taking into consideration my role in rescuing her parents.

"Ramiro was always the more social out of the two of us. I focused pretty heavily on my job, and that was it. I'd hang out with him, but aside from that, I wasn't big on company socialization."

"Any particular reason why?" I ask.

She shakes her head. "I'm not a people person. I'm better with computers."

"Except with Ramiro," Dylan comments.

"Except with Ramiro," she repeats. "He was just different. Focused at work, and fun outside of it. He pushed me out of my comfort zone, and I enjoyed it."

"Were you two romantic?" A tendril of completely unnecessary jealousy snakes through me. Likely just because she's a beautiful woman, but it's unwanted, so I shove it aside.

"No. He wanted to be, but I just didn't see him as anything more than a friend."

"I'm assuming he wasn't happy about that?" Dylan asks.

"Not at first, but he got it." She narrows her gaze. "Is this my story or your interrogation?"

"Both. Continue," I tell her as I withdraw my small notepad and pen from my front pocket.

"Anyway, Ramiro called me out of the blue and told me that he needed to talk to me right then. He said we had to meet and it couldn't wait until Monday morning. It was Saturday," she adds. "I was on a date, but it wasn't going well, so I told him I got called into work and asked that he drive me home. He did, and Ramiro was sitting on the steps when he dropped me off."

"I'm assuming he didn't care to see you get out of another man's car," Dylan says dryly.

"To be honest, I don't think he even saw me get dropped off. It wasn't until I was right in front of him and I'd said his name twice that he even looked up. And even then, he seemed surprised I was back."

"Did he appear to be visibly upset too? Or just distracted?"

"Both? He seemed upset and super distracted by whatever it was."

I make a note on my notepad.

"What did he want to talk about?"

She starts to cross her arms but hisses in pain when she moves her injured arm. I note the way she favors it. *She was shot,* I remember, mentally kicking myself for that not being the first thing I did when we got here.

"Let me look at your arm," I tell her, pushing up from my seat and setting my notepad down on the table.

"It's fine. I just rewrapped it."

I eye her. "I'm good with injuries in the field." My gaze nearly shifts to Dylan, but I keep it trained forward. Many of the wounds I've dealt with were his. My stomach still churns when it slips into the forefront of my memory. Even after we'd rescued him, he'd been a man with a death wish, running into situations without thinking them through.

"Fine. But you're wasting your time." She pushes off the door and heads into the kitchen, taking a seat on one of the barstools.

"Noted. So what did Ramiro want to talk about?" I wash my hands then head back over and start unwrapping her arm.

"He said he believed someone in the company was using their access to remove certain protections." She speaks through gritted teeth, clearly in pain with every slight movement.

I remove the wrapping then gently pull the gauze pad away.

The skin surrounding the bullet wound is an angry shade of crimson. The edges are swollen, and upon closer inspection, I see a glint of glass buried in the injury. No bullet though. And from the angle, I'd say it just grazed her. My guess is the glass is what's causing the infection. The wound can't heal.

"Have any run-ins with a pane of glass?" I question, momentarily shifting the direction of our conversation.

"Maybe. Why?"

"There's a chunk of glass buried in your arm. It needs to be dug out before the injury can heal properly." I raise my gaze to her pale one and note that her face has paled even more. "Dylan can hold you, so you don't move."

"Not necessary," she retorts. "Do what you need to do."

"It's going to hurt."

"I'll survive. Probably. But if I pass out, you do *not* have my permission to take me to a hospital or anywhere outside of this cabin, capisce?"

"Capisce," I reply with a smile. "Though, I guess you wouldn't really know, would you?"

She glares at me. "You'll regret it if you do." She takes a deep breath and faces forward. "Do it."

After reaching into my field pack, which has an excellent arrangement of first aid supplies, thanks to my little sister, Doctor Lani, I retrieve a pair of gloves and a pair of pointed tweezers.

Dylan moves closer, likely to steady Alice in case she starts having issues once I've started trying to remove the glass. Depending on how deeply it's embedded, it could be just as painful as removing a bullet.

"Okay. Ready?"

"Ready." Alice shuts her eyes tightly and holds her breath.

"It's important to keep breathing," I tell her as I gently

grip the backside of her arm. My entire hand wraps around her upper arm, so I'm able to use my thumb and fingers to gently pull the skin apart just enough to get a better look inside.

"I'm. Fine," she hisses.

I look up at Dylan and give him a slight nod. He moves in behind her. We've seen it in the field: The injured person will start holding their breath to try to keep the pain at bay. Then, to compensate, their breathing becomes rapid and shallow, they hyperventilate, and they pass out.

"Here we go." As carefully as I can, like a real-life game of Operation, I guide the tweezers into her injury.

She hisses again.

The glass is deep enough that I have to move past some tissue before closing the tweezers around it. "I've got it, okay? Going to pull it out now."

Alice doesn't respond, just offers a single nod. She's breathing again, taking deep, steady breaths.

Keeping the balance of moving quickly but also doing what I can to avoid damaging the tissue any further, I pull the glass free. The shard is far larger than I thought it would be, nearly a quarter inch long, and shaped like a dagger.

Alice sways in her seat, and Dylan reaches out to steady her with gentle hands on her shoulders.

"I'm good. Sorry." She takes a deep breath. My twin

releases her. I glance up at him, noting the darkness in his gaze. Physical touch—aside from occasional hugs from our parents and siblings—always brings that darkness back.

It costs him greatly every time he has to step outside of his carefully crafted bubble.

After grabbing a fresh piece of gauze, I press it to her injury. "Hold this with your good hand."

She does, and for a brief moment, her fingers brush mine. A shiver runs through me, desire that hits me so fast I'm sure I imagined it.

"That's huge." She studies the glass, pale gaze widening.

Get it together, Tucker. "Yeah. Thick too." I set it on a piece of napkin. "It's long enough you likely scraped your bone too. You really need to be on antibiotics." I reach into my pocket and withdraw my cell.

"What are you doing?"

"Calling my sister. She's a doctor. I'm going to have her call something in for you."

"Oh. Okay. Cool."

I tap Lani's contact then put it on speaker because I imagine it'll put Alice at ease, knowing she can hear everything that's being said.

"Brother mine, what can I do for you?" Lani greets after the second ring.

"I need some antibiotics called into a local pharmacy. You can put it under Dylan's name."

"Excuse me? Why do you need antibiotics?"

"Infected wound in an upper arm."

She groans. "Please tell me neither of you got shot. You guys are magnets for bullets, and this is getting ridiculous. I mean, you've only been gone, what, twenty-four hours?"

"Hey, never been shot here, remember?" I joke. "And it's not for us. There was a piece of glass stuck in Alice Sterling's arm. About a quarter of an inch long and wedged close to the bone. I'm worried the infection will be deep. I don't want the prescription under her name just in case she's being monitored. Same with mine."

Lani is quiet for a moment. "Alice Sterling? You found her?"

"We did. And you're on speakerphone."

"Text me the location, and I'll make the call. Since I'm on speakerphone, I will also add this. Alice, I don't know whether or not you killed anyone, but if you hurt either of my brothers, I will personally hunt you down and make it look like an accident. Got it? Cool. Love you guys, bye!" She hangs up without waiting for a response from Alice or us.

Dylan chuckles.

"I like her," Alice replies with a grin. "Seriously, she sounds great."

"She is great." I text Lani our location then ask her to choose a pharmacy in the area.

"Okay." Setting my phone aside, I reach into my pack

and withdraw a bottle of sterile saline. "Can you grab a towel from the bathroom?" I ask Dylan.

He nods and heads down the hall, Delta on his heels.

"Not a big talker, is he?"

"No."

"Kind of strange you guys are twins, given how different you seem to be."

And because any answer I give will open a can of worms we've sealed shut, I don't reply at all. Dylan comes into the room with a towel. He offers it to me, so I gently lift her injured arm and slide the towel beneath it. "You can remove the gauze." She pulls it aside, and I rinse the injury with saline.

She hisses and shuts her eyes tightly.

"Sorry," I mutter as I set the saline aside and pull out a bottle of Betadine. "This is going to hurt."

"Because every moment leading up to this has been vacation," she quips.

"Fair enough." I gently dab the injury with the Betadine, carefully avoiding getting it directly into the wound. Then, I apply a patch of sterile gauze and lightly wrap a self-adhesive bandage around her arm. "Done."

She gently raises and lowers her arm. "It still hurts, but it feels better. Thanks."

"You're welcome." I head into the kitchen and dispose of the dirty gauze, bandages, and the piece of glass. Then, after washing my hands, I head back into the living room. "Now that your arm is probably not going to fall off, how about you continue?"

"Probably?"

"I'm no doctor," I add with a shrug.

"Solid point, Mr. Hunt." Alice takes a deep breath. "So as I said, Ramiro was distracted. He told me that someone was trying to steal information and we needed to patch it up."

"Why was that shocking?" Dylan questions. "It's your job, isn't it?"

"Which is what I thought. But with how weird he was acting, I knew something else was up. He insisted I write something we could install directly into the system via the server room. He said it was the only way to protect what they were trying to steal."

"Any idea who *they* were?" I ask.

She shakes her head. "Though I now suspect it's someone inside of Web Safe."

"Why do you think that?"

"Because it was a member of the security team who shot Ramiro. It's not unusual for us to access the server room, yet he didn't even bother asking why we were in there before he started shooting."

I open my mouth to ask her for a name, but my phone buzzes, cutting me off.

Reaching into my pocket, I withdraw it. Dylan does the same with his, letting me know it's a group text. Which means things just escalated.

I open the message.

Bradyn: Check your email. Now.

CHAPTER 10
ALICE

"What are we looking at?" I question as I step up behind Tucker.

Neither of them has said a word since they read whatever message came through on their phones. Tucker just grabbed his laptop and took a seat at the dining room table while Dylan moved to his right side.

"I'm not entirely sure," Tucker replies, then pulls up an email with a video attached. I lean in closer as he makes the video larger, only to find myself staring down at security footage from Web Safe.

"That's the server room," I reply. It's grainy. But I'd know that room anywhere. Hope surges through my system. Are we about to find proof that someone is dirty? Is this somehow going to free me from running for my life?

Tucker hits play.

Seconds tick by with nothing, and then—Ramiro sprints

into view of the camera. *No.* Grief hits me square in the chest, nearly knocking me back a step. This is from the day he died.

I come into view of the camera, dark hair braided tightly over my shoulder.

"That's not right," I say. "My hair wasn't braided." Even as I speak, I watch in absolute horror as the video version of me raises her weapon at Ramiro and fires. *Bang. Bang.*

He falls backward onto the ground, hitting it while I raise the gun in my hand toward the camera, and fire again.

The screen goes blank.

The whole thing takes all of five seconds, but those seconds contain the power to erase my entire life. Even though the only truth is that we were in the server room together the night he died.

"No. That's not right." I step back.

Dylan and Tucker both turn toward me, their expressions furious, as though I'm enemy number one.

"Looked pretty clear to me," Dylan says. "You killed your friend. I wouldn't want to tell the truth about it, either. You had to know that we'd figure it out though. So what was your plan?"

Tucker is quiet.

"No. *None* of that is right. My hair wasn't braided. I had a former foster mom who braided it so tight my brain felt like it was going to pop, so I never braid my hair. I hate it. And I would never have hurt Ramiro. Someone manipulated that video. You have to believe me." My voice cracks with barely contained emotion.

Tucker doesn't answer, just shifts his attention back to the phone. "The email was forwarded to Ramiro's uncle from someone at Web Safe. It's being sent to the police right now, which means every agency in the country is coming for you."

My stomach churns, nausea burning me up. This cannot be happening. They're framing me so they can bury the potential data breach. "This cannot be happening," I mutter aloud. "Give me that video, and I'll prove it's a fake."

"Hand over evidence to you so you can manipulate it? Not a chance," Dylan replies.

I glare at him. "If I'd killed Ramiro, do you really think I would have gone back to save my parents? Or that I would have let both of you walk in here?"

Dylan turns to Tucker. "Any sign that video was tampered with?"

"I need my desktop. It has better computing power."

"Where is it? Let's go get it," I say, desperate to get to the bottom of this. I adore Ramiro's family. And now they're all going to think I murdered him.

"In Texas."

"Oh." *Of course it is.* Which means I'll have to trust them enough to leave this place with them. "Is that where my parents are?"

"Yes." Tucker looks at Dylan.

"I didn't kill him."

"You understand that this footage says otherwise, right? And unless I can prove you didn't kill him—"

"If you prove it's legitimate, then feel free to turn me in. But I'm telling you that it's not. And if you can't prove it, I can. I'm betting my life on it." Panic thrums through my veins. I *need* them to believe me. Because if they don't, I'll lose the only semi-allies I have in this fight.

If the leak that Ramiro found is as bad as he seemed to think it is, it will cost thousands of lives—at least—and bankrupt more businesses than I can count.

And that's only the beginning.

"How about you tell us the rest of the story," Tucker says. "Then we'll decide where to go from there."

"Fine. Okay." They'll believe me when they hear it… right? *They have to.* My gaze shifts to Dylan, who's eyeing me as though I'm going to jump at him and yell "boo!" any minute now. I try to think back to where I was before the email, finally remembering we were just approaching what Ramiro came to tell me.

"As I said, Ramiro was visibly upset and distracted. I asked him to elaborate, but he told me we had to go inside to talk. That it wasn't safe out on the street. So we did. Once we got into my apartment, he went through and unplugged my computer, television, router, any electronic device that was plugged into the wall. Then, he took my cell and his cell phone, as well as both of my laptops, and shoved them into Faraday bags he'd brought with him."

"So he was paranoid," Tucker comments.

"Very. The only things left plugged in were my lamps and appliances. He even went through with an RF detector and checked for bugs. Interestingly enough, he found three of them hidden in two of my lights and an electrical outlet."

"Your apartment had been bugged?"

"Yes. To be honest, had he not found anything, I probably wouldn't have believed him. It seemed so outrageous at the time." I rub the heel of my palm against my chest as the image of him lying dead assaults me again.

"Any idea who would have placed the bugs and why?"

"To be honest, I haven't even had the time to give it any thought. Everything spiraled from there, and a place I'm not staying at the moment wasn't high on my priority list." I take a deep breath and then continue. "Uh, he told me that he'd been out with two of the guys we work with, and they'd told him that they'd found two security threats that popped up overnight."

"Doesn't that happen all the time? Isn't that the purpose of companies like Web Safe?" Dylan questions.

"Sure. But these two hits were *identical and* had been placed in two different companies with nothing in common. Low-level ones too. They were protecting nothing more than basic employee information."

Dylan continues staring at me like I grew a third head.

"A hacker is going to typically target similar companies. Two separate hackers will have different coding techniques. It's like a thumbprint," Tucker says.

"Exactly," I reply. "And why bypass higher-profile companies with more important information? Ramiro thought that maybe it was a test. They were trying to see if they would get caught. But the next day, he said he patched three more breaches, all with the same code, all formulated at the same time. He tried to trace the origin location of the attack but kept hitting a wall. Which is why he came to me. He believed that someone in Web Safe might have been selling access to hackers. They punch a hole in the security, the hacker gets in, and then they seal it back up. He wanted me to write code that would prevent the hole from ever being punched."

"Did you help him?"

"Of course. He was frantic. There were bugs in my apartment. Things were looking incredibly suspicious. So I changed, and we drove over to Web Safe. I logged into my computer and opened up the companies he claimed had been patched. But there was no sign anything had gotten into the system. There was no patch work."

"Patch work?" Dylan questions.

"Coding to repair the breach," Tucker replies.

"Yeah. There was no sign that anyone had ever tried to access the information. Which, of course, made Ramiro even more paranoid. The only way that would happen is if someone who *knew* our coding language repaired it. But there was no log of it in the system."

"You keep all the records?"

"Every breach. Every patch. Full transparency," I reply. "It's possible that the repair was done by the night crew— they tend to not update records until right before they leave —but Ramiro was insistent. So, with all of those pieces, I did what any good friend would do, and I tried to prove him right, hoping that I would, in turn, prove him wrong and put his mind at ease."

"Seems like a lot of panic over something that you deal with on a daily basis," Tucker comments.

"Which is exactly what I thought too. Even considering the bugs in my apartment. I mean, that could have been anyone trying to get access to our clients. It's happened before, and our security has handled it."

"Employees have had their apartments bugged?" Dylan questions then shares a look with Tucker.

"Yes. A time or two. We deal with the type of accounts that would crumble the economy if they're breached. And that's not even including the military contracts or law enforcement information we protect. We're a target. It's just understood."

Dylan shrugs.

"Anyway, as I was trying to find any trace of the hack, a door opened, and our head of security—a man by the name of Wilbur Huck—and one of our lower-level bug chasers, as we call them—Shawn Brackers—came into the room. Normally, that's not a big deal. We have a skeleton crew that monitors the systems at night. But Ramiro panicked, turned off my monitor, and tugged me under the desk."

Dylan and Tucker exchange a look, but they don't say anything, so I continue.

"While we were under there, Wilbur told Shawn that it was time to move forward. That their clients weren't going to be happy if they didn't deliver on time. Shawn said that the accounts would be as promised at the agreed-upon time and they would just have to be patient. He said that moving too quickly would set off too many red flags."

"So they were planning something," Tucker says.

"Yes. Something big. We stayed under the desk until we were sure they were gone, but it was then that I realized what was happening. Or, at least, what the evidence was pointing to. Ramiro was right. They were purposely putting holes in the security surrounding certain companies so hackers could get in and steal the information. Then, they can claim innocence while clients lose everything. Bank numbers, routing information, employee social security numbers. The name of every single federal employee in the region. Names of people in witness protection. Anything that Web Safe protected was at risk."

"Did you turn them in?" Dylan questions.

I shake my head. "I wanted to, but Ramiro said we

needed more proof. Wilbur Huck is the brother-in-law of the man who founded Web Safe. We couldn't be sure they weren't in it together."

"So you went at it alone."

"I went home and wrote a wall of code that would shield every single Web Safe account. Then, the next day, we went to work like nothing was wrong. But at closing time, Ramiro and I stayed behind so I could install the code directly into the server room. Deploying it meant we didn't have to worry that they would Swiss cheese the accounts before we could find proof."

"Web Safe is a high-level cybersecurity company. You truly believed you alone could put something in place to protect all of those accounts? Tucker asks.

I turn to him. "I'm very good at what I do, Mr. Hunt. And I knew it wouldn't last forever, but I'd hoped to have enough time to gather what we needed. Right as we were finishing the installation, Darren found us. He opened fire, and Ramiro shoved me behind a tower before pulling out a gun."

"He was armed?"

I nod. "I didn't even know he knew how to shoot, let alone that he owned a gun. He tried to shoot back but got hit in the chest." It all plays out in my mind with horrific detail. "His gun fell, so I dove for it, and that's when I got hit." A tear rolls down my cheek, and I wipe it away with the hand of my uninjured arm. "He died, and I returned fire on them, using all but two rounds. Seeing no other way out, I shot out the glass of the second-story window and jumped."

"You jumped out of a second-story window and got nothing but glass in your arm?"

"I landed on an awning and bounced off. So aside from the glass and some bruises, I was fine."

Both of the brothers look skeptical. But the truth is on my side. They'll see that, won't they? *God, please let them see the truth.*

"What happened then?" Tucker asks.

"I ran. As hard and as fast as I could." Reaching into my front pocket, I withdraw a thumb drive. "This is the patch I wrote to secure the accounts. I had to rip it out without ejecting, so there's no telling whether it's still usable. But you can look at it and see that I was trying to fix it. Not steal anything."

Both men are silent, and I can tell from their expressions that they're processing everything I've told them. The question now is: Will they believe me? Or turn me in for being a cold-blooded killer?

"Two days ago, you were wide-eyed and terrified. Now, I find out you not only shot out a second-story window to escape, but you also seem relatively calm for a person in your position."

I turn to Tucker. "Two days ago, I accidentally killed a man. That would put any decent human being into a shocked state. As for the server room, it was a matter of survival. Something I'm relatively adept at, thanks to my past. As for my disposition right now—you're right. I'm not scared. I'm *furious.* They killed my friend, sent people after my parents, and now are trying to frame me for some- . thing I would *never* do."

"Don't forget they supposedly bugged your apartment," Dylan adds.

I glare at him. "I tend to take things in stages, and, as I said, since I'm not currently residing at my apartment, the surveillance has no direct effect on me at the present moment."

Tucker crosses his arms. "I'm not one to refute evidence that's placed right in front of me. However, given your story and the sensitive nature of what Web Safe protects, I do think it's worth looking into."

"Thank you."

"We're doing this my way, though," he says. "And if you so much as present even the slightest risk to my family or me—I won't hesitate to eliminate that risk."

Read between the lines. I go after his family, he'll put me down.

I hate that he doesn't trust me, but I can be grateful he's not turning me over…yet. "Fine. We'll do it your way."

CHAPTER 11
TUCKER

I've spent every moment since I got home yesterday trying to rip this video apart. But whoever forged it did an incredible job ensuring it would pass even the highest level of scrutiny. I lean back in my chair and groan, then roll my shoulders.

Everything aches from sitting in this chair for so long.

At my feet, Tango looks up at me, clearly hopeful that my movement means I'll be getting up and he'll get some outside time. Which, to be honest, wouldn't be the worst thing in the world. Sunlight has a way of resetting me when I've spent far too long indoors.

Maybe in addition to 'plugging into computers' as Dylan says, I'm solar-powered. The thought brings a smile to my face, as does Tango's hopeful brown gaze.

"All right, boy, you've worn me down. Come on."

He jumps up as I do, then stares at me, almost annoyed, when I pause in the kitchen to grab a glass of water.

I've been at this for sixteen hours and barely even surfaced for food. Even then, the only reason I ate is because Mom brought me a plate and practically force-fed me breakfast. Since it's nearly four in the afternoon, I imagine she'll be coming around again soon—this time to make sure I don't skip dinner.

The air is warm, the sun still bright overhead as I make my way out onto my porch. From here, I can barely see the round pen just off the back of the barn where Nova, Elliot's wife, is working with one of our newest horses.

She'd been a homicide detective before washing up barely alive in our creek a couple of years ago. Now, she's a valued member of our team, a sister, and an expert with troubled horses. Even more so than the rest of us. She just has that touch, I suppose.

I take a seat on the porch steps as Tango runs around, doing what I call a "puppy freak-out" as he rolls in the grass and retrieves a stick to run around the yard with it. There are no fences, but he remains close.

As I'm sitting here, Bradyn comes over the hill on the back of his horse, Rev. He offers me a wave then guides Rev over toward me before dismounting and tethering his horse to the post in front of my house.

It's a new addition, something we added a few months ago in front of each of our homes, so when we're out and about, we can swing by for a restroom break or a quick drink.

"Hey," he greets, coming to sit in the chair beside me.

"How's the ride been?"

"Good. I found some loose fencing in the southeast pasture. Got it tightened up." He removes his leather gloves and sets them beside him. "Any update on the video?"

I take a deep breath. I hate that I haven't made any progress. Anything that will put Alice in the clear. "No. But I'm telling you, Bradyn, I just don't see her as a killer."

"I know you don't want to," he says. "But she could be lying."

I shake my head. "I feel it in my gut." As of now, Alice is currently sitting in a holding cell in the Pine Creek sheriff's station. She hasn't been booked but agreed to be held there until we could be sure she's not a threat to us or our families. Her parents were less than thrilled, but we told them that we were hoping to get her out within twenty-four hours.

A clock that is quickly running out.

At least there, she's under constant guard by Gibson Lawson, Pine Creek's newest sheriff, and someone we've known since we were kids. He'll keep her safe and out of the system until we know what we're dealing with.

She'd gone willingly too, in exchange for a chance to sit at my computer and pick apart that video on the off chance I couldn't prove it to be a fake.

"You really think she's innocent?"

I consider. "I really do, Bradyn. You should have seen her the night they came for her parents. She was terrified after what happened in that alley."

"Truly terrified or a really great actress," he adds.

"No. Because if she were acting, she wouldn't have dropped the front. She's moved past the shock and into anger. For her friend, her parents, her life—I just don't see a killer behaving this way. There are tells, you know? And Alice has none of the tells."

"We can't hold her forever," he tells me. "Eventually, we'll have to make the call. I'll leave it up to you."

"I'll go pick her up today. I'll offer to let her stay in my guest room. Then we can monitor the exterior of my house to make sure she doesn't leave." Since her parents are currently occupying the only extra studio cabin we have for our ranch hands, and I don't trust her enough to let her stay in my parents' guest room, mine is the next best option.

"Sounds good. But you need to watch your back too. I don't want you getting so close to this that you're not thinking clearly."

Since I can read between the lines, I arch a brow and look over at him. "I'm not romantically interested in the woman," I tell him. "So there's zero chance of getting distracted."

He doesn't even try to hide the fact that he doesn't

believe me. "No? You seem awfully interested in clearing her name."

"Because I believe she's innocent. I'd be doing the same if it were anyone else in her situation. Just because you, Elliot, and Riley all found love on the job doesn't mean I'm the same. I have no interest in a relationship—of any kind."

Bradyn shrugs. "Fine. I'll drop it. Let me know if you find anything, okay?"

"Will do. You guys are monitoring Web Safe's movements?"

"I spoke to Wilbur Huck this morning and let him know we were hired to find Frank's missing nephew. I left out Alice Sterling's name, but he was furious when he discovered the video of her shooting Ramiro had been leaked."

"I'm leaning toward the belief that he leaked it himself to make sure we didn't believe her story when we found her. If he's as deeply embedded in this as Alice says he is, then he'll be doing everything he can to cover his tracks."

Bradyn nods. "Honestly, that was my first impression too. We just need to decide whether or not she's actually guilty. And if she's not, then we need to find out the truth about what she and Ramiro Caine stumbled into."

THE PINE CREEK sheriff's station is relatively small with only two deputies, Sheriff Gibson, and a receptionist. I offer her a wave now as I step into the station. Gibson glances up through the glass window in his office then sets down whatever papers he was reading before heading out into the main area.

"Anything?"

"Nothing concrete," I tell him. "Though I'm certain she's innocent. I'd like to go ahead and take her out."

Gibson looks unconvinced. "Look, if she's not innocent, and I let a killer walk free—"

"I promise she's not going anywhere. But I could use her help. If someone from Web Safe did this, chances are good that she can prove it."

"How do you know she won't manipulate the footage to prove she's innocent?"

"Because I'll know," I reply. "Can you take me to the holding cells?"

Gibson hesitates only a second then nods. "Sure thing." He withdraws a set of keys from his pocket then unlocks a door at the back before pulling it open and leading me down a white hallway. Once we reach the end, I note two empty cells, with the third containing Alice.

She's lying on a cot, staring up at the ceiling.

"Don't get too comfortable," I say.

She practically leaps off the cot, crystal eyes wide and bright. "Did you find out who did it?"

"Not yet. But I'm working on it. You ready to get out?"

Her pale gaze narrows on me. "You're letting me out even though you have no proof that I'm not a cold-blooded killer?"

"I don't believe that you killed Ramiro," I say. "Though if you'd rather wait around—"

"Nope. No offense, Sheriff, these really are great cells. Excellent customer service." She retrieves her jacket from the cot, slips back into her boots, then gets up and starts toward the door as he unlocks it. "Thanks." She takes a deep breath.

"You're welcome," he replies with a tight smile.

"Are you hungry?" I ask.

"Starving," she replies before looking at Gibson again. "Again, no offense."

He chuckles. "None taken." Then she turns to me. "Lani came by and checked her arm, then cleaned and redressed it. She said that it's looking better now that she's on the antibiotics. But I'm to remind you that Alice is not— and these are Lani's exact words—to be anywhere in the vicinity of danger until Lani gives the all clear."

I laugh. *That's so Lani.*

"Like I told the good doctor, we'll do our best," Alice replies. "Won't we, Tucker?" Alice kneels down to lace up her combat boots.

I arch a brow. "Sure thing."

Gibson holds up his hands. "It's out of my hands now. I just hope you're right," he says to me.

"I am," I reply.

"Great. See you guys later." He heads down the hall, and I wait until Alice is done lacing up her boots before we follow.

"He hopes you're right—would that be in relation to my innocence?"

"It would."

"So you're the only one who believes me." If she's hurt, she hides it well.

"Pretty much. And I hate being wrong, so I really hope you're telling me the truth."

She eyes me with mild annoyance. "Would I tell you if I weren't?"

I smile. "Fair enough." Pulling open the door, I let Alice into the main room of the sheriff's office before following her out.

"So how far have you gotten on the video?" Alice asks.

"Not far. Whoever did it, does good work."

"I know who it likely was," she says, then waves at the receptionist. "Thanks again for the cookies, Jenny, they were delicious."

Jenny's entire expression lights up. "You're welcome, Alice. I hope to see you around! Though preferably not behind bars."

Alice laughs. "Me too. See you around!"

We step out onto the sidewalk, and I'm still staring at Alice.

"What?" She brushes her dark hair over her shoulder.

"I thought you said you weren't social."

"I'm not usually. But when you're stuck in a cage with no one to talk to, you improvise. Jenny is really sweet too, so that helps."

"They let you have cookies in jail?"

"Cookies and—get this—coffee." Her eyes go wide, and she smiles before turning her attention back to the street. She looks completely different despite spending the night in jail. Like the weight of the world has been lifted off her shoulders.

"You're in better spirits this morning."

"I had a talk with God and was reminded that, 'though a mighty army surrounds me, my heart will not be afraid.'"

"Psalm 27," I comment appreciatively.

"You know it?" she asks.

"I do. Well." It's literally tattooed on my chest. Though she'll never know that. *When evil people come to devour me, when my enemies and foes attack me, they will stumble and fall.* I got it right after I rescued Dylan. A reminder that, no matter how deep the waters are, God won't let me drown.

"It's probably my favorite of the Psalms," Alice says.

I can't tear my gaze from her as Bradyn's voice echoes in my mind. *"I don't want you getting so close to this that you're not thinking clearly."* Even as I think them, though, I shove the thoughts aside. *I am not getting too close.* She's just interesting, that's all. I'm allowed to be intrigued, right? That's not a crime.

No, but murder is.

"Do you like burgers?" I ask, shifting my attention away from thoughts that have no business being in my head.

"I love burgers. Especially if there are onion rings involved."

"I can help with that. Come on." I lead her down Main Street and toward the café.

"This place looks like it belongs in a Hallmark movie."

I laugh. "It's a great little town, that's for sure."

She turns as two teenagers trot their horses down the road, likely working with the animals in preparation for our town's fall parade, which takes place the first weekend of October. It might be nearly two months away, but they start early around here.

"A western Hallmark, for sure. Do you have a cowboy hat?" she asks, turning to me. "I bet you do."

Smiling, I reach for the door to the café. "I do. Now, do you want to discuss my boots or dive into the best burgers in the south?"

She pauses for a moment and takes a deep breath, then turns to me, a gorgeous smile on her face. "It smells like they're the best. And the boot discussion can definitely wait until I've eaten."

CHAPTER 12
ALICE

Tucker Hunt is not at all what I expected.

I mean, he's great with computers—which I did expect, given everything I read—but there's so much more to him. The guy is funny, strong, kind, and that's not even mentioning the absolute delight it is to look at him.

All lean muscles and bright blue eyes.

Keep it together, Alice, you have a murderer and hacker to catch.

As we've sat here in the café, I've seen him talk to *everyone*. And I mean everyone. The waitress—who he called Talia—as well as her husband Conner, who works back in the kitchen. Then he spoke to not one but two teenage girls who came in with "technical questions" we all knew they threw together when they saw him in the window.

They're not the only ones either. Everyone who caught sight of him in the window swung in, either to ask him questions about different things he's helping with around town or check in on his family.

The guy is apparently a celebrity here in town. Or at least, that's what it feels like.

"You sure seem popular," I comment.

He grins, and a small dimple pops out at the corner of his mouth. "That happens when you grow up in a small town."

"And go to war? Become a hero? Step up to run a search and rescue company where you continue playing the hero?"

Something darkens in his expression. "Something like that."

"I don't mean anything by it," I reply. "Seriously, no sarcasm here. I just find it interesting that you're so incredibly well known around here yet appear to be so humble."

"Appear to be?" He arches a brow.

"It could be a façade. I'll know once we've spent more time together." I smile at him, feeling so incredibly light compared to how I felt even a few hours ago. This peaceful lunch, where I can momentarily pretend we're just friends catching up, has been exactly what I needed.

"Let me know if you figure it out," he jokes back. "As soon as we're done here, we'll head over to the store and get you some more clothes, toiletries, things like that. Then we'll head out to the ranch. I guess our moms have really hit it off, so they're cooking dinner together. We can swing by and see them before heading to my house."

"That would be great." Even though I'm dying to get my hands on his computer and find out who's trying to frame me, the desire to see my parents is even greater than the desire to clear my name. I take a deep breath. Since there's not much else to talk about, I decide to pry a bit into the life of the man in front of me. "So tell me, Tucker Hunt, what *was* it like growing up in such a small town?"

"Great, actually. I mean, it had its challenges. Everyone knows everyone and all that. But in the same way, we all support each other. Like a big family."

"I like that. I always thought the idea of a small town was great."

"Never lived in one?"

I shake my head. "My parents and I lived in Sacramento when I was little. After that, I bounced around homes all through California, but none of them were small. Once my mom and dad adopted me, we stayed in San Diego."

"When I was a teenager, I used to dream of the big city," he confesses with a laugh. "But I knew I never really wanted to move."

"Yet you joined the service. Special Forces, right? Army?"

He arches a brow. "Did your research, huh?"

"I did."

Tucker nods appreciatively. "I wanted to see the world. Three of my older brothers were already in the service, and I was just in awe of them. They were superheroes in my eyes. Strong men off to save the world. So, I enlisted right out of high school."

"Your twin brother went in too, right?"

Tucker's expression darkens. It's a storm that passes over his face but is gone just as quickly as it came. "He did. What got you into computers?"

Touchy subject. Got it. I file that away for later. "My dad. He loves computers, gaming, and all that. I'd been with them for only six months before they bought me a computer. That's when I knew it would stick."

"Computers?"

I shake my head. "The family. I'd stayed with other families over the years, but no matter how well I behaved, I kept getting shuffled back. By the time I met the Sterlings, I was so jaded that I actually ran away once. It was right after that when they bought me the computer." I smile, the memory a heartwarming one. "They sat me down, and I remember thinking to myself, 'Well, here we go again. Time to go back,' but they started going over internet safety with me. I don't even know if I remember everything they said. I just stared at them, completely shocked they would want me."

"They seem like great people."

"They're the best," I reply with a smile, as Talia walks up with our food.

"Here we go. A cheeseburger with onion rings and ranch dressing. And a brisket burger with french fries, a side of mayonnaise, and ketchup."

"Thank you, Talia," Tucker says.

"You are welcome. Anything I can do for you guys?"

"Nope, we're good, thanks," he replies.

"You're welcome," she tells us then turns and leaves the table.

"Can I say grace?" Tucker asks.

"Go for it." I close my eyes, fold my hands, and bow my head.

"Lord, we thank You for this food. Please let it nourish our bodies and grant us the strength we need for the day. Please guide us as we move through the next few hours and lead us to the truth. I ask this in Jesus' name, amen."

"Amen," I reply, then crush an onion ring into an onion oval and dip it into the ranch dressing. I nearly groan with delight as it crunches in my mouth. I am *so* hungry. It's been over a week since I had anything that didn't come in a bag.

Glancing up, I can't help but stare at Tucker in horror as he mixes the ketchup *into* the mayonnaise, then adds black pepper to the concoction.

After a few moments, he glances up and sees me staring. "What?"

"What in the world are you doing?"

"Mixing the best dipping sauce in the world."

"Um. No. That, my dear Tucker, is an abomination."

"An abomination?" He finishes mixing the concoction with a fry then eats it before retrieving another fry and dipping it into the ketchup and mayonnaise mixture. "Don't knock it before you try it." He holds it out to me, and I stare at it.

"I've done some questionable things in my life. Trying that will not be one of them."

He doesn't sway. "Come on, Wonder, don't be scared. What, you can jump out of a second-story window, but you draw the line at tasting new food?"

I take a deep breath. "Fine. But you get to apologize if this makes me sick all over this pretty diner." I pluck the fry and stick it into my mouth without giving myself a second to think about it. The flavor hits my tongue, and I have to genuinely chew slowly because—oh my—*how have I been eating french fries without this?* "That is— wow. Okay, Tuck, you win."

His answering grin is so beyond attractive that my heart flips in my chest. *Oh, no. No. I can be attracted—I mean, look at him—but I will* not *be distracted.*

"I won't say I told you so."

"Humble man," I reply then steal another fry and more of the sauce.

Tucker laughs, clearly not at all bothered by the fact he

barely knows me and I'm already stealing his fries. "So, I know you said you prayed, which is why you're doing so well now. But I have to say—you're holding it all together quite impressively for a woman whose life has been turned upside down."

I take a bite of burger and wash it down with some sweet tea. "I learned a long time ago that life will often kick you when you're down. More often than not, really. But there's always a brighter day ahead."

"That sounds like a story."

I smile. "It is."

"Care to share?"

Chuckling, I take another fry. "The night of my thirteenth birthday, I snuck out of the foster home I was staying in. I was still in Sacramento at the time, so I took a bus over to the cemetery where my parents were buried." I take another drink. "I remember just sitting there in the cool grass, crying my eyes out because I was so completely alone. Everything ached. My heart, my head from the crying—my legs from walking as far as I did to the bus stop. The things I'd seen while I was either with families or in the system haunted me."

The memory is still clear as day to me, so as I sit back in the booth, it's as though I'm watching it play out right in front of my eyes.

"At some point, I fell asleep. I'm not sure how long I was out for, but when I felt someone shaking me, it was right before dawn. The sun's rays were just starting to sneak over the horizon." I smile as I recall what happened next. "It was a man who woke me up. Mr. Samuel," I say, recalling his name. "He asked me if I was okay, and I just started crying again. I don't even know why, but the tears just wouldn't stop. He sat down beside me and took my hand in his, then just held it. And as the minutes passed, my pain began to dissipate. My heart didn't hurt as bad, my body didn't ache, and the weight of everything just seemed less."

Tucker is watching me carefully, absorbing every word I say.

"After I stopped crying, I realized he'd been talking the entire time. I asked him what he was saying, and he told me he was talking to God and asking Him to take my pain. I told him that I didn't understand, and I asked him who God was and why He would care enough to want to take my pain away."

"No one ever talked to you about God?" Tucker asks.

"Nope. I can't remember my parents ever talking about Him—granted, I was young when they died—but none of the foster families I was in ever spoke about God." I recall the warmth of the sun on my face as we sat in that cemetery, right in front of the stone bearing my parents' names. "Samuel was kind. He told me that God is the Creator of the universe. That He formed each and every one of us with His hands then sent His Son Jesus here to save us. Naturally, I was fascinated. I asked him so many questions; I don't even remember them all." I smile as emotion wells up in my chest. "I just remember he was so kind, and he answered every question I had. We sat there as the sun rose over the horizon, and I hung on every word he said. Then he handed me a book and told me every answer I'd need for the rest of my life can be found in it."

"The Bible."

"The Bible," I repeat. "It was old and worn, but I still have it. It's actually one of the few things I grabbed from my apartment before I ran. Anyway, he told me that everything was going to be okay. That God's timing is perfect, and He loves me more than anything. Samuel walked me to the bus stop, said goodbye, and told me that, if I ever felt lost, to pray. And that, as long as I stand on God's Word, everything will be okay. That very same day, after the foster family called to have me sent to a troubled teen group home, I met the Sterlings." My smile spreads. "And everything began to look up. So whenever I feel overwhelmed or consumed, I pray. And it's by His grace I'm making it through everything I'm dealing with right now. Because if it weren't for Him, I would have given up the second Ramiro's life ended." As I speak the words, the image of Ramiro lying dead on that floor pops into my head.

I can still feel the sting of my bullet wound.

Feel the heat of the server tower at my back.

The fear coursing through my veins.

I eat another onion ring, hoping the distraction will pull me back to the present. And thank God it does.

"God has gotten me through a lot too. All of us, really." He takes a drink of tea. "I'm glad you're leaning on Him."

I nod in response. "About a year after I started living with the Sterlings, I asked to go back and see my birth parents' graves. They agreed without hesitation, and when I got there, I asked around about Samuel. I figured he had to work at either the funeral home or the church nearby, but no one had heard of him. Honestly, I think some people thought I made him up. I mean, a man wandering a graveyard at dawn with a Bible, preaching to strangers?" I laugh. "They thought I'd dreamed him. But I *know* he was there. And not just because I have a worn Bible to prove it."

Tucker smiles softly. "Maybe he was an angel."

"I've definitely had that thought."

"I believe God works in many different ways."

I smile at him. "Amen to that."

CHAPTER 13
TUCKER

"My baby girl," Jemma coos as she rushes out onto the porch the second we pull up in front of my parents' farmhouse. The older woman wraps her arms around Alice, and her daughter does the same. They stand there for a few moments, completely silent, just holding onto each other.

The door opens again, and Fred steps out. Without a word, he joins in on the hug, wrapping his arms around both his wife and daughter. It's a heartwarming moment to see family reunited…most of the time.

A familiar ache blooms in my chest, so I rub the heel of my palm against it in the hopes it'll chase away the memories of the day we brought Dylan home.

"I just put a fresh pot of coffee on," my mom calls from the still-open doorway.

"Thank you so much, Ruth," Jemma replies as she takes

her daughter's uninjured arm and leads her into the house. "This is our Alice." The Sterling matriarch is positively glowing with joy as she stands beside her daughter.

My mom smiles. "Alice, it is lovely to meet you. I've heard a lot of amazing things about you."

"Thanks. It's really great to meet you too, Mrs. Hunt."

"Please, call me Ruth. Come on in." She ushers all three of the Sterlings inside.

"We'll be there in just a second," my dad tells her then heads over toward where I'm standing near the porch railing.

My mom offers an understanding smile before heading inside with them.

"Everything all right?" I ask. I may not be a teenager anymore, but that doesn't mean I don't recognize my dad's "we need to talk" face. It's just as clear now as it was back then.

He doesn't respond right away, just glances back at the door and leans against the railing. "You're sure she's innocent?" he asks. "I saw that video. It looked incriminating enough to have her behind bars."

"It's a fake. I just have to prove it." Even if I had doubted her before, our time at the diner would've changed my mind. Not because of the story she told me, but because of the *way* she told it. The love she had in her eyes when she spoke of God and how He is keeping her together. She's not a woman capable of murder or treason.

If only the police would take my word for it.

He sighs. "Then I trust your gut, son. Just—please be safe. We've had a lot of close calls in our family, and I'm terrified it's not going to be a happy ending one of these days."

"We're all good, Dad." I clasp a hand on his shoulder and offer a reassuring smile.

He takes a deep breath then runs a hand through his silver hair. "Is there anything I can do to help?"

"Just pray that we can figure this out so Alice and her family can return to some semblance of normalcy."

"That, I can do."

"THIS IS AN EPIC SETUP," Alice says, jaw dropped, as she surveys the wall of monitors in my office. "Like, seriously, I could live in this room."

"Thanks." I've always been proud of my setup, but for some reason, right now, even with as impressed as she looks, I'm feeling a tad self-conscious. Not because I think mine is subpar by any means, but when compared to the resources Web Safe has, it definitely pales in comparison.

"These are all areas of the ranch you have cameras on?" She points to the security footage on the wall-mounted monitors.

I nod. "With what we do, we've had a few times over

the years where we've needed to keep clients here to protect them for a time. That, and some trouble we had last year, when someone paid people to cause trouble on the ranch, means we've upped security."

"Someone paid people to come mess with your ranch?"

"They did."

"Wow. They must not have wanted to live in this world long. Five brothers—all with Special Forces training living on the same piece of property? This place must be untouchable."

"We have our weaknesses," I admit. "And with as many acres as we have, there's plenty of blind spots. We've just done the best we can with protecting the places that matter most."

"The people," she says with a soft smile.

"Exactly."

Our gazes hold for a moment, and I find myself unable to look away. She blushes and tears her gaze away from mine.

"Do you all live here on the ranch?"

"We do. My parents deeded us all an acre apiece to build our houses on, and we all pitch in around the ranch. Though Bradyn pretty much runs things."

"Your eldest brother?"

I nod.

"That's so great. What a cool way to grow up." She steps back toward my computer. "And this is gorgeous."

Alice runs her fingers over the top of my desktop in the way a mother would run her fingers over the face of her child. Or so I imagine they would.

"I built it last year," I blurt. "The computer. My old one went to Riley. His wife uses it for work now."

"That's awesome." She smiles at me. "So, you have at least one married brother. Do you have someone special in your life? I noticed only one coffee mug on the counter."

I run a hand over the back of my neck as heat climbs over the skin. "Three of my brothers are married, Riley being the most recent one to stand at the altar. Uh, I'm single, and so are Dylan and Lani." *Why is this making me so nervous?*

"No southern belles catch your eye?" she asks. She's being playful, but for some reason, it's hitting a bit harder. *Is she prying?*

"I'm not actively searching."

"Broken heart on the mend?"

"Just not looking," I tell her, trying to keep my tone level when it feels like it's thirty degrees hotter in here than it actually is. Besides, it's not a complete lie, though it's not the truth either. "I'm pretty busy with work and the ranch. There aren't many women who would be patient with all of that, and I'm not one to put only part of me into something. When I do find that someone special, I need to be able to dedicate a whole lot more of me to the relationship than I can now."

"Honorable. Not a lot of men think like that."

"I'm not like a lot of men."

"I get that feeling." Her pale crystal gaze locks on mine, and for a moment, the rest of the world simply fades away.

Then, the front door opens, breaking whatever tension was between us.

"Tucker, you here?" Dylan calls out.

"In here." I clear my throat. *Get it together, Hunt.*

Tango rushes in first, brown eyes wide, ears forward, tail wagging. He slams into my legs and does a circle, then sits so I can pet him. "Hey, boy," I reply with a laugh.

"He was not up for being distracted anymore," Dylan says as he comes into the room. His gaze lands on Alice. "Miss Sterling."

"Dylan. It's just Alice, please."

He doesn't respond to her before shifting to me. "I wanted you to know Web Safe made a move on Frank."

"What kind of move?" I step forward, a bite of anger surging through me. All I can think about is what they tried to do to Alice's parents.

"Accused him of hacking the system and leaking that security video. Apparently, Find Me is currently doing what it can to thwart a warrant being issued for their system. Web Safe is requesting a thorough vetting of Find Me's systems for proof that it was used to hack in and steal that video."

Anger burns through me. They're lies. All lies in an

attempt to distract us now that Bradyn told Wilbur we were trying to find Ramiro. My guess is that the bruisers taken from Alaric's custody also told whoever hired them that I have the Sterlings.

"There's no way Frank or anyone at Find Me could have gotten into that system." Alice crosses her arms. "And Web Safe knows that."

"Of course they know it," I say as I cross my arms too. "They're just looking for another route to take if they can't pin the data hack on you."

"If they get into his system, they can plant information that makes it look as though he did what they're saying," Alice says, eyes widening.

"Which is why he asked me to come talk to you, Tucker." Dylan fully faces me. "Frank wants to know if there's anything you can do to hide the more sensitive information in Find Me's database. Names, ages, pictures of the people they've saved. You're the only one he trusts." He casts a side-eye at Alice, who holds up her hands.

"You don't trust me. Got it. I'll make myself scarce for now." Alice leaves the room. Clearly curious about our new roommate, Tango trots after her.

As soon as she's gone, I turn toward Dylan. "She's innocent."

"I'm not saying she isn't, but given that she's wanted for murder, based on fairly clear video footage, I'm also not open to trusting her at the moment."

"Treating her like a criminal isn't right, Dylan." My brother has trust issues. There's no denying that, but for some reason, the fact that he refuses to show Alice any trust is irritating me. A lot more than it would be if it were anyone else.

Dylan takes a deep breath. "Fair enough. I'll apologize on my way out."

I nod. "Thanks for taking care of Tango. I didn't want to take him into town, and leaving him here alone just seemed mean."

"No problem. He ran off quite a bit of energy, so he should be crashing in a few hours."

"Good to know. I'll get to work on Frank's database. Depending on how good Web Safe is, I might be able to design a way for the information to be invisible to them; that way, they can't get it even with a warrant."

"I'll let him know." Dylan heads out of the office, so I follow him. Alice is sitting on the couch, petting Tango, who is lying lovingly beside her. "I'm sorry for being rude," Dylan says. "It's not my intention to make you feel like a criminal."

"It's all good. I'd be untrusting of me too. But I promise you, I didn't kill Ramiro. He was my best friend."

Dylan shrugs. "Tucker thinks you're innocent, so who am I to argue?" He turns to me. "See you both at dinner later?"

"See you there."

With one final nod at Alice, he leaves my house and closes the door behind him.

"You and your twin are two totally different people," she says again.

I sigh, looking at the door. "We didn't use to be. Come on, I could use your help with this. We need to make sure Frank Loyotta's company doesn't become exposed. I won't let them be collateral damage in this fight."

CHAPTER 14
ALICE

"Nice work." Tucker leans back in his chair and glances around his monitor to where I'm sitting at a plastic fold-up table.

I shut my laptop and grin. "Couldn't get in?"

"Nope. His company should be covered now." Tucker stands and rolls his shoulders. "One problem down."

After I started my program to prove the surveillance video of me murdering Ramiro is a fake, we started immediately working on protecting Frank Loyotta's company—something we've been at for nearly three hours as we worked to bury everything we can behind a firewall that is invisible to anyone who *isn't* looking for it.

We just have to hope that whoever looks through the system won't be expecting it. The information available is all basic—administrative employee information, their books, all that. We were careful not to hide anything that would make it look as though there was information missing. But the victims Find Me has rescued, the names of their rescuers, and anything else that should be protected are hidden.

My stomach churned when I scanned the ages of some of the victims they've rescued from traffickers over the years. If I could do anything in this world with the snap of a finger, it would be to put an end to that horrific nightmare so many suffer through.

"I know we're having dinner in an hour, but—coffee?" Tucker's question pulls me from my thoughts.

I check the status of the video decryption, frustrated that it still hasn't finished. "Yes. Please. A vat of it."

He smiles. "You got it."

I follow him out of the room, and Tango raises his head to look at us. "*Hier,* Tango," I say, using the German word for 'here' since that's what I've noticed Tucker using.

The dog jumps up and happily trots over toward me as I follow Tucker out into the hallway.

"Do you speak German?" he questions as he puts grounds into the basket of his coffeepot. "I heard you call Tango."

And then, I realize that Tango is a service animal, and we're not supposed to command someone's working dog. "Oh, sorry. I shouldn't have called him. He's a working dog—"

"No, it's fine. I was just surprised you used the

command. Wasn't sure it was because you've heard me use it or you actually speak German."

"Fluently," I reply. "I took it in high school, then again in college. After I graduated, I spent a summer in Munich with my parents. It was a dream trip."

"Munich is gorgeous."

"You've been?"

He nods. "A few times. Once was an extended layover, once was for a job, and the third time was by accident."

"How do you accidentally end up in Germany?"

He laughs. "It's a long story."

"We have time."

Tucker presses a button then turns to face me. "I jumped out of a plane at the wrong time."

"I'm sorry—you *what?*"

He grins, and my stomach does that ridiculous little flip it does whenever I see his dimples. "We were training, and I was supposed to be dropping into Salzburg. The coordinates were off, though, so I missed the jump and ended up in Munich."

"I cannot even begin to understand one's desire to jump out of a perfectly working plane."

He chuckles. "It's a skillset I hope to never have to use again. How about you? Aside from speaking German—anything random you like to do?"

"I'm an excellent yarnist."

"Yarnist?"

I laugh. "Crochet. I love to crochet."

"Crochet? As in a hook and yarn?" He snaps his fingers. "I get it now, yarnist. Cute."

"It was something my mom taught me when I had trouble sleeping. The movements soothed my nerves. After that, it just kind of became habit. While I was waiting for a program to run or watching a video, I'd crochet. There was one year I made an obscene number of beanies."

Tucker laughs, and my own smile spreads. "That's amazing."

"Maybe when all of this is done, I'll make you a beanie as a thank you for clearing my good name."

"Maybe." His smile falls just a bit, as though he didn't want to be reminded that we're only together because of a false murder charge. The coffeepot beeps, so he retrieves two mugs and sets them down on the counter before filling them up. "Do you take anything in yours?"

"Milk and honey if you have it."

"Honey?"

"Don't come at me, mayonnaise and ketchup."

"Hey, you said it was delicious." He hands me a glass jar with amber honey.

"Doesn't mean it's not weird." I lift the wooden lid, which has a honey stick attached, then drizzle it into my coffee before mixing it up. "This looks delicious. And incredibly fancy. Mine typically comes in a plastic bear."

He chuckles. "It's from our bees."

I offer him the jar. "Your bees?"

He nods. "We have twenty-two hives here on the property."

"You are living the dream, Tucker, do you know that?" After putting some milk into my coffee, I offer him back the gallon. "Is that from your cows too?"

Tucker snorts. "No. It's from the dairy farm on the other side of town. We do grow our own vegetables, and all the meat we eat is raised here on the ranch."

I continue staring at him. Not because I doubt what he's saying but because I have apparently stumbled into my dream life. My parents and I always talked about how badly I wanted to leave the city and homestead. They, unfortunately, don't share the same fascination with country living as I do, but that never stopped them from sending me the occasional real estate listing for land in California.

Land that was *way* out of my price range, of course.

"What?" he asks.

"Nothing. It's just like I said; you're living the dream." I take a sip of my coffee, savoring the honey-and-milk-flavored caffeine jolt as it dances on my tongue. "This is delicious."

He eyes my mug and the container of honey on the counter. "Okay. Fine. You tried mine, I'll try yours." He sets his mug down, adds some honey to it, then retrieves the milk from the refrigerator. As he adds it to his mug and stirs, I slip the gallon back into the fridge, then stand there, waiting for him to try it.

He eyes it in what is probably the same way I eyed the mixture at the café earlier. Then he takes a drink. A few seconds pass with his expression unreadable. "That is *really* sweet."

I laugh. "You can add less honey next time. But it's good, isn't it?"

He takes another drink. "It's good."

I beam at him, delighted that I was able to get him to try something new too. "The program should be done in the next half hour or so, but I would love to get outside for a bit if that's okay."

"Absolutely. I can show you a little more of the ranch if you'd like. Then we can swing over to my parents' house for dinner."

"That sounds awesome." I take a drink of coffee. "Do you have mugs that travel well?"

<hr>

"This is the main horse barn," Tucker tells me as we step inside a large red metal barn. The horses that are inside immediately call out and stick their long faces over the gates. My heart somersaults with joy.

Literally my dream.

"Hey there," I greet the first horse as I run my hand

over her midnight-colored face.

"That's Midnight, my sister-in-law Kennedy's horse."

"Fitting name for a pretty—girl?" I ask, glancing at Tucker for confirmation. He nods. "Very pretty girl," I coo again then continue moving down the aisle. A dark brown horse sticks its face out as I pass, so I pause and run my hand over the white star on its forehead.

"That's my horse, Jax."

"Hi, Jax, it's nice to meet you." He snorts in response and bumps his nose into my arm. "I think he likes me."

Tucker clears his throat. "Yeah, I think so too. Uh, so are you hungry? I can smell the brisket from here."

"Same." My stomach growls. "And yes, very hungry. I know we ate only a few hours ago, but it feels like it's been forever." I pet Jax again, then slowly turn and make my way back down the breezeway, noting the empty stalls. "Where are the rest of the horses?"

"Either being ridden or out to pasture. We have the utility vehicles we use daily for just getting to and from our houses, but unless it's a big job, we utilize the horses for everything that doesn't require a tractor."

"How many horses do you guys have on the property?"

"Twenty-seven."

"That's a lot of horses."

"We rescued most of them. Horses that were deemed a lost cause or were so badly abused they could barely be handled. A good portion of them came from slaughterhouses."

"Slaughterhouses? That's horrible!"

"It is. We try to save as many as we can. A lot of the ones we've saved are on other ranches or in rescues around the country."

I stop in my tracks and stare at him. "Really?"

He nods. "My oldest brother, Bradyn, is great with them. He and Kennedy have kind of taken over that portion of the ranch."

"Kennedy is his wife?" Tucker nods, and we begin walking again.

"Wow. Tucker Hunt. A hero of men and horses."

"I do what I feel God calling me to do. He gets all the glory."

"Amen to that. It's really great what you guys have going on here," I tell him as we step out into the fading sun.

"We love it." He shoves his hands into his pockets as we cross the gravel driveway that separates his parents' home from the main barn. He drove me all around the ranch, including some of the pastures where the cattle are kept.

I've seen gardens, chickens, the beehives—it's all so amazing. And even as much as I love technology, I'd happily step away from it to be in a place like this. Then again, Tucker hasn't had to give it up. Maybe there's hope for both someday.

We're just heading up onto the porch when a truck pulls into the drive. A tall, muscled man with dark hair and bright hazel eyes climbs out of the driver's side. He moves around to open the door for a petite blonde, and I'm captivated by the beauty of both of them. The man is a Hunt brother, there's no doubt about it. Even if I hadn't done my research on the family, I would've recognized him as one.

They all share certain ruggedly handsome features and dark hair, though this man's hair is a bit longer than the others. Based on what I dug up about the family, this is Bradyn Hunt, the eldest brother, and his wife, Kennedy.

She offers me a bright smile as Bradyn opens the back door and lets his dog jump out. "You must be Alice," Kennedy greets.

"I am." I shake her offered hand. "And you're Kennedy."

"I am," she replies. "Which means you've done your research and already know my husband." Bradyn and his dog climb the steps.

"I do. Nice to meet you, Bradyn Hunt." I offer him my hand.

"You too," he replies. His voice is slightly gruffer than Tucker's, his expression too. I get the feeling that Tucker is the more relaxed of the brothers, and I honestly can't wait to meet the rest to prove that hypothesis one way or the other.

Two down, two to go.

"Is this—Bravo?" I ask, hoping I'm right on the phonetic-alphabet naming. When I say his name, the handsome German shepherd looks over at me, ears perked.

"It is," Bradyn replies.

"You're a handsome boy too," I say to the pup, who wags his tail so fast his entire body shakes alongside it.

Tango jumps forward, clearly jealous of the affection Bravo is getting, and the two start wrestling.

As they're running around chasing each other, a UTV drives up and parks alongside the truck. A large dog jumps out of the back and joins the fray as another Hunt brother— this one Elliot—climbs out, his baseball cap on backward. A woman with fiery red hair climbs out of the other side, and the two link hands as they head up the porch.

"This is Elliot and his wife, Nova," Tucker tells me.

"It's nice to meet you both," I greet. "I'm Alice." I have to actively fight against the urge to step back just so I can stare at the three of them side by side. *These brothers were undersold by their files. These men are straight warriors. Like the kind I'd see in a movie, planning an all-out assault on a compound where the odds are stacked against them.*

"You too," Nova says with a friendly smile. From what I learned about the family, I know she's a former detective with Dallas P.C. and now works alongside the brothers in their company. Most of the missions she does are with her husband Elliot. Which, even given the nature of their business, is super romantic.

"Alice," Elliot greets. "I hear we're trying to clear you of murder."

"Elliot," Nova scolds. "Sorry, he doesn't have much tact."

I let out a light laugh. "He's not wrong. I'm working on shredding the false video they released. I have faith it will all come to light. Just a matter of when."

Elliot offers me a nod, and we all turn as Dylan pulls up to the house in a black truck. He and Delta jump out. Honestly, he looks more relaxed than any other time I've seen him as he makes his way to the porch. Is it because his brothers are here?

"Got that fence patched," he says. "Riley's getting cleaned up; then he and Jules will be over." Dylan turns to me. "Alice."

"Dylan."

With a final nod in my direction, he heads into the house.

"He's a bit on the quiet side," Kennedy tells me.

"So I've noticed."

"Shall we head inside?" Tucker asks, clapping his hands together. "I'm starving and would love to con Mom into a taste-tester's bite of banana pudding."

CHAPTER 15
TUCKER

Alice *shouldn't* fit so well.

Yet I'm sitting here, watching her chat with Lani as though they've known each other since forever. She and Kennedy have a riding date for tomorrow, apparently, and my parents are already discussing the three of them joining us for church on Sunday.

Sunday? That's, like, three days away.

We'll surely have this all figured out by then, right?

My stomach twists, and I take another bite of dinner even though I was full a long time ago. I need the distraction though, because right now, it's all I can do to keep from staring at Alice Sterling as she interacts with my family as though we're all old friends.

"You doing okay?" Dylan asks me quietly. He's sitting to my right, with Riley at my left. Alice is sandwiched between Lani and Kennedy, across from me and two chairs down.

"Fine. Why?"

"Call it twin-tuition. And you're not your usual chatty self. You seemed fine earlier. Did something happen?"

"No." I sigh. I should keep my mouth shut, especially given how he feels about Alice. But I've never been one to lie to Dylan. Not when asked a direct question. "I'm just catching feelings that I don't want to have."

"Catching feelings?" Dylan arches a brow. "That's an interesting way to phrase it. How old are you again?"

I glare at him. "It's something Lani said the other day. Shut it."

Dylan grins, but I notice that it doesn't reach his eyes. Honestly, it's so rare that a smile does these days. Every now and then, I get a glimpse of my twin before his suffering, but most of the time, he's this other version of himself.

Guarded and broken. Barely pieced together.

"How about you clear her of murder before you catch those feelings?" he advises.

"Working on it. She's running a program on the video right now. It should be done by the time we get back."

"And if that comes back the same as every other check you've done?"

My heart is heavy at the mere thought. I *feel* that she's innocent. But—what if I'm wrong? Will I turn her in?

I know the answer. Despite how I'm starting to feel, I

will turn her in because, if she *did* murder Ramiro, then it's the right thing to do.

"I'll do the right thing," I reply. "But it won't come back the same."

"If it helps, I hope you find something too. And as for the *catching feelings*—ridiculous expression, by the way— you could catch worse ones."

I snort. "Thanks, Dylan."

"Who's ready for dessert?" Mom announces as she stands. "I made banana pudding, minus one bite," she adds, glaring at me with a knowing look. "Jemma baked the vanilla cookies that are inside from scratch."

"Sign me up for a bowl!" Riley calls out.

Beside him, Jules laughs, and I can't help but notice just how much my brother's wife has changed over the last year and a half since they met. Her haunted gaze is lighter, her smile easier to come by.

Will that be Dylan someday?

Will unexpected love heal him too?

I look at Alice, and for the first time, my vow to not find love until Dylan learns to love again is nearly too heavy to carry. But I just can't stomach the idea of being happy when he can't be.

My throat constricts, a desire for fresh air suddenly so strong I cannot ignore it. So, pushing up from my chair, I say, "I'll be right back," then head out of the room and onto the front porch.

The night air is still hot, but it's fresh as I draw it into my lungs and lean against the porch railing. For years now, I've been haunted by the knowledge of what Dylan suffered through.

I know that there will never be a day that goes by where I'm not reminded of everything those monsters stole from him. My hands clench into fists, and I drop my head.

Lord, please take these thoughts from me. Please cleanse them from me, Lord. Please take this pain. And please, God, place Your Mighty Hand upon my brother and heal him. I ask this in the name of Jesus. Amen.

Behind me, the door opens and closes softly.

"It's a gorgeous night," Jules says as she steps up beside me and rests her palms against the sturdy porch railing.

"It is."

"I see the weight you're carrying," she says, cutting straight to the point of why she followed me out here.

I turn toward her, surprised. Jules and I have always gotten along—she's great—but we've never really had any in-depth conversations. She's far too guarded for that.

"Forgive me for overstepping; I just notice it because I recognize the same look in your eyes that my grandfather had in his for a long, long time." She smiles softly.

After she was kidnapped and assaulted, she turned to alcohol to cope and ended up in and out of rehab. Her grandfather stood at her side through all of it though, even as he didn't know the truth about what happened to her until right before he died.

"He'll see it someday too," she says. "If he doesn't already."

"I just wish I could get him to see that his life didn't end in that jail cell."

Jules reaches out and gently touches my shoulder. "He will. But you can't do what my grandfather did, Tucker— don't let Dylan's pain keep you from being happy. You can take care of yourself even as you care for him too. Put your oxygen mask on first and all that."

"Thanks, Jules." The burning in my throat intensifies as I fight to keep the pain at bay. It wasn't me who suffered, but my heart and soul broke that day all the same. And the truth is, oxygen mask included, I'd put Dylan before myself every single moment of every day. Just as I know he'd do for me, which is why he can never know the vow I made to myself.

"You're welcome. I'm going to go get some banana pudding. I just wanted to check on you." She heads toward the door.

"Hey, Jules?"

"Yeah?" She turns toward me, one hand on the door handle.

"I'm thankful God brought you into our family. And that Riley wasn't stubborn enough to mess it up."

She laughs. "I thank Him every day for bringing me here too."

"THAT WAS the best dinner I've had in *ages*." Alice takes a seat behind her computer.

I step up beside her and watch as she unlocks her computer. "Yeah. It was good."

She glances over her shoulder. "Are you okay?"

No. "Fine. Just ready to see if you managed to crack this video wide open." I force a smile. *What if she didn't? What if I'm wrong? How long can I keep looking for the truth when the evidence is staring me right in the face?*

"Same." She opens the program, and all of my hopes go up in flames. "It's not possible." Alice scrolls through the results, but they're right there—right in front of my face.

Valid.

The video is valid.

It was not tampered with.

Alice turns toward me. "Tucker, I promise, that is *not* me in that video."

"We've run it through every program we have, Alice." I cross my arms. "I think it's time you start telling me the truth."

"I *am* telling you the truth! Put it up on your screen."

"Alice—"

"Just do it, okay? If you still don't believe me, I'll call the sheriff myself."

Cheeks red, she's staring at me with such conviction in her eyes, I just don't see how she could be lying.

So without arguing further, I cross over toward my computer and log in, then turn on the projector and send the image onto the large screen on my wall. I play it, watching the murder play out right in front of me.

"Pause it," she says.

I do.

"First of all, I never wear my hair in a braid."

"Alice, that is not enough—"

She whirls on me. "I told you. I had a foster mom who would braid my hair every day, but she'd braid it so tight I'd get a headache. Ever since then, I literally cannot braid my hair. I just don't do it." She gestures to the shirt. "And this—is not my shirt. I was wearing a black long-sleeve shirt and gray slacks that night. You know how I know? Because they were my favorite pair of pants, and I had to throw them away, thanks to the blood. I wasn't wearing a pencil skirt and a white blouse. I never wear skirts. Another fun side effect of a traumatic event," she snaps. I don't dig, but the anger at what she's insinuating infuriates me.

Even still, I bury it down because, right now, all that matters is proving she didn't murder Ramiro, even though everything points to her doing so.

"All circumstantial."

"Yes, but it's the truth." She groans. "I don't know how they did it, but I'm telling you—this is *not* me."

"I don't see how they could have faked a video good enough to have both of us stumped." Even as I stare at the screen with the results right in front of my face, I *know* she's innocent. But how do you prove something you know to be true when the evidence is literally pointing toward it? It might as well be a large, flashing neon sign that reads 'murderer.'

"I don't know either." Alice crosses her arms and turns toward the computer. "But I'm not lying." She takes a deep breath then faces me. "Look, if you want to take me in— fine. Do it. I won't stop you. We had a deal. You let me prove the video was a fake, or I let you have me arrested. I couldn't prove it." She's staring me down, daring me to make that move. "But I'm *not* guilty."

I told Dylan I would.

I said that if it came back valid, I would turn her in because it was the *right* thing to do. So why does the thought of doing so—of following through on my word— feel wrong?

"It's late," I tell her. "Nothing can be done tonight."

Alice stares at me. "How do you know I won't run?"

"Because I'm your only hope, and you know it."

CHAPTER 16
ALICE

I can't sleep.

Not even a few minutes. I *know* this video is a fake, but even as I sit here staring at it, rewatching it over and over again, I'm even starting to wonder how it's possible. That woman is not me—the braid, the clothes—but she *looks* enough like me that, in this grainy footage, it might as well be me.

And Ramiro—he's wearing the same clothes. A gray T-shirt and dark jeans. My chest aches, so I rub the heel of my palm against it, then get up and walk to the large picture window overlooking the ranch. The moon is high tonight, illuminating the world beyond this pane of glass in silver.

Does Tucker stand here often? Does he take in this scene every day and on nights when he can't sleep? I glance down the hallway where he said his bedroom is. Is he sleeping now? Or unable to sleep like me?

"Because I'm your only hope, and you know it."

He's not wrong, which is why I'm still here. If he wakes up in the morning and chooses to still turn me in, then I'll have to face that. But I know that, even if I'm cuffed and hauled away to be shoved in a cage, he'll keep looking for the truth.

Because I may not have known Tucker Hunt long, but he strikes me as a man who won't rest until he knows—without a doubt.

My computer dings, so I take a seat behind it again and check my email.

One new message from Logger91. *Logan.* Quickly, I open it, my heart pounding. Did he find something? There's no message or subject line, just a voice memo attached as a file. I stare at it a few moments, honestly wondering whether or not I should wait for Tucker to open it.

What if this is the key piece of evidence that will clear me?

Then again, what if it's only another red herring with my name on it?

And with that in mind, I decide it will be better if I hear it first, just in case. If it's not helpful, I can keep it to myself—for now. But if it's something that helps, then I can get Tucker to stop looking at me like I'm a liar.

I tap the attachment, and my entire screen freezes.

It pixelates, starting from one corner to the other as the virus takes over the computer byte by byte. Why would Logan—and then it hits me.

Logan wouldn't maliciously hack my computer. But someone else would. Someone who knew that I went to Logan for help. Which means everything on Tucker's network is at risk.

Without waiting any longer, I rush to Tucker's bedroom and bang on the door. "Tucker!"

He rips it open seconds later, bare-chested and sleepy-eyed. "What is it?"

I'm momentarily stunned by the sight of his muscled chest. Of the tattoo right over his heart. *Psalm 27.*

"What's happening?

His sharp words snap me back into reality. "My computer is being hacked."

I step out of the way as he rushes down the hallway and into the room. "Is it connected to the network?"

"Yes."

He turns on his heel and rushes down toward his office. As soon as he's inside, he rips the power cord to the router out of the wall—his attempt to keep whoever is hacking my computer from accessing anything on his database.

As soon as it's shut down, he moves to his computer and removes it from the internet completely. Even though it's not connected, he needs to sever that connection just in case.

"Alice, are you there?" Logan's voice echoes down the hall, and I freeze, my gaze locking with Tucker's.

"How—"

"I don't have time to wait. I have to believe this is getting to you."

I sprint out of Tucker's office and down the hall toward my computer. The screen is black except for a blinking light in the center.

"I'm sorry for the theatrics, but I couldn't risk anyone else getting their hands on this. At least this way it'll be harder for them to know—" He trails off. His tone is strained, and even though I can't see him, I can imagine his worried expression.

"Who is that?" Tucker demands.

"My friend," I say. "Logan."

"Look, I don't know what you and Ramiro got into, but it's big. I did some digging like you asked, and they're watching me." He whispers that last part. "I found bugs in my apartment the day after we met. That's what prompted me to really start digging. Now they're saying you killed Ramiro in the server room. That the drive-by was a cover for the investigation. I know you didn't do it even though I saw the video. You never braid your hair. The idiots didn't get it right. They didn't get the details—" He trails off.

I glance back at Tucker, whose jaw is set as he listens.

"I know you too well to believe that you would ever hurt anyone. They told me to eliminate contact with you.

That if I was talking to you, I would be implicated as part of it. But because I care about you, I need to warn you: things are changing here. Big-time. They're cleaning house. Seven patch workers have been fired. They're saying that the information was stolen by you, and they don't know the depth of the breach yet. I imagine I'm next, but they haven't—" A loud bang echoes through the line. "They're here. I'm out of time. I need you to know that you're onto something. Keep pressing, Alice. You're the smartest person I know, and if anyone can figure this out, it's you. Huck—" Another loud bang. "He's in on it. But he's not the only o—" A gunshot. I flinch. "I pray this gets—" he trails off, his tone strained as if he's fighting to even speak now. "Always lov—"

The message ends.

My heart is in my throat.

Tears roll down my cheeks.

"No. No." I rush toward my computer and start hammering keys, even though I know it won't work. Whatever he used locked it down completely. Not surprising since Logan was a white-collar hacker when he got out of the army. It's why Web Safe hired him.

"Alice." Tucker grabs my hand, and I whirl on him.

"No! He was only in this because of me! I asked him to get involved! He's fine. He has to be fine." I charge forward, and Tucker stops me by wrapping his arms around me. The sound of the gunshot echoes in my mind.

I couldn't even see it this time, but I can picture it easily enough.

I've lived through one tragedy; it's not hard to visualize another.

Bullets all work the same. Tearing through flesh and muscle, destroying the spark of life that once resided within. Spots invade my vision as I try to suck in breath after breath, yet find none. Why is this happening? Why?

"Breathe, Alice," Tucker tells me. He holds me against his strong chest, and I can hear the steady beating of his heart. Doing my best to focus on it, I let the sound of his life ground me in this moment. *Thump, thump.*

"He wasn't involved from the beginning," I whisper. "I asked him to keep an ear to the ground for me. Tell me he's okay, Tucker. Please. Tell me that was something else."

"I won't lie to you, and I don't know. But if you give me a minute, I can put out feelers."

I nod then pull away from him. Tucker walks back to his bedroom, returning with a shirt on and his cell phone, which is already pressed to his ear. "I need you to do a check on someone." He looks over at me.

"Logan Tarmac," I tell him. "He lives a few blocks from my apartment. Works at Web Safe."

"Logan Tarmac," he repeats. "Yeah. Thanks. Call when you know something." He ends the call then shoves his phone into the pocket of his sweats and crosses over toward me. In a tender gesture, he puts both hands on my shoulders. "Let's have some coffee, okay? A buddy of mine is going to go check on him. He's a homicide detective with the LAPD."

"Okay." It all feels surreal. But who knows? Knowing Logan, he's probably just fine. I bet we'll all laugh about this one day. Once the smoke is cleared and everything goes back to normal.

I follow Tucker into the kitchen and take a seat on a bar stool as he preps the coffeepot.

"They're here. I'm out of time."

He'd known they were coming, which is why he'd written the virus to deliver the message. He probably killed his computer in the process, just as he did mine. My chest aches, and I rest my head in my hands.

Why is this happening to me?

Lord, why?

"Are you okay?"

I don't even try to hide it. I'm barely clinging to sanity as it is. First, losing Ramiro, and now, maybe Logan—what's next? Will they find their way here and finish the job with my parents? Will they bring war to the Hunts' doorsteps? "No."

"Then talk through it."

"I don't know what there is to talk about."

"You said that you asked Logan to get involved."

I nod. "Aside from Ramiro, he was the only one I could trust at Web Safe."

"What did he do for them?"

"When he got out of the army, he spent his time hacking into databases and reporting their weaknesses. Specifically in regard to virus protection software companies."

"Which is how he knew to hack your computer rather than just send a message. It'll scramble it. Make it nearly impossible to trace."

I nod. "I asked him to keep his ear to the ground, but I never imagined he'd—" I trail off, my chest aching. "I can't lose him too."

I expect Tucker to pry. To ask who Logan was to me and what else I said to him. So when he walks around the counter and takes a seat on the barstool next to mine, turning my chair to face him, I'm honestly a bit surprised.

And then he says, "'Teach me how to live, O Lord. Lead me along the right path, for my enemies are waiting for me. Do not let me fall into their hands. For they accuse me of things I've never done; with every breath they threaten me with violence.'" Remember the Psalm, Alice." He takes my hands in his.

"I don't know why I thought I could do this. I can't take on a company like Web Safe. They have people *everywhere*. Government contracts, law enforcement—why did I think I could do this alone?"

"You're not alone," he says to me.

"You're just another body that can pile up, Tucker. If

you were smart, you'd turn me over to the police and never think about me or this case again."

"We don't know that he's dead, Alice. Just breathe, okay? If we find out they got to him, then—"

"Then what? You'll do as I suggested and turn me over? They already killed Ramiro, likely Logan, nearly got to my parents. How many more people have to die before I realize that this isn't a fight I can win? I'm not David, but Web Safe is certainly a Goliath." I'm rambling, but I don't know what else to do. The world is steadily spinning out of my control.

The coffeepot beeps, so Tucker gets up and fills two travel mugs with coffee. "Go get some shoes on. I want to take you somewhere."

"This is not the time."

"I think it's the perfect time. We're waiting for answers, and there's nothing we can do right now except keep our heads and pray."

CHAPTER 17
TUCKER

Seeing Alice frantic and terrified that she's lost another friend was the wake-up call I needed. She's not guilty. Any shred of suspicion I had after seeing that video validated is gone. Vanished.

I doubt the woman has ever even double-parked.

She's silent beside me as we drive the UTV to my favorite place in the world. Tango is behind us in the bed, excited to be getting out. It's still dark, barely five in the morning, but the sun will be rising soon, and I'm hoping with it, we'll get happy news.

Or at least, not terrible news.

The fact that Alaric still hasn't called me back is a bit concerning, but I'm trying to remind myself that it takes time to drive in LA traffic, no matter the time of day. He'd assured me he'd go himself, and that'll take time.

I pull the UTV to a stop beside the river that runs

through our property. Then I shut the engine off so we can hear the water rushing through the riverbed. For me, the white noise is a soothing way to drown out the worries. Here's hoping it works for her too.

Tango jumps out to explore a bit, just like he always does.

"Logan and I dated for about six months," she says, speaking for the first time since we left the house.

I hate the bite of jealousy because it's not at all how I want to feel. And it's completely unwarranted. "I figured as much. Though the length of time was what I wasn't sure on."

She offers me a half smile. "He's a great guy and was a fantastic boyfriend. Treated me to nice dinners, helped me move into my apartment, and bought me flowers. Aside from the jealousy he felt over Ramiro, he was the perfect boyfriend."

"Yikes. Didn't like the best friend? That's a no-go."

I get another smile out of her. "Yeah. I tried to assure him that he had nothing to worry about, and I guess I get it —I knew how Ramiro felt about me. But I couldn't bring myself to turn my back on him. Not when he'd been there for me when I first started at the company. And Ramiro was always respectful of my relationship with Logan."

"That's good."

"He was a great man." She takes a sip of her coffee. "They both were."

"None of this is your fault."

She turns to me. "Until that message came in, you were going to have me arrested for murder."

"I was thinking about it," I reply with a grin. Truth is, I'd already made up my mind that I wasn't going to turn her in. Even if it meant keeping something from my brothers for the first time since I ate Riley's last chocolate Easter egg in the seventh grade. "The truth is, I believe you're innocent, Alice. I feel it in my gut. I just don't know how to prove it."

"We need to stop focusing on proving my innocence and start pushing to uncover what they're trying to hide."

"I agree."

"I'm not sure how we do that without getting into Web Safe, though."

"We'll find a way."

Silence descends around us, with nothing but the rushing water and crickets to fill the air. Even Tango is silent as he watches the water, probably looking for shadows of fish moving beneath the surface.

"You know, I never questioned my career choice. Not even for a second. But these days, I'm honestly wishing I'd just gone into graphic design like I wanted to in the first place."

"Graphic design?"

She nods. "I did a little on the side when I was in high school and college."

"What made you go cybersecurity instead?"

She falls silent for a moment then turns to me, tears shimmering in her eyes beneath the bright moon overhead. "I wanted to do good in the world. Even if I couldn't be out there fighting crime, I wanted to help."

"Kind of seems like you're doing both now." I bump her with my shoulder, and she smiles at me. But that smile fades almost as quickly as it came.

"If he dies, I'll never forgive myself, Tucker. It'll be my fault. Just like the man in that alleyway was my fault."

"Alice, that man attacked you."

"I still took a life. Someone's son."

"Alice." She closes her eyes tightly, and a tear rolls down her cheek. "Look at me." Because I sense she won't do it on her own, I break one of my rules and reach out to gently touch her face. The contact sends a jolt through me, recognition that this woman means so much more to me than she should in such a short amount of time.

As Dylan has been joking lately—it seems we Hunts fall hard and fast.

A thought I shove aside because I *cannot* be in a relationship. Not now, and maybe not ever. Regardless of private oaths to myself, Alice needs me to remain focused. She needs me to protect her and pursue the truth—not fall in love. Still, I stroke her cheek with my thumb and turn her face toward me.

When she opens those crystal eyes, her pain is a punch

to the gut. "Even with what he would have done to you, you still didn't mean to kill him."

"Fine. What about Logan?" Her bottom lip quivers. "He had nothing to do with this. I asked him to keep an ear to the ground. To let me know if he saw or heard anything."

"But you didn't ask him to intervene, right? To ask around? He did that on his own."

She closes her eyes again and takes a deep breath, as though it's all she can do to keep from falling apart. "That was Logan. He never could leave something well enough alone, and I should have thought about that before asking him. I was just so desperate for an ally. For someone to help me get my life back. I didn't stop to think about what that would mean for him."

"Alice. Listen to me. If Logan—" I trail off. "If he's gone, then that's not your fault. Do you blame Ramiro for what's happening to you now?"

She opens her eyes. "Of course not."

I drop my hand. "Ramiro brought you into this. He's the reason you're involved. So if you don't blame him, then do you really think Logan would blame you?"

She hesitates. "I'm alive. Logan's not."

"If something had happened to your parents. If I hadn't gotten there in time. Would you have blamed Ramiro then?"

"Of course not."

"Then stop blaming yourself for something that's not your fault."

Alice takes a deep breath. "I'm trying to remain positive. To keep my head on straight because I know, at the end of the day, none of this matters. Our happiness isn't promised here. But it's so hard, Tucker. It's so hard to keep my head up when all I want to do is give up."

"I won't let you give up," I tell her.

"No?" she asks, turning to face me again.

Seconds of silence pass around us as we watch the sun rise above the hills. "Not a chance, 404Wonder. You're stuck with me until the end."

THREE CUPS of coffee and a shower later, and my cell is finally ringing.

Lord, whatever happens, please help me help her. "Hunt," I answer.

Alaric's initial hesitation tells me everything I need to know.

"When?" I ask.

"ME is estimating his time of death to have been right before five in the morning."

"So, right after we got that message."

"We found him near his computer. Two bullets to the back. Another to his chest. There was blood smeared all over his keyboard, and whoever did it ripped his hard drive out then shredded his apartment looking for something. They were in and out quick."

Pinching the bridge of my nose, I step out onto the porch. "Any idea who did it?"

"We're running prints we found on the scene, but my guess is they belong to him. The killer was in a rush but not messy."

"It has to be Web Safe."

"Fine, but we have no proof. Aside from the word of a woman whose face is currently plastered all over the news here in California."

"I know." Turning, I face the sliding glass door right as Alice steps into the kitchen. She stops in place when she sees me, and the expression on my face must speak volumes because her hand falls to her side, and she closes her eyes. "I'll find you something."

"Just be careful. These guys went after Loyotta's company and managed to get a search warrant for Ramiro's apartment as well as his mother's residence. They've got friends in high places. Though you already knew that."

"They searched the mom's house? When?"

"First thing this morning. I just found out myself."

"It would help if we knew what they were looking for."

"It would, but until then, all we can do is keep following the evidence where it leads us. I'll let you know if anything comes up from the scene."

"Great. Thanks, Alaric."

"Sure thing. I'm sorry for her loss."

"Thanks." I end the call and hesitate for a moment before stepping into the house. How do I do this? How do I tell her that another one of her friends is dead?

With my heart aching, I close the door behind me and turn toward the living room. Alice is sitting on the couch, her Bible in hand, while Tango is sitting at her feet. She looks up at me.

"He's gone."

It's not a question, but I nod anyway. "I'm so sorry, Alice."

She swallows hard, and her eyes fill. "He deserved better."

"We'll find out who did it, and we'll bury them." I set my phone on the end table then set her Bible aside before kneeling at her feet. I grip her forearms gently, stroking the undersides with my thumbs.

"We know who did it. Proving it is the hard part."

"Hard—yes. Impossible—no." I pull her in and wrap my arms around her in what's supposed to be a quick hug. A way to help her feel not so alone. Instead, the brush of her body pressed against mine makes my heart race.

She feels so right. In every way.

Which is only one of the many reasons I need to solve this case and put some distance between us. Otherwise, I stand to break a lot more than a promise I made to myself.

CHAPTER 18

ALICE

I've never had to look far to find God. But right now, it feels as though He's completely out of reach. My throat burns from the tears I've shed over the past few hours. Tears because I practically led my friend straight into the slaughterhouse when I asked him for help.

Tucker can say whatever he wants, but the truth is, Logan wouldn't be dead if I'd never asked him to meet me at that coffee shop. Fired? Maybe. But he'd died trying to get me that message, and because of the way he sent it, we can't even use it as evidence.

I know he was trying to make the contact untraceable, but man, I wish he would have used an attachment instead. Even given the risk.

The pew is soft beneath me, its blue cushioned seat comfortable even though I've been sitting here for the better part of an hour. Dylan is somewhere behind me, lingering close enough that he's there if there's an issue, but far enough away that I get privacy.

God, what do I do?

Closing my eyes in an attempt to stop another wave of tears, I sit in the silence of the small church, wishing I could feel God right beside me. Wishing I could hear His voice tell me why this is happening and what good could possibly come from the deaths of two people who were so important to me.

"You look troubled."

I open my eyes as a man with salt-and-pepper hair sits beside me. He's wearing slacks and a pale blue button-down shirt. "You could say that."

"This is a good place to be when you're troubled." He holds out his hand. "Pastor Gabriel Ford."

"Alice Sterling."

"Aah." He arches a brow. "The infamous Ms. Sterling."

"I'm infamous?"

He laughs. "Around here, you are. Small town and all that."

"I'm actually surprised the FBI hasn't shown up to arrest me yet. It's not as though I'm lying low."

"Low enough," he replies. "Most everyone in town knows you're being protected by the Hunts. Since we'd trust them with our lives, we know you wouldn't be here if you were actually everything the news claims you are."

"Everyone does seem to adore the Hunts."

"They're great people. And the kids—though they aren't really kids anymore—have done more for this town than can ever be paid back."

I think of Tucker. Of how he's choosing to believe me even though the evidence says otherwise. He's keeping the video a secret from his brothers, something I'd begged him not to do but he said is necessary—for now.

"I can't feel Him," I whisper. "He feels so far away right now."

Pastor Ford gestures toward the Bible in my lap. "This looks well-read."

"It was a gift."

"May I?"

"Of course."

He takes the Bible from me and opens it to the first page. "'To Alice. May you never lose sight of Him.' That's a lovely inscription."

"I've had it since I was thirteen."

Nodding, he offers the Bible back to me. "I've come to understand that when we can't feel Him or hear His voice, it's because we're too focused on our next steps when we should be giving it all to Him."

"I lost two of my closest friends and very likely might lose my own life soon."

He's silent a few moments. "I'm so sorry for your losses."

"I trust in God's plan, Pastor. I have since I was thirteen. But right now, I'm struggling to see what purpose this all has. Ramiro and Logan were good men. They didn't deserve to die."

"Does anyone?"

I shake my head. "No, but—" I trail off.

"I wish I had an easy answer for why this is happening to you, Alice. Truly, I do." He glances back at Dylan. "Or why bad things happen to anyone." Facing me again, he takes the Bible once more. "We have this. His Word and His promises that, when this life is over, the pain we suffer with will be no more."

"I know that God can take tragedies and make something beautiful out of them, but I'm struggling to see the beauty these days."

"Then fight to see it," he tells me. "Read your Bible and pray—incessantly. Take up the sword of the Spirit and fight."

"What if I'm not strong enough?"

"You are," he says. "Because you have Him. The enemy attacks because he fears what's inside of you. He will tear everything in your life down because he wants to break you. Don't let him. Fight, Alice."

Tears burn in the corners of my eyes, and I clutch the Bible to my chest.

"God is with you even now. Even when you can't hear Him and He feels completely separated from you. He's not.

Lay your pain at His feet, and allow Him to carry you when things get too hard."

DYLAN IS silent as he drives us back out of town. Delta lies in the backseat, just as quiet as his owner, though he stares out the window like the happy boy he is. The two make quite a pair—the broody soldier and the happy pup.

"Thanks for taking me."

Dylan grunts in response.

"I'm sorry if I pulled you away from something."

"It's not a problem," he replies, casting me a friendly look. Not quite a smile, but not a scowl either, so I'll take it.

Silence descends around us again. "We couldn't find proof that the video is a fake."

As casually as he would be pulling into a parking lot, Dylan pulls over onto the shoulder and turns to face me. "What?"

"The video. It's not what really happened, but every program I've run on it has come back saying it hasn't been tampered with."

Dylan's hazel eyes—the same shade as his mother's—darken. "Tucker failed to mention that."

"He was ready to turn me in. Every reason why that

can't be me in that video is circumstantial, and I know that. A few hours later, we got the message from Logan."

Dylan remains quiet for a few moments. "Why are you telling me this?"

"Because you and Tucker—all of you, really—don't strike me as people who keep secrets from each other. And I don't want to be a source of discontentment between you. If you want to turn me in yourself, I understand. I'll go willingly."

It's completely true. Because even with everything Pastor Ford said about fighting, I don't have the energy to keep running for long. I have no doubt that even if I'm killed—or jailed—Tucker will find a way to bring the truth to light.

My life—in the grand scheme of things—doesn't matter. Not when there are other lives on the line should the hackers manage to get their hands on the information they're looking for. Truthfully, they might already have it, though my gut says otherwise. They wouldn't have killed Logan if they have everything they need.

Dylan pulls off the shoulder and begins driving again. "I trust Tucker," he says. "If he believes you're innocent, then I won't argue it."

"I'm worried he's going to get in over his head too." It's the first time I've vocalized it. But knowing what they did to Ramiro and Logan—what they tried to do to my parents

—Tucker is getting closer to this by the second. What if he's next?

Dylan snorts, catching me completely off guard. "Alice, my brother has been in over his head since the moment he met you. However, there's no one—and I mean *no one*—more capable of figuring this out. Besides, as he's said, he's never been shot. Too fast for bullets." I get a sideways grin from Dylan, and for a brief moment, the mask of pain he wears slips away, and he looks more like his twin than he has since I've known them.

I find myself smiling in return. "Let's hope he stays that way. I don't want any of you to get hurt because of me."

"You let us worry about us. This is hardly the first situation we've been in like this, and I can guarantee it won't be the last. No matter how many times we should've died, we're still standing. Let that bring you at least a little peace. I have a feeling you're going to need it."

CHAPTER 19
TUCKER

I've been staring at this video so long my brain hurts. After drinking some herbal tea and going for a quick workout, I'm back at it, determined to discover *how* they managed to make it look as though Alice killed Ramiro when I know she didn't.

She's been gone most of the day, wanting to spend some time with her parents after the discovery that Logan was killed. Then Dylan texted me about two hours ago, letting me know she'd asked to go to the church. Since he was there, he took her.

Which I'm grateful for because I can't bring myself to tear my gaze from this video. I *have* to find something. Anything that will give her hope. So far, no matter how many times I replay it, I can't see past what they want us to see.

Which is Alice, raising a weapon and murdering Ramiro Caine.

Tango raises his head, ears perked, as the front door opens. *"Hier,"* I say, then head out into the hall. Alice stands at the end of it, her Bible in hand. As Tango rushes over to greet her, she bends down and pets him while he sits at her feet and stares up at her as though she hung the moon.

My boy adores her.

Just like I do.

This has to stop.

"How are you feeling?"

"Honestly, a bit better." She takes a deep breath. "I told Dylan about the video."

Frustration shoves the attraction burning within me to the side. "That wasn't your place."

"Actually, it was." She sets her Bible down on the table and crosses her arms. "I won't have you lying to your family on my behalf. We either do it honestly, or we don't do it at all."

"It wasn't a lie. I just didn't tell him."

"Omission is still a lie when information like this is withheld."

She's right. And the fact that she told Dylan only makes my feelings grow. "Well, he's going to be a delight to deal with next time I see him."

Alice smiles—it's small, but there. "Actually, he was really kind. I think he appreciated the honesty."

"Dylan's like that."

"What have you been doing? Any more news on Logan?"

"Nope. I've been staring at the surveillance video, looking for a break, but so far, I've got nothing." Turning on my heel, I head back into my office. Alice follows with Tango trotting right alongside her.

The video is paused on my projector screen, zoomed in on the grainy woman holding the gun. I can't make out features, just her dark hair and general stature.

"We've stared at that video, run every program—we need to start figuring out what Web Safe wants."

"I know. But I can't help but believe this is a part of it. It's all connected. I mean, how did Ramiro figure it out in the first place when everyone else at Web Safe seems to be completely in the dark? Why did he go to you? He could have gone to the authorities, could have gone to the CEO of Web Safe. Yet he went to you to fix it before reporting it."

"He was afraid. He had no idea how many people were involved."

I turn toward her. "But *why* did he suspect anyone else was involved? You don't go from finding something like that to automatically assuming the worst."

Her expression shifts slightly, brows furrowing. Is she catching what I'm trying *not* to say? "I don't know."

"Which is why we need to crack this video. If we can break this, then we can hopefully trace it. Follow the lead all the way back to Web Safe." I hit play again, and the video continues from the moment both Alice and Ramiro come into view. She raises her gun and fires. "I just don't see how they—" I trail off, my gaze landing on Ramiro. Pausing it, I move closer, then lean in and study the grainy form lying on the ground. "Hang on." Retrieving the phone from my pocket, I tap on Dylan's contact information.

He answers on the first ring. "Yeah?"

"Come back, I need your opinion on something."

"On my way." The call ends, so I tap Loyotta's contact.

"Loyotta," he answers, tone gruff.

"What tattoos did Ramiro have?"

Alice's eyes widen, and she turns back to the screen, moving in so close that part of the image is shining on the back of her head.

"He didn't have any," he replies. "Why?"

"I don't think the video they sent you is of Ramiro."

"How is that possible? It looks just like him."

"It's grainy," I reply. "They knew what we thought we were going to see and used that to make us see what *they* wanted."

"What are you getting at?"

"I don't know, but I'll get back to you once I do."

"Let me know what I can do to help."

"Take another look at that video and focus on him. I know it'll hurt, but—"

"I'll do it." He ends the call, so I shove the phone back into my pocket.

"Ramiro didn't have any tattoos," Alice says. "He always wanted one—we'd even talked about getting one together but never did."

"Tucker?" Dylan calls out as he opens the front door. Tango jumps up off his bed to greet him and Delta.

"In my office," I call back.

Seconds later, Dylan walks into the room.

"What do you see here?" I ask him. I don't want to give him any more details than that because I want his impression without my influence.

My twin leans in toward the screen to get a closer look, careful to stay out of the way of the image. "A tattoo," he replies. "Partially hidden by the collar of the shirt. How did we miss that?"

"Because we weren't looking for it. We'd already assumed it was him in this video. But Ramiro had no tattoos," I tell him. "If we had a body, we could confirm it with the coroner." As of now, Ramiro's body has yet to be recovered. Another anomaly. Why leave Logan's body in his apartment but keep Ramiro's hidden?

"Does that mean someone else died too?" Alice asks.

"Not necessarily," Dylan replies.

The wheels in my mind are turning a million miles a

minute. "That's why we couldn't prove it's a fake. It's not." I stare at the screen. Even as I narrow in on the grainy face of the woman on the screen—she looks *strikingly* like Alice. But if that's not Ramiro on the floor, then we know that's not Alice.

"Someone staged this." Dylan crosses his arms. "Because they knew you'd debunk a fake."

"But that person really looks like me," Alice says. "Even looking at her now—it's blurry, but the size, build, hair length—it's all the same. Aside from the braid and her choice of wardrobe, that could be me."

"They went through a lot of trouble to frame you for this murder." I turn to Alice. "I need to know who could have played those parts. Anyone else at Web Safe who looked similar enough to you to pull it off? Anyone at work who wouldn't have an issue doing something that would get you locked up?"

"You think it's someone who works for them?" Dylan asks.

"Yeah. They wouldn't have trusted anyone else enough to bring them in. They would've wanted these two to remain close."

Alice considers, chewing on her bottom lip as she does. I have to look away as desire hits me out of nowhere. *Get it together, Tucker Hunt. You're not a lovestruck teenager. You're a grown man trying to keep her out of prison for murder and treason.*

"I don't—wait." She tilts her head to the side, even as her gaze is distant. "Maybe one. But her hair is blonde, not black."

"It could be a wig," Dylan replies.

"Oh, good point! Kara Beverly. She's had it out for me since I took the promotion she was hoping for. But we're the same size. Even shared a few outfits before she decided she hated me."

I shift my attention back to the screen, feeling a bit more hope than I have since receiving this video. Our first actual lead. Now all we can do is pray it'll lead somewhere. "I guess it's time to see what we can get out of good old Kara Beverly then."

CHAPTER 20
ALICE

"Here you go," Dylan says as he climbs back into the car with a tray of coffees.

"You might be my favorite twin at the moment," I tell him, sending a side-eye to Tucker, who glances back at me through the rearview mirror. Ever since I came clean to him, Dylan's been a lot friendlier with me. Something that came in handy first thing this morning when Tucker tried to leave me behind.

"I told you it was safer on the ranch."

"And I told you that you're going to need me if you want any actual answers."

He'd been adamant that leaving me behind was the best option. Honestly, the only reason I'm here is because he was worried I'd find my way here despite their warnings. That, and Dylan came to bat for me and said it was better for them to keep an eye on me anyway.

So here I am. Sitting in the backseat of Tucker's rented truck outside Kara's apartment, waiting for her to get home from work.

Work. I barely even remember what it felt like to wake up in the morning, drink coffee in peace, and head into work. The routine feels as though it was a lifetime ago.

I take a sip of coffee.

"So what's the plan after she arrives? Are we going to follow her into her apartment and demand answers?"

"We don't have to follow her since we know what the apartment number is," Tucker retorts.

I roll my eyes. "Obviously."

"We're going to see if we can persuade her to come forward," Dylan tells me. "If we can do that, we have a witness. One thread that will lead to everything unraveling."

"But if Web Safe paid her to keep quiet—" I take another drink of coffee. "She's not going to give them up easily."

"We'll figure it out," Tucker replies. "Hopefully, she won't take too much convincing."

A white sedan pulls up into the spot labeled with her apartment number, and Kara climbs out, wearing a pencil skirt and a gray blazer. *Kara.* Just seeing her makes my blood boil. I know she hates me, but Ramiro was always kind to her. How could she do that to him? How could she protect the real killer?

"That's her," I tell them.

"I don't suppose I can convince you to stay in the truck, can I?" Tucker asks. "You are wanted for murder."

Dylan snorts and climbs out.

"Not a chance." I shove the door open before he can put the child locks on me—because I don't doubt for a second that he would—and climb onto the sidewalk. The air is warm, the sun beginning to sink, as we make our way up to the front door of her apartment building.

"Stay out of sight," Tucker tells me as he reaches out and presses a button beside her name on the panel next to the main entrance.

I nod and step out of view of the camera.

"Yes?" Kara's voice fills my ears. "Oh, hi, what can I do for you?" Her tone switches to flirtatious, and I have to clench my hands into fists.

Back off, I want to warn her. Which, of course, makes no sense. Tucker's not mine. Not in any way, shape, or form. If he decides he wants to date a woman who frames people for murder, well—that's on him.

And it's that final thought that has me realizing just how ridiculous I'm being.

Get out of my head, intrusive thoughts.

"Hi, Miss Beverly. My name is Tucker Hunt, and I was hoping I could ask you a few questions. I'm trying to find information on a woman who used to work with you. Alice Sterling? I'm investigating her involvement in a murder."

"Alice. Yes, of course. I'll buzz you right in."

"Great, thanks." I can hear the smile in his voice, and jealousy churns in my gut.

What is happening to me?

A buzzer goes off. "Come on," Tucker says.

I step out and notice how he's blocking the camera with his body, just in case she can still see. We move into the building, and I climb onto the elevator first, keeping my head tilted down so the baseball cap I'm wearing shields my eyes.

With my hair tucked beneath it, and baggy clothes on my frame, it'll be harder to identify me—but not impossible.

A few seconds tick by, and the three of us stand in silence until the elevator reaches the top floor. Dylan's eyes are closed, his hands clenched into fists. There's a bead of sweat on his temple.

Tucker looks just as nervous, though his gaze is trained on his twin.

I watch the exchange, Tucker's words from a few days ago running through my mind. I'd commented on how different he and Dylan are, and he'd said they weren't always that way. So, what happened? Was it the stint Dylan did as a POW that fundamentally changed him? Or something else?

The elevator doors open on the seventh floor, and Tucker climbs off first. Dylan holds the doors open and waits for Tucker to signal us forward. Then, we make our way down the hall before stopping just outside her door.

Both Dylan and I remain off to the side, so she can't see us through the peephole.

Tucker knocks.

My heart begins to pound.

Is this the moment where I learn the truth? Or will she call the police and have me arrested before she says anything? Oh, man. Why did I insist on coming? *Lord, grant me strength, please. Help me.*

"Well, hello, Mr. Hunt. Please come in." Kara's flirtatious tone frustrates me further.

"Thank you, Miss Beverly. I have my brother and another member of our team with me. Is it okay if they come in too?"

She leans around the door, but I keep my hands in the pockets of my baggy jeans, my head tilted down to the ground. My guess is she only sees Dylan and is more than happy to invite the third stranger in because of the good looks the other two share.

"Absolutely. Come on in." She steps inside, and Dylan follows first with me coming right behind him. Tucker manages to block my body somewhat as we move in, so she doesn't get a clear look at my face. "Can I get you guys anything to drink? Beer? Wine? Something stronger?"

"No, thanks. We don't drink," Tucker replies.

"Like, at all?"

"Not a drop," Dylan answers.

"Ooh, good boys. I like it."

I roll my eyes, wishing I could face her and watch that flirtatious smile fall right off her face when she realizes who I really am.

"Miss Beverly, we have reason to believe that Alice Sterling is not guilty." Tucker jumps right in.

Kara snorts. "She's guilty."

"You seem so certain—why?" Tucker asks.

"Because I know her. She grew up troubled. Her own grandparents didn't even want her. Then she was in and out of foster homes—you know how that goes."

Anger sings in my veins, and I have to clench my hands into fists to keep from giving myself up.

Kara continues, "I warned Ramiro to stay away from her, and had he not been so obsessed with her, he might've listened. But she had him wrapped around her finger until the day she put a bullet in him. And now she got Logan too. He was a tall drink of water, that one. Too good for her." She clicks her tongue. "Yet he trusted her too, and now look where that got him—dead."

That does it. "You're lying!" I yell and whirl on her, ripping my baseball cap off as I do. The anger pulsing through my veins is new—even for me. I've had a temper before, but this—this feels feral. And the satisfaction I feel when I see the horrified expression on her face brings me more joy than it should.

"You—you brought a murderer into my home!" she yells, lunging for her phone.

Unfortunately for her, Tucker's faster. He withdraws a black box from his pocket and shows it to her. "Your phone and internet are down," he tells her. "This is a signal scrambler. You won't be able to call anyone."

Kara pales, her eyes widening. "Wh-what are you going to do to me?"

"Nothing," Tucker replies. "We just have some questions. Can we sit?" He gestures toward her couch, but her gaze flicks between me and him.

"I'm not here to hurt you, Kara," I growl. "Besides, we *both* know I'm no murderer."

"No, we don't," she snaps. "You killed Ramiro. I saw the video. We all did."

"That you helped them make!" I yell, clenching both hands into fists again. *Anger gives a foothold to the devil.* I repeat Ephesians 4:27 in my head over and over again. But even as I have it memorized, I cannot keep that anger from burning through me. My entire life is on the line here, and she had a part in my downfall. My friends are dead, and she's helping to cover it up. As far as I'm concerned, she might as well have pulled the trigger.

Anger gives foothold to the devil, I think again, then take a deep, steadying breath.

"I don't know what she's told you," Kara says, "but she's a killer. And possibly a thief. I know that something was stolen from the server room the night she killed Ramiro. They won't tell us what, but we've had to scour the systems, trying to find any other vulnerabilities."

"They said something was taken?" I ask.

"As if you don't know," Kara sneers.

"Miss Beverly, we know it was you in that video."

At Tucker's words, Kara freezes in place, her face paling slightly.

Got you.

"I don't know what you're talking about." Kara crosses her arms.

"We know that Ramiro Caine is not in that video. The man who was shot in that video has a tattoo. Ramiro had none. We have all the evidence we need to take it to the police."

"Then why don't you?" she asks, tone dripping with venom.

"Because we're not interested in what you faked," I tell her, stepping forward. "I want to know *why* Ramiro was killed."

"You tell me. You're the one who shot him."

I take another deep breath, trying to still the waves of fury within me. How can she stand there and face me down, knowing what she did?

"If you won't talk to us, we're going to be forced to take what we have to the police. You'll be dragged in for questioning; then whoever is using you to help cover this up is going to get really antsy." Tucker crosses his arms. "Do you think they'll want to risk letting you tell the truth?"

Kara's gaze switches to him. "Again, I have no idea what you're talking about. Now, you can leave my apartment, or I will scream as loud as I can. The phones may not work, Mr. Hunt, but I assure you, my lungs do."

Tucker uncrosses his arms and shoves his hands into his pockets. "Just remember we gave you the chance to come clean," he says then reaches out and straightens a photo frame on her shelf. "If you decide you want to talk, here's my number." He retrieves a business card and offers it to her.

She takes it, likely just desperate for us to leave.

"As soon as you're gone, I'm calling the cops."

"As soon as we leave, we'll be contacting them," I reply. "Even if I have to turn myself in to get them to take this case seriously, I will. Ramiro and Logan deserve justice."

"On that, we can agree," she sneers. "They both could've done better than you. Something I told them right up until the day they died. Tragic, really, that they both lost their lives."

It takes all the strength I have to turn away and not slam my fist into her smug face. And as we walk down the hall to the elevator, then take it down to the parking lot, I repeat the verse in my head over and over again.

Anger gives a foothold to the devil.

Based on what's happening to me now—I'd say the enemy is having a field day with me. But I refuse to let him win.

No matter what, I will keep my eyes focused on God.

For He is my light.

He is my shield.

He is my salvation.

"Fight, Alice."

CHAPTER 21
TUCKER

"Yes, I did exactly what you said to do," Kara says, her voice clear through the bug I planted in her apartment when I'd straightened that photo on the shelf. "Yes, exactly. But he said they have proof that it's me in that video. You promised me that you'd protect me."

It's nearly eleven at night, and though she made a call right after we left, it wasn't to the police, and it wasn't until right now that she'd gotten a return call—something she was definitely not happy about, given all the muttering she did while pacing around waiting for it.

"If they take me down, I'll tell the truth," she threatens. *Bad move, Kara.* "No, I don't care what you say. You promised me. I did what you asked and now—" She falls silent. *Man, I wish she'd put it on speakerphone.* Knowing it's not Alice in that video is enough to clear her of the murder, but if we don't know who put Kara up to it, we can't solve the rest of it. "Fine. I'll see you then. Goodbye."

I hear her phone hit the counter relatively hard and mark the time the call ends. I have no idea who was on the other line, though I imagine it was Wilbur Huck. He's the only one with high enough clearance to pull off what Alice is saying they're trying to pull off. Plus, he's the one Logan claims is in on it.

Wilbur Huck.

Since we recorded this call without a warrant or permission, the information I overheard won't be admissible in court. However, it helps us to get closer to finding the truth because now we know that Kara is involved. She's a lead, a thread to tug until the rest of the truth falls out.

My gaze drifts to the couch where Alice is sleeping. She passed out from exhaustion about an hour ago, and I covered her with a blanket. Try as I might, I haven't been able to keep from looking at her from time to time.

She's just so beautiful. So kind. Though not incapable of anger, that's for sure. I'd genuinely thought I was going to have to hold her back when she'd lunged for Kara. Part of me toyed with not holding her back and letting her have that outlet. Who knows, maybe it would've gotten Kara talking.

It's not right—but the thought did cross my mind.

Dylan is sleeping—or what he calls sleep—which is really him lying in bed, catching thirty minutes at a time.

It's the most he's gotten since we pulled him out of that prison. Instinctively, I glance toward the door.

It's not uncommon for him to be thrown into a full-blown PTSD episode in those brief moments he gives up control to rest. More than once, he's come at me with a knife or other weapon he managed to get his hands on.

Never a gun though.

My guess is that's because it was an old, rusted knife he was carrying when we found him. He'd nearly taken Riley's hand off with it because he'd been so disoriented he couldn't even recognize us. And in those moments, in Dylan's mind, he's still in that pit.

As it does whenever that particular memory assaults me, the knot in my chest tightens, and I rub the heel of my palm against it. I lower my head, trying so hard to breathe through the ache.

"Are you all right?"

I nearly jump out of my skin at Alice's voice. "When did you wake up?"

"A few seconds ago." She keeps the blanket wrapped around her shoulders as she drops into a kitchen chair beside me. "So are you?"

"I'll be fine." I take a deep breath and offer her the earpiece. "Kara got a return call," I tell her.

Interest piqued and topic of conversation successfully changed, she takes the earphones and presses one side to her ear as I hit play. The expressions that play out on her face showcase the battle she's fighting against her own anger.

It's something I can relate to.

"Does that help us?"

"Unfortunately, it was recorded without a warrant, so it's not going to do us much good unless we can find out who she was talking to and get that information to someone we can trust."

"Which, in this state, is no one. Web Safe has contacts all over the place." She runs her hands over her face.

"We'll figure it out. We're going to head back to the ranch first thing in the morning. It's the safest place for you until we can get some concrete evidence. But I'm about ready to kick the doors of Web Safe in myself."

She nods. Then her piercing crystal gaze narrows on me again. "Spill."

"About what?"

"You looked like you were walking through fire when I woke up."

"I'm just tired." The lie tastes vile on my tongue. "Look, it's not something I want to talk about, okay?"

"I didn't want to talk, either, but it helps."

"Not this time." I've talked until my face is blue. To Pastor Ford, to a therapist I saw briefly…to God. Only the latter has helped, and it's still a struggle. Every day I wake up, I'm reminded of my greatest failure.

Trusting in the word of a government I vowed to serve and nearly losing my brother in the process.

<hr>

BEING BACK HOME IS ALWAYS a breath of fresh air. An early flight home, thanks to Jesper—the private pilot we use for nearly every mission—and I'm sitting on my own front porch, drinking a cup of fresh coffee, with Tango at my feet.

With Kara, and whoever she spoke to, aware that Alice is with us, it seemed the most logical choice to return to the place where it's the easiest to protect her. Here, we have security, and six of us—including Elliot's wife, Nova—who are all tactically trained and prepared for war, should it reach our doorstep.

Which, in this case, might happen. Web Safe is desperate to get their hands on Alice. And I'm starting to believe it's for a lot more than the fact that she was in that server room with Ramiro.

We have all of these questions and not enough answers.

Alice is out for a ride with Kennedy and Nova now, the three of them somewhere on the ranch. While I'm not thrilled that I'm not there too, I trust Nova to keep her safe. As a former detective and a member of our team, she's more than capable.

Besides, the ranch is the only place where I can put some safe distance between us.

Around Alice, everything is jumbled. I barely know the woman, and she's got me thinking about her every moment of every day. And not just because she's a client.

No matter how badly I'd wanted to settle down at some point, that all changed when Dylan nearly died. He needs me, and I need to be present for him. So why does Alice have my head in such a mess? Why can't I logically convince myself that jumping into anything with her would be a bad idea?

Tango gets to his feet, tail wagging, as my dad comes around the corner on foot. "Hey there, son. I thought I saw you out here."

"Morning, Dad." He takes a seat in the rocking chair beside me.

"Where's Alice?"

"Out for a ride with Nova and Kennedy."

"Aah, that's right. I think Jemma said something about that earlier. She and your mother have become insepara-ble." He laughs.

"How about you and Fred?"

"He's a good man. At the house working right now."

"They do seem like good people."

"I agree." He shifts his gaze out toward the ranch. "Things have always felt so simple here. Sure, there's a lot to do, but everything has its place. The animals have a routine, and every day is the same. When it comes to the ranch anyway." He winks at me. "Throw other people and situations like the ones you and your brothers deal with into the mix, and things get a lot more complicated."

"You can say that again."

Dad turns toward me. "What's complicating things for you today?"

"Why do you think anything is?"

"It's all over your face."

I set my mug aside and cross my arms. "This case is tangled. We have a video showing Alice shooting Ramiro, only it's not Alice or Ramiro in it. We have a dead man found at his computer and no concrete leads to follow. I've been trying to get into Web Safe's documents since we got back first thing this morning, so I can figure out what information they believe was taken. But I've hit wall after wall. Apparently, they've upped their security since the last time I broke into it."

"Is that something Alice can help with?"

"I doubt it. She told me that they have so much security in place, the important information isn't even stored online. It's in the server room with backups that are stored on site." I take a deep breath. "She's right though. We've been so focused on proving her innocence that I worry we're losing sight of what the real threat is."

"Whatever data Ramiro said they were trying to leak."

"Exactly," I reply. "But I don't see how I get to it without being inside Web Safe."

"Do you have anyone inside of Web Safe you can trust?"

"Nope. We have no idea how far up the chain the corruption goes. My guess is Kara has already told whoever is behind this that Alice is with us too, so there's no going in pretending we're just trying to help. I'm actually surprised a SWAT team hasn't shown up already."

He laughs. "That would certainly be a complication."

"Isn't that the truth?" I smile at him. "Dad, can I ask you something?"

"Sure. Anything, you know that."

"If you made a promise to yourself, but now you aren't sure that you want to keep it—" I trail off because I have no idea where I'm going from there. "Never mind. I'm overthinking."

"Tucker. I love you, but you are not the overthinker of the group. That title belongs wholeheartedly to Elliot."

I snort. He's not wrong. I'm typically an excellent decision-maker. As soon as I have the facts, I make one. No overthinking involved. Most of the time, it works out. It's the same reason why Dylan is alive today.

My decision, based on facts presented.

I knew he was alive despite what I was told. And I acted on that knowledge.

"So tell me what's on your mind."

I've never told anyone that I decided long ago that I wouldn't settle down until Dylan found happiness. I know that if I were to tell my dad now, he would likely understand but also tell me all the reasons why that's not necessary. How Dylan wouldn't want me to feel that way.

He's not wrong, but I can't bring myself to find joy when my twin suffers.

It could have just as easily been me in that cavernous jail cell, clinging to life and never knowing if I would be rescued.

"Alice."

"Ah, I suspected as much." He chuckles. "It's the look you give her when you think she's not looking. The very same one I noticed your brothers giving their wives back when they, too, were being stubborn."

"I don't want a relationship, but I can't get her out of my head."

"You don't want a relationship because of her—or you?"

"Me."

My father falls silent. "That's a bit more troublesome, then." He crosses his arms and leans back in the rocking chair. "Care to elaborate as to why?"

"Not particularly."

My relationship with my father—all of our relationships with him, really—are based on trust. He trusts me to come to him when I need to, and we can trust that he won't press until we're ready.

"I'm not sure I can offer much advice, but I can tell you that it's okay to change your mind. If you made a promise to yourself, but now you want something different, that's okay. You're allowed to grow, and oftentimes the things we think we want—or don't want—in the past are not the same things we desire in the future. Pray, and let God lead you where you need to be."

"Thanks, Dad."

"Anytime, kiddo." He pushes to his feet. "I need to go help your mother load her car for the silent auction tonight, but I want to leave you with this. If you're withholding happiness from yourself because of something you had no control over, you're not helping anyone. You're only punishing yourself."

I shouldn't be surprised that he sees right through me. The man might as well be a mind reader for all he knows. And his words echo through my mind even though I can't bring myself to act on what I'm feeling toward Alice.

Despite the promise I made to myself, she's a client. Anything more than that would make her a distraction. And distractions lead to mistakes.

In this case, those mistakes will lead to death. And hasn't there already been enough of that?

CHAPTER 22
ALICE

"Thanks for this, guys. I really needed it." I climb off of Ellie, the horse I've been riding for the past couple of hours, then gently pet her face.

"You're welcome. Horse therapy is the best," Kennedy replies with a smile.

"Only second to girls' night with pizza," Nova adds.

Kennedy points at her. "True." I watch as she undoes the cinch of her saddle, then mimic it on the one I borrowed. After sliding the saddle from Ellie's back, I set it on the tack rack then take the comb Nova offers me.

"How are you doing?" the former detective asks.

"I'm alive," I reply. "Which is more than I can say for my friends. I feel so guilty being out doing this when I should be trying to get them justice."

"I lost a close friend of mine back when Elliot and I

were trying to find out who was after me." Her smile is haunted when she turns toward me. "His name was Miles. He took a bullet that was meant for me."

"I'm so sorry."

"Thanks. And I'm sorry about your friends. But, Alice, you have to keep living. Even on the days when it gets hard—and there will be plenty of those to come—you can't stop."

I draw in a deep breath. "Everything is so messy right now. We have all these different pieces, and no way to put them together."

"When I was working a typically difficult case, and nothing seemed to fit together, I'd force myself to take a step away. Sometimes, when you make your brain think about anything else, the glue comes to you."

"It worked?" I ask her as I brush Ellie.

"Every time," Nova replies. "Don't you feel better after our ride? Even though we had to drag you out of the house?"

I laugh. "Yeah. I really do."

"See?" Kennedy beams at me.

Both women are so incredibly kind. There's not a shred of darkness in either of them. Even after everything they both dealt with. The stories that led them here to Hunt Ranch were heartbreaking, but look at all they've found since then.

Love.

Joy.

Happiness.

Faith.

It gives me hope that my tragedy might bloom similarly, even though it makes me feel incredibly guilty to think about that right now.

"Can I ask you both a more personal question?"

"Sure thing," Nova replies.

"Open book over here," Kennedy adds.

This could be a mistake. But, here goes. "How soon after you met them did you realize you had feelings for Bradyn and Elliot?"

Kennedy and Nova exchange glances then turn to me.

"I knew I loved Elliot before I even knew my own name," Nova tells me then leads her horse back into his stall. "Honestly, probably the moment I opened my eyes and saw him." Her expression takes on a lovestruck smile.

"Really?" I take Ellie's lead rope and undo the quick knot Kennedy taught me to tie this morning, then guide her into her stall.

"Oh yeah. For Elliot, it took a bit longer. But I just knew." She closes the stall door and turns to face me. "He was so kind, brave—and when I was barely clinging to life, unsure who I was or who to trust, I just knew he was there to protect me. That God sent him to me."

"That's so romantic."

She grins at me. "It was. How about you, Kennedy?"

"Mine was a bit later." Bradyn's wife laughs. "Though that had a lot more to do with me terrified I would end up getting him killed if I let him too close. Bradyn is the one who convinced me that love is worth every risk."

Lucky women. I hate that I'm a bit jealous of what they have. Not because of Elliot and Bradyn but because of the love they've found. And of them not being afraid to take that next step despite the world falling apart around them.

"Are you feeling anything for a certain computer genius?" Kennedy asks, wiggling her brows.

"What? Me? Oh no, I was just curious. You know. I'm a talker."

Kennedy leads her mare, Midnight, into her stall and closes it.

"That's not true." I take a deep breath. "Not the talker part, I'm definitely a talker once I'm comfortable with someone." I laugh nervously. "Tucker is a great man, and there is a part of me that is drawn to him. More than a part, really. But I know it's likely just infatuation. A result of being in the middle of a crisis."

Both women exchange another look.

"It's not like it was with you guys. We're not fighting our feelings. You can't fight something that's not really there."

"You just said you felt something," Nova says.

"Sure, but Tucker doesn't. He was ready to put me in jail before figuring out that the woman in that video wasn't me. This is a job for him, and if I let myself think —even for a second—that he has feelings for me, it'll make things even more uncomfortable than they already are." Just last night, he'd shut down when I'd tried to get closer.

"But he didn't turn you in." Nova steps forward. "And he didn't tell anyone that he wasn't able to prove the video a fake."

"He was waiting until the morning, I'm sure."

"No," Nova replies. "Those men have a code between them. They don't keep secrets from each other. No matter what time of night it is, they reach out. *Nothing* comes before that code. It's what's kept them alive all these years, and what helps them perform at the level they have to perform at. Tucker broke that code to keep your secret, and that means something, Alice. Whether you're ready to see it or not is something else entirely."

"TUCKER BROKE the code to keep your secret, and that means something."

Nova's words rattle around through my mind like a song on repeat as I sit on a bench outside the cabin my parents are staying in. I should have gone back to Tucker's over an hour ago, once I was done visiting with my parents, but I just can't bring myself to face him yet. Not when everything in me wants to lose myself in what I'm feeling for him.

I can't, of course. For so many reasons, regardless of what Kennedy and Nova said. But I feel like I've been waiting forever to find the kind of attachment my parents share, and now—is it right in front of me? Or am I imagining it?

The door opens behind me, and my dad steps out. He doesn't notice me at first. Just takes a deep breath and runs both hands over his face. He's exhausted. I can see it clear as day, and I feel horrible knowing it's because of me.

He turns to head my way, then stops and nearly jumps when he sees me. "Alice! How long have you been out here?"

"Since I left you guys."

"That was over an hour ago."

"I wasn't ready to leave yet," I reply then tap the seat next to me. "Care to have a sit?"

"A sunset-watching party with my one and only daughter? Sign me up." He takes a seat on the bench beside me and wraps one arm around my shoulders. I lean into him, enjoying the warmth of his familiar embrace.

It doesn't matter that Fred Sterling isn't my biological father because he's my dad in every single way that counts. God blessed me greatly with two sets of parents who loved me. Even if I lost the ones who brought me into this world, I have Fred and Jemma.

I nearly lost them too. It hits me out of nowhere, and tears burn in my vision.

"You doing okay, Ali?"

"I'm just stressed." Sitting up, I wipe my face.

"I don't see why."

I glance over to find him grinning at me. It's his trick at disarming me. And it works every single time.

"In all seriousness, my darling, you're handling this with more strength than I ever thought one person could have."

"It's all by the grace of God," I tell him. "That and Tucker told me he won't let me quit."

My dad wraps his arm around me again. "That Tucker seems like a good egg. I like him. His whole family has been incredibly welcoming to us."

"They're good people," I agree.

We sit in silence for a few minutes, and in the distance, I watch as two of the ranch hands I've yet to meet help Elliot carry hay into the barn for the horses. Every moment I spend in this place has me even more in awe than the last. The way this family works together to care for their animals and this property.

The way they care for each other.

"I know we've already told you, but I am sorry about Logan. While I didn't particularly care for him while the two of you were together, he didn't deserve what happened to him. Him or Ramiro."

"Thanks, Dad. And you didn't have to remind me that you didn't like him. I remember the Easter debacle."

"What? I beg your pardon?" He feigns innocence as he withdraws his arm and holds up both hands.

"Dad. Come on. You tripped him when he walked by the grill. I saw it. Mom saw it. You're not very good at being sneaky, you know."

His expression falls; then he smiles. "Fine. But you two were fighting, and I let an impulse win."

I laugh. "He was mad that Ramiro was there."

"I know. Hence the tripping."

Shaking my head, I lean against his shoulder again and take a deep breath. "Everything is spiraling out of control."

"It'll settle down." He presses a kiss to the top of my head.

"I hope so."

"How is Tucker being toward you? With you two staying in that house—"

Pulling away, I arch a brow. "Dad."

"What? I just want to make sure you're safe. I wouldn't be a good father if I didn't."

"I'm fine," I reply with a laugh. "Truly. Tucker is a gentleman, and when we're not sleeping—in separate bedrooms—we're working on the case."

"Just making sure. I saw how you kept glancing over at him at dinner. And that was after only knowing him a day.

You've spent nearly a week in close quarters, so I just want to check."

"Tucker's great, but we're just friends—not even that, really. I'm a client, and he's working to keep me alive."

"So are you. Great, that is. Better than, even."

"You have to say that because you love me."

"I do, but that doesn't make it any less true." He takes my hand in his. "Alice, you are the greatest thing that has ever happened to your mother and me. You are the sun in our sky, the moon amongst stars—you're our everything."

Tears burn in my vision. "Dad."

"It's true. And I want you safe and happy. That's all I want."

"Right now, I can give you safe. Happy? That one I'm not so sure about."

He squeezes my hand gently. "It'll come."

"Once all of this is over and we can go back to normal, I think I'd like to come stay with you and Mom for a while. If that's okay. Get my feet back under me."

"My darling Alice, you can stay with us for as long as you want. Forever work for you?"

Laughing, I lean my head against his shoulder, and he wraps an arm around me. We sit there together, like we have so many times before, but this time, my thoughts are not on the sunset but rather the man waiting for me on the other side of the ranch.

CHAPTER 23
TUCKER

The front door opens, and my heart leaps when Alice steps inside. She looks exhausted, but when she sees me, she smiles. And I don't miss the way her entire expression lights up when she does. *I'm in deep.*

"Hey," she greets.

"Hey. Good day?"

"A great day, considering." She takes a seat on the couch beside me.

She's close enough that her thigh brushes against mine. I clear my throat. "I take it you had fun then?"

"I did. Kennedy and Nova are great. Then I spent some time with my parents."

I'd known where she was because I'd checked security camera footage when the sun was starting to sink and she still wasn't home.

Home. When did I start thinking of this as her home? You're treading dangerous waters, Tucker Hunt.

"Awesome. I'm glad you had a good time," I reply then shift my attention back to the Bible in my lap. Whenever I struggle, it's where I run for help. The lighthouse guiding me home when I'm in troubled waters. I've read the full Bible cover to cover at least a dozen times—and then some. But I *always* find something new whenever I open its pages.

Until today. Though, to be fair, that's entirely because I'm not focusing. Mainly because the woman beside me has been on my mind for every moment of every day since the second I saw her staring up at me through that broken basement window.

"What book are you reading?"

"Psalm 3."

"'But You, O Lord, are a shield around me; You are my glory, the One who holds my head high. I cried out to the Lord, and He answered me from His holy mountain.'" She tilts her head. "I know that one. Question is, what are you crying out for?"

I push up from the couch and set my Bible aside. "It doesn't matter."

"It does matter. Look, we're sitting around, waiting for Kara to say something that will give us proof as to who's behind the setup, so it's not like we don't have time."

"I don't have time for this conversation." My tone

sharpens because we're getting way too close to me coming clean about everything I'm feeling.

"Why?" She gets up and follows me into the kitchen. Frustration ebbs at me. *Why can't she just drop it?*

Anger gets the best of me. "Because you're a client, and discussing my personal life is not relevant to this case. No matter how nosy you are about it," I snap, and the moment the callous words leave my lips, I regret them. She's lost her two closest friends and had her entire life turned upside down, and I'm so wrapped up in my feelings about her that I can't even respond respectfully.

Alice crosses her arms. "Fine. Understood." She turns on her heel.

"Alice, wait—"

She whirls on me. "I'm not unaccustomed with the idea of lashing out to protect secrets. I practically trademarked the idea. You want to keep your personal life private? Fine. I get it. I'm a case—a client, as you so eloquently put it. We're not friends. I'm not crashing in your spare bedroom because I want to be here; I'm here because I *have* to be here. Thanks for reminding me of that." She turns on her heel again and marches down the hallway.

I groan and run both hands over my face. *Way to go, Tucker.*

My cell rings, so I withdraw it, so frustrated with what just happened that I don't even check the readout. "Hello?"

"You need to get Alice out. Now," Dylan says, his tone

rushed. "Pack light. The driveway is blocked, and you're going to have to ride out."

"What do you mean?" Adrenaline pulses through my system. It's nearly dark. Why are they here now?

"You've got a team of tactical officers headed this way. Gibson called to warn us, said he couldn't reach you on your cell, but they have a warrant for her arrest."

"Just hers?"

"Apparently, though I imagine your name will be added shortly. They're on their way, Tucker—get her and get *out.*" He hangs up the phone, and I rush down the hall toward the spare bedroom.

"Alice, we have to go, now."

She rips the door open. "I'm not interested in going anywhere with you."

"Then feel free to wait on the porch for the tactical team that's on their way. That way, they don't kick in my pretty front door."

Her eyes widen, and she pales. "What? They're coming?"

"Yes. And unless you want to end up in handcuffs, we need to go—now."

"Okay."

"Shove whatever you need into a backpack, and let's go." Without waiting for her response, I turn and rush toward my hall closet. Ripping the door open, I withdraw my go bag.

It stays packed with essentials, spare rounds, protein bars, two life straws for water filtration, a medical kit, a fire starter, and thermal blankets, as well as some freeze-dried food packs and other miscellaneous supplies.

After that, I grab my radio and toss my cell phone onto the couch. The radio will reach the end of the property line, then I'll need to find a burner phone to make contact.

By the time I've done that, Alice comes out with a small backpack over her shoulders. Eyes wide, she looks genuinely terrified. I certainly can't blame her. The same people after her now are responsible for two deaths already—and who knows how many others.

Someone beats on the door. Knowing it's Dylan, I don't bother to check.

"How did we not know this warrant was coming?" I ask him.

"No idea, but they have it. Gibson called Beckett, and she's looking into it for us. It really doesn't matter though because they're coming for her." He hands me a black phone. "I bet she doesn't even make it to a jail cell."

The thought terrifies me. "I can't take anything they can track."

"They won't trace this one," he says. "It's a spare I keep." He pauses, and that familiar haunted look returns to his gaze. "Just in case."

I shouldn't be surprised that Dylan has a burner in his

possession, but I'm definitely grateful for it. "You're not coming?"

"Not this time. It'll raise suspicion if I'm not here too. I'll contact you as soon as the coast is clear. Only had time to saddle one horse. You'll have to share. Ride out, get to the safe zone, and I'll get in contact with Jesper and have him arrange something to get you out."

"Got it. You know what to do with my computers?"

He nods. "I'll get it done."

Dylan's not great with physical contact, but I pull him in for a hug anyway. "Love you, brother."

"Love you too." He pulls away, then steps aside as I rush out onto the porch, Alice on my heels.

My boy Jax is waiting, saddled, with saddlebags on his back.

"Food," Dylan says. "Mom ran outside and shoved it into the bags while I was on my way here." His phone rings, so he puts it on speaker. "Yeah?" he asks.

"They just turned onto the drive," Elliot says. "Bradyn is intercepting them to buy time, but he won't be able to delay them long."

"We're on our way out," I tell him.

"Good. Stay safe." The call ends, so I cross over toward where Jax is tethered and unwrap the reins before wrapping them once around the saddle horn.

"Give me your backpack."

She does as I ask, so I use a cord to secure it to the saddle bags while keeping mine on me.

"You climb up first," I tell her.

Without hesitating, Alice slips her boot into the stirrup and climbs onto the animal's back. I climb on behind her, wrapping one arm around her waist, the other gripping the reins. I can't even process the emotional turmoil sitting so close to her will throw me into because my only thoughts are about getting her to safety.

I look to Tango, who's sitting on the porch. Without knowing what's coming, taking him with me is a risk, but I don't like going anywhere without him. When he's not there, it feels like a part of me is missing. But if we end up caught and taken to jail, they won't hesitate to turn him over to animal control. "Keep Tango with you, okay?"

"I will," Dylan replies as he crosses over to place a hand on Tango's collar so he can keep him from following us. "Go. Now."

With one last look at Dylan, I apply pressure with the heels of my boots to Jax's side and click. I don't turn around when I hear Tango's panicked whine, though it breaks my heart.

I cling to Alice, and she holds onto the saddle horn with both hands as we race back behind the house and into the trees as fast as Jax can take us. I avoid the gravel, since the ground here is strong enough that it shouldn't show hoof prints.

I'll change course at the creek just in case, but my hope is we'll have enough time and distance that they won't know where to start looking for us.

WE RIDE for just over three hours, putting as much distance as we can between us and the main part of the ranch. After crossing the creek and heading in the opposite direction, then switching back and correcting course, we've finally arrived where we need to be.

It's situated at the property line between the Hunt Ranch and the Johnson's place—a neighboring ranch family who is less delightful than acid rain. But they keep to themselves and will *never* willingly let anyone search their place—police included.

According to a text I got from Dylan an hour ago, the federal agents who showed up are still on the premises, searching each and every one of our houses, including the cabins that belong to our ranch hands. They tried to question both Jemma and Fred—even threatened to arrest them if they didn't cooperate—but one phone call from Beckett Wallace, a no-nonsense attorney who has come to our rescue more than once, and they backed down.

For now.

I slow Jax down then stop him completely and climb

off, holding him as Alice climbs down and stretches her legs.

"That was intense. I don't know how people did it back when cars didn't exist." She gently pats Jax's shoulder. "You did so good, boy."

"We'll camp here tonight. Shouldn't light a fire just in case, but we should be safe."

"Should be?"

"If they scan the ranch, looking for thermal signatures, we'll be found."

"Great." Alice reaches into the saddlebag and withdraws a bottle of water. She tosses one to me then opens the other and pours it into a collapsible bowl Dylan must have slipped into the bag as well. She fills it with water and offers it to Jax.

Another reason to adore her. That she'd tend to animals before caring for herself just shows how absolutely selfless she is.

"What's next? You said camp, but after that?"

"Dylan can't risk calling Jesper while the police are there. So he'll likely wait until the coast is clear. Then we can arrange to meet him somewhere down the highway. He'll pick us up, and we'll be able to get out."

"But then what? I can't keep running forever. I won't. This has to stop. One way or another."

"We're going to have to change up our strategy."

"Which means—"

The answer is one I wouldn't have considered until now, because it breaks at least two dozen laws—probably more. But I just don't see how we get anywhere unless we risk everything. "It's time to break into Web Safe and find out exactly what they're keeping from us."

CHAPTER 24
ALICE

I was never one for camping outdoors. In a cabin with a locked door and running water? Sure. Sign me up. But being outside always felt like it would leave me feeling too exposed. Like anyone could come up from behind me and I wouldn't even know they were coming.

However, being out here with Tucker, I can honestly say I feel relatively safe. He's constantly watching, staring off into the distance as though waiting for the cavalry to come bursting through, weapons drawn, cuffs out.

"Why didn't you bring Tango?" I ask curiously. Since they're working dogs, I was surprised when he left him behind.

"I don't know what we're going to be dealing with. There are certain missions that are best if he sits out."

"Like breaking into Web Safe?"

He grunts but doesn't verbally respond. In fact, he's

barely said two words to me since announcing that he plans to break into Web Safe. Which, I feel I should remind him, is a suicide mission. I just don't see how we walk in there and still live to walk back out.

Because I can't stand the silence, I clear my throat. "Did you do a lot of camping as a kid?"

"My dad thought it was important to teach us how to survive off the land. We'd go out on a Friday with nothing but the clothes on our backs and a pocketknife."

"Really?"

He nods. "Served us well when we joined the military."

"That's impressive."

"It's survival," he replies. "Though at twelve, I admit I thought it was a waste of my time."

I laugh. "I can imagine that." Tipping my face up toward the sky, I look at the stars. They're so bright out here, with no city lights to drown them out. The air is warm around us, almost like a blanket, so I lie back in the grass. To my left, Jax continues to graze happily, his saddle and bridle left near a tree. Now he has a halter on, its lead rope tethered gently around a fence post near where we're sitting.

"How about you?" He takes a seat beside me. In the fray of our escape, I gave up being mad about his outburst. Whatever he's dealing with—it's his burden to carry. And I know an awful lot about not wanting to share one's pain with the world.

"Aside from the cabin you found me in? Nah. We never really camped. I did sleep outside a time or two when I was in between foster homes though."

"That must have been tough."

"It wasn't great," I admit. "But I learned to be resilient."

"Positive spin on a negative situation."

"That's all we can do, right? Look for the light amidst the dark? I'm trying to remind myself of that."

He shifts his gaze away from me and starts toying with a small stick he picked up off the ground in front of him. "I'm sorry I snapped at you earlier."

"Tucker—"

"No," he interrupts. "There's no excuse; it wasn't right. I'm just—I'm struggling, Alice. And I don't know what to do about it."

"Struggling with what?"

He takes a deep breath then turns to me, eyes so bright they almost seem to illuminate from within. "You."

"Me?" Guilt slams into me hard and fast. *I shouldn't have involved him and his family. Now he's out here on the run with me, and he's going to end up just like Logan and Ramiro.* "I'm sorry, Tucker. I know this is a lot. Asking you to help with this. I ripped you away from your family—" I'm silenced when he cups my face and pulls me in to press his lips to mine. I stiffen for a moment, unsure what to do, but a heartbeat later, every single muscle in my body turns liquid, and I sink into him.

As his lips move against mine, my heart hammers behind my ribs.

I grip his strong shoulders, needing something to hold onto or risk losing myself completely.

The kiss is tender, soft, a meeting of lips in a gentle whisper, but it's so loud. I'm deafened by the beating of my own heart.

Tucker pulls away, though his hand remains on my face.

"Oh," I whisper.

His blue gaze searches mine. Is he looking for anger? Frustration over the kiss? Because he'll find *nothing* but desire to do it again.

Because I *need* him to know that, I grip the front of his shirt and pull him in again. He buries his hand in my hair, and the kiss-induced buzzing in my head takes away all rational thought over why this is probably a bad idea.

He pulls away again. "We need to stop. I need to breathe." He pushes up and steps away from me, hands on his hips. "I'm sorry, I—"

"I kissed you too, Mr. Hunt." I push to my feet too. "So I'm what's been bothering you? Because you're attracted to me, but I'm a client? Do you guys have rules or something?" I think of the code Nova and Kennedy talked about.

Is this part of it? But then, how did they end up with their husbands?

He's quiet, his back turned toward me.

"Tucker?"

"I made a promise to myself a long time ago." He turns to face me, eyes closed. It's a few moments before he opens them.

"What kind of promise?"

Tucker crosses his muscled arms, and I can see that he's battling with whether or not to be honest. Should he trust and tell me? Or is he unwilling to be vulnerable?

"You don't have to tell me."

But he's already lost to his past. I can see it in his distant gaze.

"I'll never forget the day a chaplain showed up at my parents' house. I could hear my mom's scream from the barn." He shakes his head. "Bradyn, Elliot, and Riley were with me too, and we all sprinted toward the house. The black SUV had government plates, and I just knew what they were there to say." He takes a deep breath, and I remain quiet. "They told me Dylan was dead. That my twin brother was killed in action, and they didn't even have a body we could bury." A tear slips down his cheek.

I remain rooted to the spot despite my desire to run toward him. But I sense that any interference from me will shut this conversation down before he gets whatever it is off his chest.

"I told them they were wrong. My gut told me that Dylan was still alive. I just knew it. They insisted I was wrong. That I would come to terms with it and we needed to make arrangements for a funeral." He shakes his head again. "My parents started coming to terms with it, but I never did. My house wasn't built at the time, so I was sharing an apartment with Riley in town. I remember going home and spending two straight days online, searching through databases I wasn't supposed to be in—looking for anything to prove I was right."

"And you found something."

He nods. "I managed to find the orders he was given, which gave me his location. I hacked satellites and got footage of him being arrested and taken into a gated compound guarded by a militia in South America."

"What happened then?"

"I told Riley, Elliot, and Bradyn. Then, together, we told our parents that we were going to bring Dylan home. Dead or alive, he was coming home." Tucker wipes the tears from his cheeks. "That was the first mission Hunt Brothers Search and Rescue went on, and it was the only mission Lani and our father ever took with us."

"They went?"

He nods. "Lani was in med school, but we knew that Dylan would likely be injured, and we wanted a medic on sight. My dad insisted on coming too and hired a private plane to take us there."

"Jesper?" I met the former fighter pilot when he flew us to and from California. Super interesting guy and beyond loyal to the Hunts.

He shakes his head. "Jesper came later. This guy went to our church and was a member of my dad's men's ministry. He passed away suddenly about a year after we brought Dylan home."

"I'm sorry."

He doesn't directly respond to me, just continues staring out into the trees.

"What happened when you got there?" I ask when he doesn't continue.

"We rented a house on a private beach, one that could be easily protected should anything happen. Then my brothers and I set out, fully geared up and ready for war."

Which they found, I think to myself. That is, if Tucker's expression is telling me anything.

"Bradyn and Elliot took the front while Riley and I came around the back. By the time we'd cut through the chain-link fence and reached the back door of the compound, chaos had already begun. Alarms were going off; armed soldiers were running through the halls, prepping for a fight. We thought they'd seen us, but then—" He trails off. "We reached the lowest level of the compound just as two men hauled a third out of a hole in the ground." His expression is furious now, the tears streaming down his cheeks in rapid succession. "It was literally a gaping hole. Dark, damp—the man was so skinny I could see his ribs, and what I could see of his skin that wasn't covered in blood and bruises was so pale it looked thin as paper." Tucker's voice breaks. "They threw the man to the ground—he was cuffed—but when he came up, there was a rusty knife in his hand. He charged, and one of the men fired." Tucker pauses. "I'll never forget that moment. Everything slowed down. Riley and I sprinted forward just as Dylan fell backward into that hole."

"Oh, Tucker—" I can't even begin to process the emotions burning through me right now. The pain he must have felt in that moment, watching his brother they'd come all that way to rescue possibly dying right in front of him.

"As soon as the two soldiers were no longer a threat," he growls out, "Riley and I descended into that pit. There were wooden stairs leading down, and Dylan was at the bottom. Dead bodies lined the sides, bodies of the fellow soldiers he'd served with. Men he'd loved as brothers, whom he'd been forced to watch decompose in the months he was held there. He was bleeding out on that floor, but when he saw us, he was so panicked that he charged at Riley, slicing out with the blade and nearly taking his hand off. We had to pin him to the ground and—"

Tucker closes his eyes, and even though I'm not sure it's what he wants, I move forward and take his hand. He grips it, fingers threading through mine. His hand is trembling beneath my touch, so I place my other hand on top, hoping to add another layer of comfort as he relives what was likely the worst day of his life.

"We had to keep him chained like an animal as we dragged him out of that cell. The things they did to him—We'll never know the extent, but they changed him forever. Dylan is no longer the same man he was, and I don't know that he'll ever be."

"What's the promise you made?" I ask him after a few seconds of silence. "You told me that you made a promise to yourself."

Tucker turns to me now, bright blue eyes glittering with tears. "That I wouldn't let myself be happy until Dylan can be."

Tucker's words haunt me as I replay them in my head. I've always been a visual person, able to play out books in my head as though they were a movie on a screen. It's a skill I was grateful for until now.

Because I can see Dylan in that hole.

I can feel Tucker's pain.

Riley's—all of theirs.

The youngest of all five brothers was held captive, tortured, beaten—who knows what else, all while the government he'd served turned their back on him because there was no proof of life. Did they even bother to truly look? Or did they just assume? Given Tucker was able to figure out his brother was alive with—what was likely at the time—limited resources, I'm guessing he wasn't deemed worthy of the risk it would present to rescue him.

But for Tucker to make a promise to not find happiness until Dylan? That breaks my heart. And not just because—at the present moment—I would very much like to be that happy but because I imagine Dylan would hate that his brother is suffering on his behalf.

I may not have known the Hunts long, but I've spent enough time around them to know that they all love each other very much.

"You made a promise to yourself that you wouldn't be happy until Dylan is?"

"Yes."

I know I need to choose my words carefully, that if I don't, I risk pushing Tucker away. "Does Dylan know?"

"No one does. Just like no one outside of our family knows what I just told you about Dylan."

I can read between the lines: *I trust you. Don't let me down.*

"I won't say anything," I tell him.

"Thanks." He shoves his hands into his pockets.

"But just for the record—I think not choosing happiness for yourself would only further torture Dylan."

"He's my twin. And I can't abandon him."

"You think choosing happy would mean abandoning him?"

Tucker steps away. "Look, I'm a 'give it my all' kind of

person. Work? I throw everything I have into it. Same thing with the ranch. But if I were to get into a relationship, then—"

"You'd give it your all, and you worry Dylan will feel alone."

Tucker shakes his head. "Every other one of our brothers is married."

"Lani's not."

"He's *my* twin. I need to be there for him. I should have been there for him."

"Tucker." I squeeze his hand. "Given the army's policy on not allowing siblings into the same unit together, my guess is there was no option for you to have been there."

"They waited four months before telling us he was dead."

"What?" I ask, absolutely horrified.

"He was tortured for four months before any of us even knew he was missing." He shuts his eyes tightly and shakes his head. "Look, I'm not trying to make this about him. The fact is I am enthralled by you, but I can't—I shouldn't have kissed you. I'm the one who started it, and I'm sorry."

"I'm not." I release his hand, not at all offended because I know his struggle has nothing to do with me. "It was a great kiss. Even if a relationship doesn't come out of it, a memory certainly will. Me getting kissed by the handsome and elusive Tucker Hunt beneath a blanket of stars." I press my hands to my heart. "Put me in a black-and-white movie and watch me swoon."

Tucker's expression lightens just a bit. Which is exactly what I was going for. "You're not angry with me?"

"Why would I be?"

"I made a move on you, then told you—quite literally in the same breath—that I can't do a relationship."

I shrug. "You said you can't be in one until Dylan's happy. So the way I see it, I just need to find what makes him happy. Then we can see what this really is." I gesture between us.

Tucker grins. "That easy, huh?"

"That easy." I stretch up on my tiptoes and press a kiss to his cheek. "Seriously, though, Tucker, great kiss. And I'm not mad." It's hard to hide pain from someone as observant as Tucker, but I manage. The truth is, I *am* hurt.

Hurt that he's struggling so much.

And hurt that there's nothing I can do about the rejection I feel even as I know it's not about me.

***

THE CELL PHONE beside me buzzes, so I answer it just as Tucker instructed me to do before handing over the position of group sentry and grabbing some sleep. "Hello?"

"Where's Tucker?" Dylan asks over the phone.

"Hello to you, too, Dylan. Tucker's asleep. I told him

I'd take watch halfway through the night, and he told me to answer if the phone rang."

"Hi." Dylan is silent for a moment. "You both need to get moving. Tell him to meet me at the intersection of Pine and Cedarwood at dawn. He'll know where it is. And tell him to leave Jax in pasture twelve. Elliot and Nova will pick him up and bring him back to the barn."

"Will do. We'll see you then." I end the call then stand and cross over to where Tucker is sleeping soundly. His eyes are closed, his head resting on his curled-up elbow. He's lying on top of the thermal blanket—same as I was when I slept—and even though I know I should be waking him, I can't help but sit and stare for just a moment.

Like this, without the battle hanging over his head, he looks almost peaceful. Serene. I hate that I have to take that from him by waking him up and plunging right back into the fight.

"If you keep staring, I'll be forced to turn you in for stalking."

"Add it to my list of charges." I smile. "How long have you been awake?"

His blue eyes open. "Pretty much the whole time."

"Really?"

He nods. "I'm not the greatest sleeper anyway."

"I told you I would keep watch."

"And you did. What did Dylan say?" He sits up.

I'm a bit frustrated that he didn't get sleep when he

could, but I let it go—for now. "To meet him at the intersection of Pine and Cedarwood and to leave Jax in pasture twelve. He said Elliot and Nova will pick him up."

"When?"

"Dawn."

Tucker looks up at the sky. "We'd better get going then." He stands, stretches, and as he holds both arms over his head, I get a glimpse of a tan, muscled abdomen. *Oh, boy.* I force my gaze away and work on folding up the thermal blanket.

"How far away is this meetup?"

"About a half hour to pasture twelve," he says. "Then we'll have to walk the rest of the way, which will be about another forty-five minutes or so."

"Gotcha."

He reaches into the bag and tosses me a protein bar. "Breakfast of champions."

"Hey, I practically lived on protein bars even before all of this. They were my go-to after the gym. Chocolate chip cookie dough. Which also happens to be my favorite flavor."

"Hates marshmallows, loves chocolate chip cookie dough." He flashes me a smile that makes my stomach twist into knots. "Noted."

Oh, man.

Tucker crosses over toward Jax and offers him a bit of water before sliding the saddle onto his back and placing a bridle over his large head. Together, we repack the saddle bags and are on the horse's strong back within ten minutes of getting that call from Dylan.

I'm seated in front of Tucker, his arm banded around my waist, the other holding the reins. We rode exactly like this yesterday, but it feels different now.

Probably because of the passion his kiss ignited in my soul. The desire to spend more time with him, to get to know *him.* And, I can admit it to myself, the need to feel his lips on mine again. To know if there's something that will last once we've gotten past all of the danger.

Is he feeling the same way? Or are the walls he successfully put up last night blocking out all feelings?

Keep it together, Alice. You've got bigger problems.

"So the plan—you said we're going to Web Safe?"

"Do you think you can get us in?"

I consider his question, thinking through every logical way that I could get the two of us past security and into the server room without anyone being aware. And there's only one route I can think of that might work—if protocols haven't changed.

"There's one way—maybe. Web Safe changes all protocols every few months just to make sure things stay secure. But right now, trash day is on Saturday mornings."

"Trash day?"

I nod. "The bins are rolled out with bags on top of them before being rolled back into the building. If we can get between the liner and lie flat at the bottom of one of those bins, they'll walk us right past security checkpoints and straight into the basement."

"You want me to lie down in the bottom of a trash bin?"

I turn my head and grin over my shoulder at him. "Afraid to get dirty, Mr. Hunt? I assure you those bins are relatively clean."

His gaze drops to my mouth for just a moment, and my pulse kicks it up a notch. *Man, I want to kiss him again.*

He shifts his gaze forward once more. "How would you know they're clean?"

"Because I've done it before. Back with Ramiro. It was a game we'd play. Who can get into the building first without using the typical routes."

"Is Web Safe aware of the vulnerability?"

I shake my head. "The only one who knew was Ramiro. I beat him by fifteen seconds."

Tucker is silent for a moment, but his arm tightens around my waist as he pulls me closer against him. "Then we'll give it a try and pray protocols haven't changed."

"We're going to need prayer if we're going to pull this off." I continue to lean against his chest, not pulling away even as he loosens his arm. Because this closeness is stirring feelings within me that I've waited years to find. The kind of heart-stirring affections toward a man who loves God and respects me that could lead to something more.

Something worthy of a lifetime.

CHAPTER 25
TUCKER

Exhausted, I step toward the edge of the property line and stare down the gravel road. As soon as I'm sure it's clear, I wave Alice out of the trees. She moves out alongside me, and we begin walking, staying close enough to the edge so that, should I see any trouble, we can disappear into the thin border of trees.

I glance over at her, and my gaze instantly drops to her mouth.

That kiss.

She'd wondered why I couldn't sleep, and while it is true that I'm not the greatest sleeper, it was really the memory of her lips on mine that had me up most of the night. Everything about Alice calls to me.

Her strength. Kindness. Her love for God. She's everything I've ever wanted. My dream woman. The person I would love to spend the rest of my life with.

But the timing is wrong. Or, at least, that's what I have to keep telling myself. One more taste of Alice, and nothing else will matter. I'll throw out that promise I made to myself and jump in headfirst. It'll be Dylan who will pay the price. And he's suffered enough.

"You said trash days are Saturdays?" I ask, hoping to redirect my focus from what I can't have to surviving the problem I do have.

"Yes."

"Which means first thing tomorrow. What time do they put the bins out?"

"Usually about seven in the morning. It's still a risk, though, Tucker. I want to make that clear. Anything we do here could land us in a lot of trouble. If you'd rather find another way, we can."

"I'm open to suggestions, but as of now, I'm not finding any. I spent a lot of time trying to get into their systems, but they're locked down. Our best bet is to get into the server room then get out as quickly as possible."

A truck pulls around the corner, and since I recognize it, I don't bother rushing into the trees. Dylan pulls off to the side and climbs out.

"You both okay?" he asks.

"Better now," I reply, tossing my backpack into the bed of his truck then reaching over to take Alice's from her.

"Are my parents okay?"

"They are," Dylan tells her. "I thought your dad was

going to punch the lead detective though," he grins. "It was rather amusing."

Alice laughs softly, some of the stress melting out of her expression. "Dad has a bit of a temper when it comes to our family being at risk."

"It was well-deserved. Trust me." Dylan turns to me. "Jesper is waiting at the airstrip. As of now, I don't think we have to worry about police intercepting the plane, but we need to move fast just in case they catch on."

"Then let's get going." I open the back door for Alice, waiting as she climbs in before closing it and climbing into the passenger seat. "Tell me about the search. They get anything from my computers?"

"Nope. Swapped the hard drives before they got there. Aside from some ranch reports, they got nothing."

"You keep spare hard drives?" Alice asks.

"I do. Anytime there's a potential threat, I swap them so sensitive information doesn't end up in the wrong hands."

"And so there's no proof of Tucker accessing websites he shouldn't be," Dylan adds.

"That too," I agree.

"Smart," Alice replies. "Did you ever hack Web Safe?"

I turn around to look at her, a grin on my face. "Do you really want me to answer that?"

"You did? When?"

"Back when they first got started. They wanted to know if there were any weak points, so I tested it out."

"They asked you to?"

"Nah. But I did send in an anonymous report, then waited a bit before hacking in again."

Alice laughs. "You're the ghost."

"Huh?"

"You're a bit of a legend at Web Safe. The hacker who managed to slip past firewall after firewall right after they opened yet never took anything. You were in, then out just as quickly."

"You hear that?" I ask Dylan. "I'm a legend."

"I already knew that, brother," Dylan replies with a chuckle. For a moment, a bit of his darkness slips away, and the weight of everything we're facing lessens—only for a moment though.

"You bring any gear?" I ask, turning to check the back-seat. There are two tactical backpacks and two bulletproof vests sitting right beside them.

"Medical supplies, extra ammunition, a few extra firearms, knives, and the other necessities."

"What other necessities?"

"Binoculars, emergency kits—water, blankets, freeze-dried food."

"You make it sound like we're walking into war," Alice comments.

I turn toward her. "We are."

"Good point."

Dylan makes a right to head out of town toward the

small private airstrip we use whenever we need to travel quickly and quietly. His phone rings, so he answers it on Bluetooth. "Yeah?"

"Where are you at?" Bradyn questions through the speakers.

"On the road, brother. Nearly to my destination."

"Good. They're getting antsy. Threatened to arrest all of us if they discover we're harboring Alice."

"Where do they think I am?" Tucker questions.

"Out looking for her," Dylan answers. "Though Kara did tell them that she was with us when we came to see her. So they're likely not buying that story. At least, not for long."

"This is such a mess." I pinch the bridge of my nose.

"Agreed. Let me know when they're wheels up," Bradyn says then ends the call.

Dylan takes another turn. "What's the plan now?"

"Since I can't access their digital records, and Alice says that everything of any importance is stored directly on the server with *no* outside access, we're going to have to go into Web Safe."

"You're going to break into a top-security company while also on the run and hiding from every law enforcement agency in the country?" Dylan whistles. "That's a bit on the reckless side, Tucker. And that's coming from me."

He's not wrong. It's a major risk. But when all the cards are stacked against you, sometimes you have to break the house down and start all over again. Going back to the beginning is the best way to figure things out. And everything started in that server room when Ramiro Caine was shot.

That's where we'll find our answers—I'm sure of it.

"Did you happen to grab that patch you wrote?" I ask Alice as I turn around in my seat to look at her.

She nods and withdraws the thumb drive from her pocket. "It's never far from me."

"Good. Then we'll install that while we're at it. Make it impossible for them to steal anything."

"I can come with you," Dylan says. "Might be better if you've got backup."

I shake my head. As much as I'd love my brother to come, we have to think about the ranch as well as the optics. If he suddenly disappears, then they're going to really buckle down looking for me. They'll likely go through on their promise and throw my entire family in jail just to lure me back.

And after what nearly happened to Alice's parents, I won't risk my family—or hers.

"My guess is they're watching the ranch. If you don't come back, then they're going to start checking flight logs, which might end up leading them right to us."

"Fair enough. But I'm a phone call away. If you get in over your head, I need you to promise you'll call me, Tucker." His tone is serious, his expression the same as he glances over at me.

Most of the missions I'm on, Dylan and I do together. I keep him grounded, and he's the best one to have around when things go awry. This will be one of only about five missions we've ever done apart, but he needs to remain here to buy us time before the cops realize Alice and I aren't on the ranch and come looking elsewhere for us.

"I will," I promise, though I truly hope that's not a call I have to make.

"THIS IS YOUR CAPTAIN SPEAKING, and I'm happy to report the weather is beautiful, sky is clear, and we'll be making record time to your destination. So sit back, relax, and enjoy what peace you can find before we land." Jesper's tone is amused as he makes the callout over the private plane's intercom.

Once a fighter pilot, he walked away from the military after his third tour. Now, he flies for both us and Find Me, helping us track down the lost and bringing them home. The guy is a genius pilot and a great man.

Alice has been quiet most of the flight, sitting in the seat across from me as she stares out the window.

What's she thinking about?

Our kiss? The danger we're walking into?

"How are you doing?"

She turns toward me and smiles. It doesn't reach her eyes, but it takes my breath away all the same. "Not too bad. Just thinking."

"About?"

"All the reasons this is a bad idea. What if I'm wrong? What if they've changed protocol? I mean, we're *literally* walking right into a trap—willingly."

"If things go wrong, then we pivot. This will hardly be the first mission where things have gone sideways. We always manage to pull through. I've got plans B-Z ready to go."

"What are those, then?"

"We run. Call in the others. And go in tactically rather than stealthily. Besides, I'm the ghost, remember?" I add, hoping to bring the smile back to her face.

Instead, she turns to look back out the window. After undoing my lap belt, I walk across the aisle to sit in the seat next to her. Still, she doesn't turn to face me.

"I'm worried that this is going to end with you dead." It comes out almost a whisper, and that warmth that's been blooming in my chest since the moment we met grows.

I'm falling in love with this woman. And she's not wrong—we might not walk out of this one. Web Safe is not like the other criminals we've faced. They have a stellar reputation, and so far, we have no tangible proof that they're doing anything against the law.

"Alice—"

"No. I'm serious, Tucker. Look at Logan and Ramiro. Both of them are dead. Web Safe is untouchable. They've managed to spin it to make me look so guilty that no one will bother to look closely at them."

"All the more reason we do look closely." I reach over and take her hands in mine. They're smaller than my own and smooth, where mine are calloused from labor on the ranch. But even with all the differences, they still fit so perfectly together.

We fit perfectly together.

I withdraw my hands before I do something stupid and kiss her again.

"Dylan seems worried."

"Dylan is always worried."

"Really?"

"Yes. He pretty much lives his life planning for every worst-case scenario."

"Isn't that smart? Having a plan when things go bad?"

"Sure. But when that's *all* you're planning for, where's the time to be happy? To seek joy? To live?"

"I never worried about the worst-case scenario before. I'd pretty much lived worst-case until I was thirteen," she says. "And once I realized I'd found a home with the Sterlings, I chose to only see the good. It was a mindset change, but I find I'm regressing now because all I can think about is having to watch you die." She closes her eyes and takes a deep breath. "My mind keeps replaying what happened with Ramiro, but instead of him"—she turns to me—"it's you taking those bullets. You falling down. You bleeding out as I'm forced to watch."

Emotion burns in my chest. Desire to ease all her pain, to promise her that I'm here now. I'm alive now. And I'll do whatever I can to remain that way. Without giving it too much thought, I take her hand and press it to my chest, right above my heart.

"I can't tell you how this is going to turn out. But I can *promise* you that I am not an easy man to put a bullet in." I smile, hoping to ease some of her fear. "I've been in more combat zones than I can count, behind enemy lines with nothing more than a weapon and my faith, and I've walked away without ever taking a bullet."

"You came out without a shirt on when I thought my computer was getting hacked. I saw your scars."

"Knife wounds. Not bullet holes."

"And that's supposed to make me feel better?"

"Sure. Doesn't sound like they're using knives. I may be a magnet for those, but bullets? Please. I'm not worried about those." It's all bravado at this point, but I'm fighting to keep her anxiety at bay. We *have* to go into this with clear heads. If we walk in afraid, we very well may make mistakes.

And mistakes *do* get you shot.

She relaxes slightly. "You're so calm. I forget that you've done this before."

"All you need to know is that I'm good at what I do. And if anything goes sideways, we'll find a way to pivot, okay?"

"Okay."

I lower her hand from my chest but keep it in mine. She turns her hand over and threads her fingers through mine as she shifts to look back out the window. My stomach flips, and my pulse increases.

"If you're withholding happiness from yourself because of something you had no control over, you're not helping anyone. You're only punishing yourself."

My father's words replay in my mind, hitting me out of nowhere. Is that what I'm doing? Am I punishing myself because of what happened to Dylan? Because I wasn't there during his darkest hour? Was my promise ever about Dylan? Or was it a way to ease my own guilt because I feel as though I let him down?

CHAPTER 26
ALICE

"Looks like your theory was right," Tucker says as he offers me a pair of binoculars.

I take them and peer through the lenses as Web Safe's janitors wheel out the dumpsters. It's the *one* place where cameras don't reach. Once inside, though, we'll be under constant watch. Even sooner than that, really, since as soon as they start wheeling the dumpsters inside, they'll be in full view of the cameras covering Web Safe's back entrance.

"The trash trucks will be here within the hour. We'll have maybe five minutes to get inside, and after that—" I take a deep breath. "We'll be in the lion's den."

Tucker takes my hand and squeezes. Something he's been doing a lot since the plane ride yesterday. Not that I'm complaining, I'm here for every single gentle touch because he has a way of calming the anxious storm within me.

"It'll be okay. But if we really don't have that much time, we need to get close enough so that we can move fast. What's the closest we can risk before being spotted?"

I point toward the vacant lot behind Web Safe. "We can hide in the brush. It's what I did before. I managed to make it to the dumpsters and get safely inside within a minute."

"Perfect." He sits up and tucks the binoculars back into his backpack. He's dressed in all black, from his combat boots up to the tactical vest and T-shirt he's wearing. The vest has a set of knives tucked in the front as well as a firearm, in addition to the one holstered at his waist.

He looks ready for war.

Which, I guess, is fitting, given the circumstances. That gnawing in my gut intensifies. What if this all goes wrong? What if I lose him too?

I can do this. I gently touch the front of my own tactical vest, which is not quite as armed to the teeth as Tucker's but is complete with the thumb drive with my patch on it, as well as a secondary one Tucker wrote on the plane, using the laptop his brother packed in one of the backpacks. His version is a virus that will infiltrate the system, give him remote access, and also point out any vulnerabilities so we can trace what the hackers are actually looking for.

We install his, then mine, and then we get out.

He'd even given me a weapon, a 9mm handgun holstered at the front of my vest—just in case.

"Hey, Alice." Tucker takes my hands in his. "Listen, if you want to stay out here and keep watch, you can direct me to the server room remotely." I know he's talking about the earbuds we're both wearing. Our way of keeping in touch even when we can't see each other.

"No. You're not going in there alone."

"I can do it."

"I know you can, but you're not." Being away from him spikes a different kind of fear. One where I have to listen helplessly as he's killed, just as I had to do with Logan. "No. I'm fine."

"Okay. You're sure?"

"Yeah. I'd rather die alongside you than listen and be helpless to do anything about it."

Tucker grins and releases one of my hands to brush some hair behind my ear. "I might just swoon right here if you keep talking to me like that."

It's silly, but his playful attitude is helping ease some of my own issues. Especially when that playfulness comes with a side of flirtation that makes my heart flutter.

"Well, we wouldn't want that." I scoot out of view just in case anyone is watching in the distance before standing and shielding myself in the trees on the opposite side of the road from Web Safe.

"You're clear on the plan?" Tucker asks as he does the same and stands in front of me.

"Yes. We get in. Once the dumpsters stop moving, we climb out and make our way up the back steps and into the server room. There's basically constant surveillance throughout the building, so we need to stick to walls and disable cameras as we move."

He withdraws a device from his pocket. "This will do the trick. It'll isolate the network the cameras are on and freeze the panes momentarily. They won't see us move and shouldn't notice any interference. We'll be ghosts."

Poor choice of words. "Then let's get this over with." I start toward the small walkway that will take us down the side of the hill and to the truck parked below.

Once we're in the truck, Tucker guides us away from the shoulder and heads out onto the street. As we pull into the convenience store on the other side of the field between us and Web Safe, my anxiety has hit an all-time high.

My hands shake, my heart pounds, and as though he can sense it, Tucker takes my hand again. "Lord, we ask that You watch over us. Lead us to the truth, God, and keep us safe as we seek it. Please place your protection around us, God. Above all, let Your will be done. In Jesus' name I pray. Amen."

"Amen."

"Better?"

I take another steady breath and smile at him. "Yes. Thanks."

He nods. "Once we're in the bins, we'll need to remain silent, okay?"

"Okay."

"The earpiece is sensitive, so if you need to talk, the slightest whisper should do it."

"Okay."

He smiles at me then reaches forward over the console and gestures for me to lean in. I do, until we're only a breath apart. Tucker's finger gently touches the earpiece, and it beeps in my ear.

But he doesn't pull away.

Bright blue eyes level on mine, and his lips part just slightly.

My heart pounds.

Tucker swallows hard, and his gaze drops to my lips for just a moment. Does he feel this too? This bone-deep, soul-warming connection between us? Or is it just a basic attraction for him? "I want to revisit that promise I made to myself once this is all over," he says. "Because I'm not sure I can let you go."

My stomach flutters. "Then don't."

His hand gently caresses my cheek. "For luck." Leaning in, he presses his lips tenderly against mine. Like smooth waves kissing the shoreline, he keeps the kiss soft. Gentle. A promise of what's to come should we survive this. But even as terrified as I've been, the roaring of my heart steals every bit of fear from me. Because if I have God on my side and Tucker here with me, then what do I have to fear?

I'VE BEEN in this bin before. Curled in the bottom beneath the lining, taking slow, careful breaths so I don't move so much that the janitors notice. Then, it had been exciting. A challenge to win. An adult version of hide-and-seek, where the worst thing to happen would be Ramiro beating me.

Now there's so much more to lose though.

Tucker.

My life.

Our freedom should we be arrested.

With only the deafening sound of my pulse echoing in my ears to keep me company, I pray. Constantly. Incessantly repeating my favorite verse from Psalm 32.

"For You are my hiding place; You protect me from trouble. You surround me with songs of victory."

We're doing this for the right reasons—and that's what I keep telling myself.

We're fighting the good fight. A battle for our lives. And the Lord is beside us.

The door creaks open, and bootsteps grow closer.

Here we go.

"Then I told her that she could get lost," one of the janitors says. *Perry.* I recognize his voice. Arguably, one of the kindest men you'll meet—if he likes you. "Who is she to boss me around? They may have promoted her, but I refuse to answer to a spoiled little girl."

"She's our boss though," the other janitor says. He's younger, and while I don't know him well, I remember he started a few weeks before everything fell apart. *Keith.* "We don't have a say in that."

"Well, I'll quit before I let her order me around like she's some sort of general." He shoves the dumpster forward, and I jolt slightly, stabilizing myself as best I can with one arm against the top and my foot pressing to the bottom.

Keith chuckles. "You may not have to quit if they keep letting people go."

"They need us. Those new security guards aren't going to take the trash out, are they?"

"No. But they'll supervise us doing it," Perry mutters.

Supervise us doing it? My heart begins to pound, and my fingers dance over the firearm tucked in my vest. I don't want to use it, but if it's our lives or someone else's—

The door creaks open again, and a new person joins the group. "You took long enough," a gruff, masculine voice complains.

"You want to do this?" Perry snaps. "By all means, you can empty all of the trash cans in the entire building."

I remain as still as I can, barely even breathing.

"You going to look inside or what? I'd like to move on with my day." Perry is agitated, irritated at the interruption.

Look inside? Fear ices my veins, and I close my eyes tightly. *Lord, please don't let them see us. Please shield us from their sight.*

"Go on," the voice says again.

Relief momentarily mutes the fear as the bin starts rolling again. I count the seconds, comparing it to the time it took to get inside the last time. That way, if there's any change to the routine, I can alert Tucker. So far, though, it's been smooth sailing.

We pause, likely right before the waste room so Perry can scan his badge in. I hear the door open then wait until my bin comes to a stop.

"Hey, Keith, do me a favor and go check the bins on the fourth floor."

"Seriously?"

"Yes. I'll handle the bathrooms on floor one, but I can't remember if we emptied all the office bins."

He groans. "You got it. I'll do just about anything to not have to clean the bathrooms in this place."

"Then this is a good deal for you. Afterward, take your lunch."

"Thanks, Perry."

"Yeah. Now go. I don't want any complaints if there's trash remaining in there when everyone arrives Monday morning."

"Aye-aye, Captain." The door opens and closes again, but I remain where I am until I can be sure Perry is gone too. He always liked me, but I doubt enough that he'd risk jail time letting us go should he discover us.

"Girl, get out of the bin. You forget you told me about this hiding spot?"

Busted. My heart pounds. Slowly, I tug the cover down and sit up. Perry is grinning at me, the corners of his brown eyes crinkling in amusement. When I started working here, he'd been a gruff old man, short-tempered and frustrated. But, after a few weeks, I wore him down. We started eating lunch together once a week, and he became a sort of surrogate grandfather to me. "Hey, Perry."

"You're going to get yourself killed." He reaches out and takes my hand, so I climb out. Since I'm not sure where we stand, I don't reveal Tucker just yet.

"You don't seem surprised to see me."

"Honestly, I'm surprised it took you this long to sneak back in. With everything going on, it's been total chaos in this place. You know they put that brat, Kara, in your place? She's running the show upstairs these days."

"I'm not surprised. Are you going to turn me in?"

He arches a brow. "I guess that depends on why you're here."

"I didn't do what they said I did."

He waves a hand in front of his face. "I know you

didn't. You're no thief. I bet it's Kara who's the real thief. I never liked her. And now that she's marrying Darren—"

"Wait, Darren the security guard?"

He nods. "You didn't hear?"

"I've been a bit busy."

"Good point. Yeah, they're engaged now. Mr. Huck has pretty much given them free rein of the place. They've changed up everything and are watching whatever we do like hawks. You know us janitors aren't even allowed to go through the front entrance? Or be on any active floors during office hours?" He shakes his head. "They've got us down to two on staff at any one time, and we have three hours to clean the entire place top to bottom on weeknights."

"I'm sorry, Perry."

"I've lived through worse." He studies me. "Why are you here?"

"Because something is off, and I want to find out what it is. Ramiro died trying to uncover the truth, and I intend to find out why."

Perry nods. "Then I think it's time I take an early lunch." He smiles. "As far as I'm concerned, I never saw you."

I can't help it. I wrap my arms around him and pull him in for a hug. "Thank you so much, Perry."

"No need to thank me. You're the best of these folks. You'll make things right. I know you will."

I pull away, hope in my heart. *Thank You, Lord. Thank You for letting it be him who pushed the bins in.*

"Be safe, though, girl. They're after you. Have all the security guards on high alert. They even fired most of the staff that was here before and hired new guys. Guys who never knew you. I don't even know half of who's working here anymore. With all of our new restrictions, we hardly ever see anyone."

They hired new guards because they don't want any hesitation when it comes to catching me. Anyone who has prior interactions with me is a risk to the whole *shoot first, ask questions later* policy they seem to have these days. "Thanks for the heads up."

He nods. "You have about thirty minutes before Keith realizes I sent him on a wild goose chase and comes down to check in with me. Get out before then."

"Will do. Thanks again, Perry."

He smiles and nods again then opens the door and disappears into the hallway.

"All clear."

Tucker pulls the cover down and grins at me. "You're a constant surprise, Miss Sterling."

"Why is that?"

"You told me you're not social, yet you got close to Jenny within a matter of hours." He climbs out of the bin and stands in front of me, towering nearly a foot taller than me. "And now you have a man willing to risk his own job because he trusts you."

"Perry is a good man. Some of the others treat him like garbage because of his past, but I see him for who he is now."

Tucker strokes my cheek. "Which is one of the many reasons I find myself completely drawn to you. You're kind, Alice. No matter what life throws at you, you're not hardened by it."

"I don't see the point in losing myself to the darkness in this life when there's so much light too."

"Exactly." He releases my face and heads toward the door. "Where's the first camera?"

I have to take a heartbeat to recover from the attraction burning in my veins. "Uh, right outside the door. It points straight in here so they can monitor who's coming in and out."

"Got it." Reaching back, he takes my hand. "You ready for this?"

No. "Let's go."

CHAPTER 27
TUCKER

The back stairwell of Web Safe is quiet. With cameras on every landing and a larger than normal distance between floors one and two, I take careful steps, ensuring that the device in my hand is discovering the camera's unique digital signature before we move into view. Alice remains right behind me, glued to my side, so by the time I drop the connection to the previous camera, she's in the clear too.

It's a painstakingly slow process when there's no telling how soon a security guard will decide to take the stairs instead of an elevator.

So far, we've been in the clear.

Thank God it's a Saturday. Otherwise, I doubt we would've made it up the first set of steps.

"We're on the second floor," Alice says, gesturing

toward the number on the door. "It's the entire server floor, and it should be empty since it's a Saturday."

"Security?"

"They didn't use to monitor this floor since the server room is password protected. No one gets in without a code."

I turn toward her. "Do you—"

"I've got us covered," she replies with a smile. "They won't even know we're here. There's a camera that points through this door, then another at the end of the hall. You'll need to take them both out at the same time."

"Okay." I breathe a sigh of relief. "Then let's do this." I pause by the door, waiting for the device to read the two camera signatures. As soon as those are down, I stick the device into my pocket then carefully withdraw my firearm. Keeping it up before me, I move out into the hall-way. It's darker than the stairwell, with only dim lights overhead.

Not unusual for a server room. Since it runs so hot, they'd want to keep as much temperature control as possi-ble. The air is cooler here too—drier. Again, not unusual. A wall of glass separates us from the server towers, which are standing tall in a room about the size of my entire house.

Alice moves ahead of me now, stopping at the security panel. She types in a sequence of numbers; then the panel blinks green, and the door slides open. She flips her hair over her shoulder and beckons me to follow.

Adrenaline dances through my veins in anticipation should everything go wrong.

"Over here," she instructs and rushes toward a tower right at the heart of the room. Withdrawing the thumb drive, she plugs it into the port then pulls out a keyboard and monitor from a cabinet beside the tower.

Keeping my weapon in hand, I watch for any sign of movement. As my gaze travels around the room, I note the newly replaced windows, and my understanding of what Alice went through grows.

I doubt she even knew the gun would work on those windows. Yet she trusted in God to get her out. *Faith.*

"How's it going?" I ask her.

"I'm working on it. They've put up more walls since I was in here last." Furiously typing on the keyboard, she's the picture of focus, plugged into the task at hand. "I don't —none of this makes sense."

"What?"

"There are no holes," she says. "Honestly, the security is even better than it was before. I—"

The door opens. I rush over and plaster myself over Alice, pressing her between me and the server tower, my weapon in hand. She freezes in place, her body going rigid as more than one set of footsteps grows closer.

Frantically looking for any way out, I point to the right, and she nods. Slowly, we rotate as one unit, moving around the server tower until we're just out of sight.

"I knew you'd come back."

Alice's eyes go wide, and her face pales.

"It was only a matter of time before you showed up. You shouldn't have come back here, Alice."

She pushes past me, but I remain out of view as she steps away from the protection of the tower. "You're dead," she whispers.

Now, I come out behind her, weapon raised. The man on the other side of the tower is one I never expected to see. Alive, that is. *Ramiro Caine.*

"Tucker Hunt," he says. "Even given the circumstances, it's quite an honor to meet you. I'd ask you to kindly lower your weapon, though, as there's a large-caliber rifle pointed directly at Alice. Should you not lower it, I'll give the signal, and she'll take the hit." He raises his hand, and a red dot appears on Alice's shoulder. "Either of you will work for our current needs. Therefore, one of you is expendable."

I don't even hesitate. Slowly, I lower my weapon onto the ground.

"The vest too," he orders.

I peel the Velcro free and set it on the ground then keep both hands up. They tremble as fiery rage burns through my body. Alice grieved him. Her friend—or so she thought.

"You died. I watched you die," Alice growls, her tone strained.

"You watched me get shot," Ramiro corrects then tugs

the neck of his shirt down to reveal an angry red scar right below his clavicle.

"Why? What are you doing? Why are you doing this?"

"I'm doing what I have to do," he replies, expression sharp.

"We were friends. Best friends." Her broken tone infuriates me further.

"Do you have any idea what you've put her through?" I demand.

"It should have ended that night. I tried to make things right, but I'm in too far." Ramiro looks from her to me, then back to her again. "I am sorry for dragging you into this. But now, there's no choice."

"What do you mean, it should have ended?" Alice questions. She takes a step closer, and I move in right behind her, ready to yank her to safety should things escalate any more than they already have.

"Your patch was supposed to fill the holes I left. If they had, then the hackers wouldn't have gotten into the systems. But they did, and since the test worked, now we have to follow through. If I don't, they'll kill my family. Don't you see?" He takes a step closer. "I don't have a choice."

"There is *always* a choice," Alice says. "You chose wrong. Did you kill—" She trails off. "Did you kill Logan?"

Ramiro's expression shifts. He goes from being almost

remorseful to hard. Unfeeling. "Logan got what was coming to him."

"You killed him." She takes a step back, right into my chest. I steady her with hands on her shoulders.

"How do you think your uncle is going to take this?" I snap, fury igniting my normally controlled temper. "He's been searching for you."

"Uncle Frank will never know. They'll never find my body, and neither of you will walk out of here. So there's no chance he'll ever find out."

"You're wrong," I reply. "And it's going to break his heart to see what you've become."

The door opens again, and an entire team of security guards dressed head to toe in tactical gear descends upon us.

I'd say this is a substantial escalation.

"Logan did put up a fight—if that helps. Took three bullets to put him down. And he still managed to send out whatever it is he sent you. We certainly couldn't figure it out."

"You murderer!" Alice lunges forward, furious tears streaming down her face.

I pull her back, holding her against me. Her entire body trembles in my hold. "Think it through," I whisper in her ear. "We've got guns on us. Don't let your anger get you shot."

Alice stills. "Fine."

I release her.

"What's the plan then, Ramiro? Are you going to kill me too?" she asks. "You said we weren't going to walk out of here. So are you going to face me down—after everything we've been through—and put a bullet in me too?"

Ramiro doesn't respond, but I can see that her words affected him—at least a little bit.

"First, we have something better planned for you." Another man steps into view. *Darren Wade.* Huck's second-in-command of the security department. He grins at me. "Tucker Hunt. He's not quite as intimidating as you said he'd be," he says to Ramiro, who locks eyes with me.

"Don't be fooled. He's deadly," Ramiro warns.

"You should listen to him," I tell Darren.

"I'm not worried. I'm holding all the cards," he says with an arrogant grin.

"What do you want from me?" Alice asks.

"I'm going to provide you with a list of accounts, and you're going to drop the firewalls so my clients can get what they need. Then you're going to plug it up so no one can tell that anything happened at all. In and out with no possible chance that anyone can trace the leak back to Web Safe."

He grins as though he's already won.

"Why me? You have plenty of people here who can do this."

"Ramiro says you're the best." He clasps a hand on Ramiro's shoulder. "He couldn't do it alone."

"But you asked me to patch the system," Alice says to Ramiro.

"He had a momentary lapse of judgment," Darren replies. "Just needed some motivation to get back on the right track."

"You won't get away with this." Alice clenches both hands into fists at her sides.

"Actually, I will."

"I won't do it."

"Oh, you will, Otherwise, I'll put so many holes in lover boy here that he'll look like Swiss cheese." He aims his handgun at me. "Do we have a deal?"

"Not a chance," I growl.

"Yes. Fine." Alice turns to me. "I won't let them kill you."

"Alice, you can't do this."

"I have to," she says. There's defeat in her eyes, and it kills me to see it.

"Great. Now, you can come with us until it's time. Come on, don't be shy," Darren says as he gestures toward the aisle they're currently standing in.

A security guard lifts my weapon and vest then steps back. Together, Alice and I start walking. Every step we take, I'm looking for a chance. An opportunity to get us both to safety, but as the guards fall into step behind us, I realize with horrible certainty—we're trapped.

And backup won't come for at least another twenty-four hours.

The only joy I have right now is in knowing that, when I miss my check-in, Dylan, Bradyn, Elliot, and Riley will level this place. And even if I'm not alive to see it? The sheer knowledge of what they'll do brings me more joy than it probably should.

CHAPTER 28
ALICE

Ramiro is alive.

And not just alive—but working for Darren.

It was all a setup.

He would have known about the dumpsters. Was he waiting for me? Is he the one who told them to hurt my parents because he knew it was the only thing that would bring me out of hiding?

I continue pacing the supply room they've placed us in while Tucker scours the shelves. For what, I have no idea. He's barely said five words to me since we got locked in here, shielded behind this door with an armed guard just outside.

We were both stripped of our weapons and any gear we brought in. We're sitting ducks. Waiting for whatever they have planned for us.

"Yes. Thank you, God."

I turn as Tucker kneels to the ground, an old laptop in his hand. "Everything in this room is useless; that's why it's here. Dead batteries, fried hard drives—they're all broken."

He beams at me. "Nothing is useless." Lifting the leg of his black cargo pants, he reveals a hidden pocket just inside the bottom of the pant leg. He removes a small black tube then unscrews the bottom and pulls out two wires.

"What is that?"

"Something of my own invention," he replies. "I call it tech life support."

"What does it do?"

He flips the laptop over and removes the battery cover, then takes both wires and connects them inside the computer. After turning the laptop over, he presses a button on the bottom of the tube. "Moment of truth." He presses the power button, and the laptop comes to life.

"How did you do that?"

He looks over at me. "Finding me more and more attractive by the minute, aren't you?"

It's ridiculous that, even given what we're facing and the fact that my dead best friend is actually an enemy who is very much alive, Tucker still makes my heart race. "Maybe."

He chuckles. "It won't last long, but it should be enough to send an SOS."

"You need network access, though."

"Don't worry so much," he says. "I've got us covered." A blue screen overtakes the monitor. Tucker types in an IP address then follows it with a few rows of code and a message.

Caine alive. A+T being held at Web Safe. BC.

He taps a few more keystrokes; then the screen fizzles and dies. Tucker lets out a breath. "Now we pray it went through before the laptop fried the life support."

Lord, please let it have gone through.

"You signed it BC."

"Bring cavalry," he replies then shoves the device back into his pocket and shelves the laptop again.

"What now?"

"Now we look for something that can be a weapon."

"We can't fight our way out of here."

"Sure we can."

"No! We can't!" I yell, panic strangling me. I got him into this mess. I walked him right into the hornet's nest so they could tear him apart.

Me.

I got Logan killed.

And now I'm going to get Tucker killed.

If his brothers come—I can't even think about that.

"How can you think that's possible?" I open my eyes, barely able to see, thanks to the tears.

"Because just like you, I refuse to bow to the darkness when there's so much light. We're alive, Alice.

Which means there's still a chance we can get out of this."

"We're outnumbered, outgunned, and have no backup."

"Which makes things a bit more problematic, but not impossible." His hands go to my shoulders then slide up my neck and cup the sides of my face. "You need to think through how you can make it look like you're doing what they're asking without actually releasing any information."

"I can't do that. Ramiro is a hacker too, Tucker. He'll know."

"Remember what we did with Find Me?" he asks. "We hid it behind a wall. Do the same thing. Hide the important stuff behind a wall. They're not going to risk spending the time it would take to sort through what they find. They're going to grab and go."

"And then what? They'll discover what I did."

"We only need to buy time for the cavalry to come," he says.

"Why? So they can die too?"

Tucker grins. "You clearly underestimate my brothers."

"There are only four of them. Five if they bring Nova—"

"Exactly. Five of them."

"Against dozens of armed security guards."

"Alice, if Dylan came in here alone, his only weapon a rusted knife, I'd still bet every dollar I have on him. And if

I have that much confidence in one brother, think about what the entire team can do together. Right now, I need you to have faith and decide how you're going to hide important information behind a wall that will be invisible to even the best hackers. Because they were right about one thing—only you can do it."

———

I'M NOT EVEN sure how long we're trapped in this supply closet, but it feels like forever before the door opens and Ramiro steps inside, gun in hand. He points it at us. "Let's go."

I don't move. "You're making a mistake."

He shifts his aim to Tucker, who growls in response. "I'm allowed to shoot him if you don't comply."

Hurt and angry, I take one step. Then another. Tucker moves in behind me, and we leave the closet. When time continued passing and no one showed up to rescue us, I lost hope that Tucker's message had gone through. It was a long shot, anyway, but now the horrible truth settles in: We're on our own.

Tucker stumbles forward, shoving me to the side. He spins and kicks, his foot hitting the firearm in Ramiro's hand and knocking it free.

"Hey!" Ramiro yells.

Tucker doesn't hesitate. He barrels forward, slamming his body into Ramiro and taking him to the ground. He rears back and slams his fist into Ramiro's face then grabs the gun and grips my arm. "Come on."

He moves so fast I barely even have time to breathe from the time we're walking out at gunpoint to running down the hall, gun in hand.

We duck into the stairwell, just out of sight of the cameras. Tucker checks the weapon, counting the rounds in the magazine. "I don't have my camera jammer, so they're going to be able to track every move we make. Think you can guide us out of here?"

"Yes. This way. We'll go out the same way we came in." I move down the stairwell, going as fast as I can to ensure no one catches up with us. As soon as we reach the bottom of the stairwell, Tucker moves in front and checks the hall.

He takes my hand and tugs me out. We race toward the doors where the janitors unknowingly rolled us in.

Hope surges.

It's right there.

Mere feet away.

And then—

Darren steps into view just ahead. Tucker rips me out of the way. A single gunshot echoes, and Tucker stills. He's frozen in place for a moment, then looks down and gently touches his stomach. Blood stains his fingertips.

A low growl cuts through the silence as Tucker raises his gun.

Darren fires again.

Tucker's body jolts.

The weapon in his hand falls.

"No!" I scream. "Tucker!" I rush forward and catch him as he sinks to his knees. The weapon falls beside him, so I lift it, letting him lean against me as I hold the weapon up.

"Pull that trigger, and we'll fill him with lead," Darren warns. "Drop it, Alice."

"Shoot him," Tucker growls against my shoulder.

"I can't. Not when there's still a chance to save you." I drop the gun, and the guards lower theirs.

"Grab him, and take him to the server room."

"No. No! Don't touch him!" I cling to Tucker, but they rip him from me then drag him down the hall toward the elevator. I lunge to my feet and sprint forward. Darren slams his fist into my gut before I can make it past him.

"Put your hands on her again, and I'll tear you apart!" Tucker bellows. He tries to fight against their hold, but with the blood pouring from his wounds, his strength is waning.

Air is ripped from my lungs, and breathing becomes an impossibility when Darren wraps his hand around my throat. "You underestimate me, Alice. A mistake you're going to keep paying for until you realize just who you're dealing with."

"If he dies, I won't help you," I choke out.

"If you don't help me, I'll ensure he dies." Darren throws me to the ground. "Now, I suggest you move quickly. Lover boy is losing a *lot* of blood."

CHAPTER 29
TUCKER

There haven't been many moments in my life when I've been utterly and completely afraid. In most high-risk moments, I'm relatively good at keeping my head. But as I lie here, slowly bleeding to death from two bullet wounds to my abdomen, watching as Alice is marched toward a computer, tears streaming down her cheeks, I can honestly admit I'm terrified.

"You know what to do," Darren orders.

Alice hesitates.

"Don't do it," I tell her. "They're going to kill us anyway."

Darren glares at me for a moment before crossing over and pressing the barrel of his gun into one of the bullet wounds. Pain shoots through my body, fire spreading through my veins and searing every inch of me.

I grind my teeth together, doing what I can to keep from yelling.

"Stop! Fine! I'll do it!" Alice yells. She rushes toward me, but Ramiro, sporting a busted lip and broken nose, grabs her by the arm and pulls her back.

"He's not playing around, Alice. Do what needs to be done so this can all be over. Don't you want this to end?"

"With you dead, sure," she snarls as she rips her arm free from Ramiro's grip then slams her fist into his chin. "Touch me again, and I'll make you regret it."

He balls his hand into a fist and starts toward her, but Darren whistles. "Knock it off. Your lovers' quarrel can wait. Do what I've asked, Alice, or I'll put a bullet right here." He presses the weapon to my temple.

I stare at her, urging her to ignore him and do what's right.

But I see the defeat in her tear-filled crystal gaze.

"Fine. Apply pressure to his wounds, and I'll do it."

Darren grins. "Fair enough. Ramiro, you do the honors. I imagine causing Hunt some pain will bring you joy."

"Not a problem." Ramiro crosses the floor, his gaze murderous. How this guy is related at all to Frank, I'll never understand. He kneels where Darren was crouching only seconds ago, then shreds two pieces of fabric from the bottom part of my shirt, balls them up, and presses them to both of my wounds with far more pressure than necessary.

I choke on a groan, unwilling to give him the satisfaction of knowing how much pain I'm in. Every second that passes, my body grows colder. If the bleeding doesn't stop, I'm not going to last long enough to do anyone any good.

Tears burn in my eyes, so I close them.

Lord, please be with us. If I don't survive, protect Alice. Please let Dylan find happiness, God. Please. I don't want to die, but if it's my time, let Your will be done. But, please, please save them.

I open my eyes right as Alice turns toward the computer.

"Good girl," Darren mutters as Alice begins typing on the keyboard.

He hovers over her, and she turns to glare at him. "I work better when someone isn't breathing on my neck."

He presses the barrel of the gun to her back. "I don't care. I'm going to watch and make sure you do it."

"I didn't realize you knew how to do anything but shoot people." Her tone is sweet but laced with venom, and it brings a half smile to my face.

That's my girl.

My girl.

Will I ever get the chance for that to be true?

Minutes tick by as Alice frantically works, and then— an explosion rattles the windows. My heart pounds. *Yes. Thank You, Lord!*

"What was that?" Darren demands.

I grin. "A family reunion."

His cheeks redden as anger replaces the arrogant expression on his face. "You keep working," he orders Alice then turns toward Ramiro. "Leave him to bleed out if necessary. Watch her, and make sure she does what I need her to do. The rest of you, with me." Darren rushes toward the exit while Ramiro leaves me and withdraws his weapon.

He moves in right behind Alice, the gun in his hand.

As soon as he's close enough, Alice spins and slams her forearm into his, knocking the gun to the ground.

"You stupid, stupid woman!" he yells as he reaches for her. She brings her leg up and kicks him between the legs. Ramiro falls forward as Alice dives for the gun.

I crawl toward her, unable to stay where I am and watch but unable to do much, either, given I've lost the use of my legs and most of the feeling in my body. Breathing is a struggle, but I have to get to her.

Ramiro grips her leg and pulls her forward. She falls, forehead hitting the ground. But she twists in his hold and slams her booted foot into his face. Bone crunches, and he falls still.

Alice gets the gun and holds it up at him, her hand shaking. When he remains still, she sprints over toward where I've fallen, unable to move any farther.

"You need to hang on, okay?" Tears in her eyes, she applies pressure to the wounds on my stomach. There's no telling how much damage the bullet did, but even if it was a through-and-through, the blood loss is so substantial; I don't see myself getting out of this alive.

"I need you to know that I—"

"No, Tucker Hunt. You keep those final words to yourself."

I smirk. "How did you know they were going to be final?" Every single word is labored, every one taking more energy than I have.

"Because I've seen enough movies." She sits down, weapon at her side, and cradles my head in her lap as she applies pressure with her hands. "You better not die on me."

"Make sure Dylan is okay."

"You'll make sure he's okay," she replies, tears streaming down her face. "I don't want to know what it's like to go back to a life without you in it."

Spots invade my vision, and what little feeling I still have in my body fades. "I—" But before I can finish, speaking becomes impossible, and the world fades away.

CHAPTER 30

ALICE

"Tucker? Tucker!" I scream his name, shaking him with one hand while I continue to apply pressure with the other. "No, no. You cannot die. God, please don't take him!" Tears stream down my face. "Please bring him back to me," I cry, cradling the man I've fallen helplessly in love with.

The door opens, so I frantically grab the gun and aim it straight ahead as I cling to Tucker's limp body.

"Tucker?" A frantic voice calls out. *Dylan.*

"Over here!" I scream, dropping the gun. It clatters to the ground. But with the brothers here, I don't need it.

Dylan comes into view, and his expression breaks. "No." He sprints toward me and falls to his knees. Tango and Delta are right behind him, both dogs panting. Tango whimpers and sniffs Tucker's hair. It breaks my heart into even more pieces.

He presses his fingers to Tucker's neck.

"I tried, Dylan. I— Please tell me he's okay."

Bradyn and Elliot come into view, Nova, Bravo, and Echo with them. Their broken expressions are impossible for me to read. Because they can't be thinking what they're thinking right now.

He can't be gone.

I cling to Tucker as Dylan looks over at them. "No pulse."

"No!" I scream. "No!" That's not possible. Nova rushes over and grips my arm, trying to pull me away from Tucker. "No. No. God, no."

Dylan lays his brother flat and begins chest compressions while Riley reaches into the backpack he's carrying and withdraws a packet. They shred Tucker's shirt open, revealing the ugly wounds.

"*Hier,* Tango. *Hier,* Delta," Elliot orders. Tango hesitates but obeys, lying down at Elliot's side beside Delta and Echo.

Nova guides me away. "Come on. He's in good hands now."

"No. I can't leave him."

"Sweetie, come on." Nova wraps her arms around me, and I collapse against her, shoulders shaking with the force of my sobs. Over her shoulder, I watch as Dylan performs CPR and Riley proceeds to pack Tucker's wounds full of gauze.

That means he's okay, right?

After all, they wouldn't try to save a dead man, would they?

They would since he's their brother. No pulse. Dylan said he had no pulse.

Oh, God, please don't take him.

Ramiro groans and starts to sit up. Anger unlike anything I've ever experienced comes over me, and I push away from Nova, get to my feet, and cross over toward him. Bradyn and Elliot are already pulling him to his feet, but I don't stop even as they hold him.

I rear my fist back and slam it into his chin.

"You did this!" I scream, then hit him again. My knuckles burn, but I reach for him again when strong arms come around my waist and pull me back.

"Alice, stop! He's not worth it." Riley hauls me back as Nova steps up between Ramiro and me. Tucker's blood saturates Riley's hands. And that crimson is *all* I can see. His blood. All over his brothers.

"If he dies, I will make you suffer," I growl at Ramiro. "I promise, I will rip you apart with my bare hands. You will pay for what you've done!"

Riley drags me back toward Tucker. "Don't focus on Ramiro. That jerk doesn't need you."

I can barely look at Tucker. He's pale, his eyes shut, body jerking as Dylan continues chest compressions.

"Focus on Tucker. He needs you right now, okay? He needs you."

Grief and fear strangle me, but with shaking hands, I reach down and take Tucker's in mine. "God, please don't let him die," I whisper. "Please."

"Medics are here!" A man yells as another man I don't recognize rushes into the room alongside four paramedics pushing a gurney.

They rush to Tucker's side, and Dylan withdraws. He places both hands on the back of his head after standing then just stares down at his twin.

"Make sure Dylan is okay."

It was the last thing he asked—the only thing he asked of me.

Trembling, I pull away from Riley and move around the room to Dylan. He turns to me, tears in his eyes. Then, he wraps both arms around me and pulls me against his chest. His entire body is trembling as though it's all he can do to keep himself on his feet.

His heart is racing beneath my ear.

"He'll be okay," I say, even though right now, I'm not so sure. "He has to be okay."

The paramedics lower the gurney then lift and place him on top as they start to work, fitting him with an oxygen mask and opening a defibrillator pack. They attach the machine to his chest and shock him.

Tucker's body jolts off the gurney, arching up as the electricity shoots through him.

I choke on a sob and bury my face against Dylan's chest. His arms tighten around me.

"We got rhythm," one calls out.

God, please.

"Let's get him loaded."

I pull away from Dylan as they raise the gurney and roll Tucker away.

"Go," Dylan tells me. "Stay with him."

Nodding, I follow the paramedics. My entire body feels numb as I move down the halls of a place I once knew so well it was practically a second home.

Three bodies have been covered with sheets in the hallway. I keep my gaze straight ahead, trying not to pay too much attention to the war zone as we move through it.

Frank Loyotta is waiting on the lower floor, talking to some police. When he sees me, his gaze darkens. He offers me a single nod then moves away from the officer he's talking to. I glance behind me as he passes then see that the brothers and Nova have brought Ramiro out. The man I thought was my closest friend wears a furious expression as he glares at me.

Wilbur Huck is kneeling on the pavement, cuffed beside Darren.

Darren looks from the gurney to me then grins. It's all I can do not to rush over there and ram my boot into his face.

But Riley is right—anger will do me no good. I need to be there for Tucker.

He's all that matters.

"Here." Dylan holds out a paper cup of coffee to me.

Even though I'm not sure I can stomach anything, I take it from him. Maybe doing something that feels relatively normal will pull me out of this immobile misery where I can't do anything but wait. It's the *worst*.

The doctor hasn't been out since Tucker was wheeled into surgery, and none of the nurses will tell us anything.

Bradyn and Riley are lingering near the doors while Elliot and Nova are sitting down on my other side. Dylan's been pacing, though now he takes a seat beside me, his own coffee in hand.

All of their dogs remain at their sides like shadows.

Except Tango.

He's at my feet, his brown gaze trained on the doors leading to the back as though he knows that's where Tucker is. Leaning down, I run my hand over the top of his large head. "I'm sorry, boy," I whisper. He doesn't even look up at me.

Sitting back in the chair, I close my eyes for a moment as the tears threaten all over again.

Four hours.

It's been four hours since the ambulance arrived. Tucker crashed twice on the way here, and both times, I prayed harder than I ever have, begging God not to take him.

"Are you okay?" Dylan asks.

I open my eyes and sit forward then take a drink of the coffee. It has no taste as it slips down the back of my throat. "No."

"He's going to be okay."

"How can you be sure?" I ask Dylan. "How can you—" I trail off, my chest aching.

"Tucker is the strongest man I've ever known," Dylan tells me. "If anyone can pull through, it's him."

"He lost so much blood." I stare down at my hands. Blood is still crusted to my upper wrists, but I did what I could to wash some of it off before taking a seat. I start picking at it now, trying to scrape the rest of the blood away.

Maybe then, it won't feel so real.

Maybe if I'm clean, I can pretend everything is going to be okay.

"He'll be okay." Dylan reaches over and gently covers my hand.

I notice how his brothers watch us carefully, how surprised they seem at his gentle touch on my hand. But with everything going on, I shove that aside for later. "I love him, Dylan." I whisper the words, almost afraid to say them out loud for fear of what will happen if he doesn't survive.

I won't just lose a friend.

Or someone I've come to adore.

I'll be losing love.

My love.

"I know you do," he replies softly.

"I'm so sorry. To all of you," I add louder. "I brought you all into this. It's my fault he's back there."

"It's not your fault at all," Nova says as she reaches over and takes my other hand. "The only one at fault is the one who pulled the trigger."

"Darren," I growl. "I want to kill him."

"No matter how badly we all want that, vengeance belongs to God," Elliot says as he crosses his arms. "And there is nothing we can dole out that can even come close to what He can do."

"I know that. But—Tucker— We were so close to getting free. It was *right* there."

The waiting room doors slide open, and Frank Loyotta walks in. His expression is hard, his eyes red. He takes his hat off and looks around. When he sees all of us sitting here, his hardened expression softens. "Any news?"

"Not yet," Bradyn replies.

He runs a hand through his hair. "I'm so sorry. I don't

even know what else to say. Ramiro told me everything before they hauled him away. I can't believe he would be capable of this. I just—" He trails off and closes his eyes as a few tears slip free. "I never would have thought him capable of anything like this," Frank says again then turns to me. "Alice, I'm so incredibly sorry for doubting your innocence."

"It's okay," I manage.

Frank nods once then continues toying with the hat in his hands. *He's nervous. Why is he nervous?* "Can I—can I wait with you all?" he asks.

"Of course you can." Elliot stands and clasps a hand on Frank's shoulder. "Please join us. We can use all the prayer we can get right now."

Frank visibly relaxes, taking a seat beside Elliot as he sits again.

The room descends into silence once again, with only the occasional faint ringing of a phone to keep us company.

Lord. I can't even finish the thought because there are no new words to pray. I've already prayed them all. Closing my eyes, I bow my head and simply focus on Tucker. The way his eyes light up when he's smiling.

The dimple barely visible beneath the thick stubble on his face.

Lord, please.

The doors slide open again, and a group of people rush inside. Ruth and Tommy Hunt come in first, heading straight for where we're sitting. Ruth's eyes are red-rimmed and swollen, her hair a mess. Tommy doesn't look much better with his hair on end as though he's been running his hands through it.

Lani is right behind them, her expression serious, eyes red from crying. Riley's wife, Jules, and Bradyn's wife, Kennedy, are with her, walking on either side like pillars of strength for the youngest Hunt. She doesn't join the rest of us though—she splits off from Jules and Kennedy, heading toward the nurse's station.

If anyone can get answers, it's her.

The brothers embrace their wives—all of them letting the weight they've been holding falter just a bit when they wrap their arms around their spouses. I gently squeeze Dylan's hand because, right now, we're all each other has.

My heart aches, and the tears come again. It's all I can do not to crumble into a puddle on the floor.

"Hey, sweetie," Ruth says as she crosses over. Dylan releases me and stands, accepting a hug from his mother.

"I'm so sorry," I tell her.

"You listen to me." Tommy kneels in front of me. "You have nothing to be sorry about, Alice. This wasn't you. Bradyn told us what you did when he called. We know that you fought off Ramiro. That you were able to get pressure on Tucker's—" His voice breaks. "We know what you did for our son. This is, in no way, shape, or form, your fault. Okay, kiddo?"

But it feels like it is.

I close my eyes and hang my head low, doing what I can to breathe.

Tommy squeezes my hand again then stands.

I feel so cold.

"Hey, Ali."

I open my eyes, surprised to see my dad kneeling in front of me, my mom in the seat Dylan was in moments ago. Seeing them brings tears, and I crumble. He brushes some of my hair behind my ear. I know he's likely angry, looking at the bruises on my face, but he doesn't ask about them.

The pain in my chest intensifies when I watch Lani turn toward us, a broken expression on her face, as I cling to my coffee cup like a lifeline. "He can't die, Dad."

"I know, honey." When I wrap my arms around him, he pulls me into his familiar embrace. My mom gently rubs my shoulders. I hold on to them, the cup of coffee the only warmth I'm feeling.

"He coded on the operating table," Lani tells us.

"Oh, God. No." Ruth leans into Tommy, and he wraps his arms around her.

"They were able to reestablish rhythm, but he's not out of the woods just yet," she says. "We need to pray—hard. Because if Tucker is going to survive, he needs a miracle."

CHAPTER 31

TUCKER

They tell me I died.

More than once.

The doctor says he's not even sure how I'm still alive. That, for all intents and purposes, I should be with the Lord right now.

It's a miracle, they keep saying. But they don't know the half of it. I saw death. In those brief moments when my heart was not beating, I felt the warm embrace, the gentle peace that settled around me. It was unlike anything I've ever experienced. Even now, it feels like a dream rather than something I experienced while my heart was stopped.

Then I was ripped back into the now. Into pain and darkness. But I will thank God for that every single day. Because it means my time isn't over yet. Barely awake, I lie in a hospital bed with a cannula beneath my nose. I'm exhausted and surrounded by the beeping sounds of a machine in the background and the oxygen being pumped into my nose, filling my lungs.

The door opens, and Lani walks in alongside my mother.

My mom covers her mouth on a sob then walks around to gently caress my forehead just like she used to do when I was a kid and sick.

"I thought I told you guys to stop getting shot," Lani says, tears in her eyes.

"First time for me, remember?" I choke out. My throat is so dry, but it feels good to speak. "Alice?"

"She's fine. In the waiting room. Doctor said you can only have two visitors at a time, and she told Mom and me to go first." Lani reaches down and takes my hand.

Knowing Alice is okay and close by eases that gnawing fear I've had since waking up. "She's okay," I repeat, closing my eyes.

"I wouldn't say okay," Lani says.

"What do you mean?" I open my eyes, my heart rate increasing to the point that an alert sounds on the monitor. I know she'd been hurt when Darren hit her. Did he do more damage than I thought? Did Ramiro hurt her after I lost consciousness?

Lani releases my hand to turn the alarm off on the machine. "Calm down. You're not out of the woods yet." She takes a deep breath. "Physically, she's fine. She's a mess, worried about you."

I recall how she'd clung to me as I slipped away. Her frantic cries. Her pleas with God to save me. Pain blooms in my chest. I raise an arm and gently rub my free hand against it.

"How are you feeling?" my mom asks.

"Tired. Kind of out of it."

"That'll happen when you come back from the dead," Lani replies. "I'm going to head back into the waiting room so I can send Dylan in. He's a mess too. He did chest compressions on you until the paramedics arrived. Riley packed your wounds. The two of them are the only reason you were loaded into an ambulance instead of a coroner's van."

My mom chokes on a sob, so I reach up and gently cover her hand with mine.

Riley would have handled that fine. He goes into work mode and blocks out everything else. But Dylan. What did that cost him? Those moments of uncertainty? Of pain?

My brother has already suffered so much, and I hate that he thought that—even for a moment—I was gone.

"Okay. Thanks."

"I'll go too. That way Alice can come see you." My mom leans down and kisses my forehead, lingering there for just a moment. "I love you so much, Tucker Hunt."

"Love you too, Mom. Love you, Lani."

She squeezes my hand again then heads over toward the door.

"Love you," Lani says. "Glad you didn't die."

I smile as they leave the room. Once I'm alone, I close my eyes for a moment. Everything is so hazy that I can barely keep my eyes open. The room spins a bit, but it subsides the longer my eyes are closed. As I drift, I think I hear the door open again, but I'm already too far under to open my eyes again.

———

BY THE TIME I surface again, I'm feeling a bit better. I open my eyes and note that it's dark outside now. Dylan is sitting next to the bed with a book in his hand.

"I didn't know you could read."

His gaze lifts instantly, locking on me. "I like to look at the pictures," he replies.

I grin. "It's good to see you."

"You too, Tuck. You had us all scared."

"Me too. How are you?"

"I'm not the one who was target practice. Two bullet holes. Man, when you do something for the first time, you go all out." His tone is sharp, strained.

"Dylan."

He leans forward and sets the book down on the table. "I'm better now," he says. "But I really thought you were gone. When I came in and saw her clinging to you, when you had no pulse—" Tears burn in his gaze. "I can't outlive you, Tucker. We have a deal."

I reach over and take his hand. "We go out together in a firestorm of bullets while we save the world. That's the plan. I remember."

He snorts and rubs tears from his eyes with his free hand. "Your girl is a tough one."

My girl.

"She is."

"She went completely feral on Ramiro. Riley had to drag her away from him."

Pride warms my chest. "Really?"

He nods. "She stayed with you on the way here too. They had to nearly restrain her to keep her from following you into surgery. It wasn't until I got here that she even let herself get checked out. Physically, she's fine."

I take a deep breath and smile, imagining Alice putting up a fight when they asked her to leave. I can picture her charging after Ramiro the same way she went after those bruisers in her parents' house.

"You love her."

His words are a punch to the gut. A reminder of the promise I made to myself all those years ago. Yet, here I am, breaking it because I fell head over heels in love with her. "Yeah."

"So, you caught those pesky feelings after all."

I laugh, then wince when pain shoots through my

abdomen. "Yeah, I guess I did. Not sure anything will come of it though."

"Why not?"

"I just— I don't know that it's the right time."

Dylan covers my hand with his. "You've been taking care of me for a long time, brother. Longer than you needed to. But I can't be the reason you refuse to be happy."

"What do you mean?" *Did Alice say something, did someone—*

"I've known for a long time that you've been putting off letting yourself be happy because of me. But my demons are mine, Tuck. They're not yours."

"You're my twin."

"And you've been sacrificing for me long enough. Come on, Tuck, don't let Alice get away because you're afraid of what could happen if you let yourself embrace what you feel for her."

A tear slips down my cheek as the weight of my brother's pain lessens ever so slightly. "I don't want to leave you alone."

"You won't. We live less than a mile apart, Tucker."

I snort. "True."

"Just do me a favor and stop suffering on my behalf. My own pain is hard enough to carry; I don't want to shoulder yours too."

I nod. "Okay."

There's a soft knock on the door right before it opens.

Alice steps in, her eyes wide, one bruised. There's a cut on her cheekbone and another splitting her lower lip. Seeing her injuries brings a fresh wave of anger over me, but it's nothing compared to the joy consuming me as I lay eyes on her again.

Our gazes hold with her standing by the door and me unsure what to say.

What do I say to her?

What if she decides she wants to stay in California?

"I'll check in a bit later." Dylan takes his book and stands, pausing right before Alice. He gently touches her shoulder and whispers something in her ear.

I'm so shocked at the sight of him touching her that I nearly miss her soft laugh. He *never* touches anyone. The darkness doesn't return when he leans in, and the smile on his face doesn't fade.

It only makes me love her even more that she puts him so at ease.

"Okay," she replies.

Dylan flashes me another smile then heads out of the room.

"How are you feeling?" Alice asks, crossing over toward the chair Dylan just vacated.

"Like I can no longer brag about having never been shot," I reply, hoping it'll bring a smile to her face. Instead, her expression falters, and tears break free. "I'm sorry, Alice, poor joke." I reach out for her, and she takes a seat on the edge of the hospital bed. There's barely a sliver of space available, but I wrap an arm around her to keep her from falling. She lays her head against my chest, fitting so perfectly against me.

"I thought you were going to die, Tucker. You did die. You crashed in the ambulance on the way here. On the operating table. They didn't think you were going to make it."

"God wasn't ready for me yet," I say softly then kiss the top of her head. "How are you doing?" I tip her face up and gently brush my thumb over her split lip.

"I'm better now."

"Ramiro?"

"In jail where he belongs," she growls. "They have enough evidence on him, Wilbur Huck, Darren, Kara, and the rest of their security team to lock them up for a long, long time. It was on the news earlier. Web Safe is going to be lucky if they can keep their doors open after this. So I guess I'm out of a job."

I laugh. "I bet we can find you something else."

"We?" she asks.

"What kind of guy would I be if I let you job hunt alone?"

She laughs then takes a deep breath. "Frank is in the waiting room. He hasn't left since he arrived. He's pretty broken up over what happened."

My heart aches for Frank. For believing he'd lost his

nephew to finding out that he was behind all of this—responsible for murder and trying to steal sensitive information, all for money.

"Did the hackers get anything?"

She shakes her head against my chest. "They didn't get anything. Your brothers got there right in time."

"They always do."

"Hey, Tucker?" She raises her head, crystal gaze bright and shimmering with unshed tears.

"Yeah?"

She swallows hard, then opens her mouth before closing it again. "I'm just really glad you survived. I don't know what I would have done if you hadn't."

"Me too."

I know it's probably ridiculous, but there's a part of me that was hoping she'd say those three words I am so desperate to hear. Three words that would change everything between us.

CHAPTER 32
ALICE

My apartment was once a safe haven for me. The place I'd wind down from a long day at work. I would sit at the table every morning, Bible open in front of me, sipping from a cup of coffee while the sun rose over the mountains in the distance.

Now it's just a place where I used to live. Where my life was predictable, my days planned out to the very hour when I would lay my head down on top of my pillow.

I place my jewelry box inside a moving box then lean down when a photo strip flutters to the ground. Bending over, I lift it and feel a familiar grief settle in my chest. Ramiro and I took these photos a few months ago when we went bowling with some of our other friends. Both of us are smiling and happy, making silly faces in each of the three prints.

Who would have thought, less than a year later, he'd be trying to kill me.

Tears burn in my vision as I toss it into the trash bag beside my dresser then turn to survey my room. Bed stripped, dresser empty, closet bare…everything in boxes.

"Hey, Ali, you ready?" Dad peeks his head into my room. "Hey, are you okay?"

"What? Oh, yeah, just remembering the past." I smile then seal up the top of the box containing my jewelry box, journal, and a few other special items I wanted close by for the move.

He comes into the room then looks down into the trash bag. "Ahh, yes. The past." He pulls the plastic strip, tightening the bag. "He was your friend at one time. Regardless of how it turned out, it's normal to grieve."

"I know. But I don't want to anymore. I want to move forward, one step at a time."

We leave my room together, and I set the box down on top of the stack already prepped for the movers who are coming first thing in the morning. Dad sets the trash by the door then turns to survey my apartment.

"You know, I remember when your mother and I helped you move into this place. Logan was there too, if I remember correctly."

Logan. "He was. Dropped a box with some pictures and broke the glass on every single one."

Dad laughs. "He was mortified."

"Replaced them all too. Somehow, he managed to get into the apartment when I was at the gym, so when I got home, I was surprised by all the new frames."

"That's sweet."

"He was." Even if we hadn't been a fit romantically, I will always appreciate Logan for the friendship we maintained even after we'd broken up.

And I'm not sure I'll ever be able to forgive myself for putting my trust in Ramiro when Logan was the one who deserved it.

"You ready to go?" Dad asks.

"I am. I could use an entire pizza in fuel too. I'm exhausted." I retrieve my purse, and Dad laughs while he hauls the garbage bag out of the apartment, leaving it beside the door for the trash pickup in the morning. After locking the door behind me, we make our way down the steps. His Subaru is parked in the spot right beside my apartment, and as I climb inside, I breathe in the familiar scent of his cologne.

After everything we went through, I knew I couldn't come back to this apartment. A fresh start is exactly what I'm looking for, and that can't be found when everything around me reminds me of the past.

"Hey, can we swing by the cemetery before heading home?"

"Sure thing, honey." Dad reaches over and closes his hand over mine, squeezing it gently.

My phone dings, so I withdraw it and smile when I see a text from Lani.

Lani: Everything is ready for your arrival!

There's a photograph of an empty living room right beneath the text.

Nerves twist in my gut, but more than that is excitement. Joy. Because my fresh start is coming as soon as noon tomorrow when my flight lands in Dallas.

Me: I can't wait. Does he suspect anything?

Lani: He's a guy…so no.

I laugh.

"What's funny?" Dad asks, casting me a smile.

"Lani. My apartment is ready to go. I asked her if Tucker knew, and she said no because he's a guy."

My dad barks out a laugh. "Us guys do tend to be rather obtuse at times."

"At times," I reply with a smile.

"Speaking of Tucker—how is he doing?"

"Better. Lani cleared him to start walking up to two miles a day and some bodyweight exercises, so he's happy about that."

"That's good."

"Yeah. I thought so. Dylan is picking me up at the airport tomorrow so I can surprise him."

Dad is quiet for a moment. "You know, your mother and I are so proud of you, Alice."

"Why? Because I'm moving away?"

He laughs. "No. Well, not just that, anyway. You're following where you feel God calling you, and that, my dear child, is wonderful."

"Did I tell you that the CEO of Web Safe offered me the director position?"

"What? Seriously?"

I nod. "I wanted to know what I was going to do before I told you guys."

"Alice, that is amazing."

"It would have been—a few months ago. Even if I set aside my feelings for Tucker, I wouldn't ever want to go back to that place. It just wouldn't be the same. Everything would be a reminder of what I lost."

"Something I understand quite well. You should know that your mother and I have been talking, and—well—we don't think Texas would be a bad place to live for two old folks on the verge of retirement."

Joy blossoms in my chest. "Really?"

He smiles. "We can't do anything right now, but within the next year or so, I think we might be able to swing a move like that."

"Dad, I would—but your life is here."

"You're our life, Ali. And if this thing with Tucker pans out, there might be some grandchildren in our future?"

Heat burns my cheeks. "Dad. I haven't even told him how I feel yet. I'd say grandchildren are a ways away."

He laughs again then turns into the parking lot of the

cemetery. After pulling into a spot and turning the engine off, he turns to me. "Even still. You are our life. Our every-thing. And we're so proud of you."

"Thanks, Dad."

"You're welcome." He withdraws what he refers to as his "car book" from his console and removes his seat belt. "Now, you go do what you have to do. I'll be here when you're ready."

I let out a light laugh and climb out of the car, then head down the aisle toward where Logan was laid to rest last week.

Every step I take feels heavy, but I need to say goodbye one more time. One final bit of closure before I can end this chapter and move into the next one.

LOGAN TARMAC is carved into cool stone, along with a pair of combat boots and dog tags. I kneel beside his grave then gently run my hands over his name.

"I haven't had the chance to tell you how sorry I am." Tears sting in the corners of my eyes. "I should have trusted you when you'd told me that there was something about Ramiro you didn't trust. I thought you were just being jeal-ous, and maybe on some level you were, but—I can't help but believe, if I'd have just trusted you, then you wouldn't be dead right now." I close my eyes, shoulders shaking. "I'm sorry, Logan. You deserved better. I should have been a better friend to you. I should have never brought you into this." My throat burns as I try my best to keep from completely losing it to the guilt. "I pray you're resting in peace with the angels now."

"I imagine he is."

I glance up, the familiar voice bringing a whole slew of emotions running through me. "Samuel?"

"Hello, Alice." He's older now, his hair more white than gray, and there are fresh lines around his eyes.

"You—how are you here?"

"I travel around here and there." He takes a seat beside me, and a familiar peace settles over me. "I am truly sorry for the loss of your friend."

I continue staring at him. We're in a totally different city than before, a brand-new area. *How is this possible?* "I don't— Thank you."

He smiles sadly at me. "You've suffered greatly in your young life, yet there is still so much light in you. Just like that first time we met. You remember?"

"Of course I remember. I looked for you after that, but no one knew who you were."

He chuckles. "I was around. Aside from this tragic loss, I take it things have worked out? On the family front?"

"Yeah. Two amazing people adopted me right after we met the last time. They're wonderful."

"That's good. I'm glad to hear it." He studies me. "There's more. You have the spark of love in your eyes."

I laugh. "You could say that."

"He a good man?"

"He is. I just have to see if he feels the same."

"I wouldn't worry too much about that. Bright things are in your future, Alice. Bright things."

"Thanks. I'm honestly not quite sure what I'm going to do next. But I'll pray about it until the path becomes clear."

"That's all any of us can do." He smiles at me.

I keep staring at him, half expecting him to sprout angel wings or disappear, but he continues sitting beside me beneath the sunlight, the chirping of birds all around us. "How are you here? Coincidence doesn't seem to cover it."

"Like I said, I travel a lot. Going where I'm needed." He turns toward me. "But I don't get the sense you're going to need me anymore. I'll continue to pray for you, Alice Sterling, and for your future. I imagine God has great things in store for you." He pushes to his feet, so I do the same. "Keep your eye on the future, and follow where He leads."

"Always. I— Wait, I never told you my last name."

Samuel simply smiles. "Goodbye, Alice."

"Goodbye."

With a smile still on his face, he turns and begins walking back toward the trees. I lose sight of him near the edge of the cemetery where the path curves behind the chapel.

Tears fill my eyes, and I wrap my arms around myself. "Thank You, God. Thank You."

"Come on, Lani. I don't need to be babysat."

"Oh, stop complaining. We're not stopping by for long. I just need to grab a few things before dinner."

"Fine. But why can't I wait in the car?" I ask as we climb the steps up to her apartment.

"Because then I wouldn't have the pleasure of your company while I looked for the perfect shade of lipstick."

I roll my eyes but grin. Lani's been practically glued to my side since they released me from the hospital and we flew back home. Up until yesterday afternoon, she was even staying in my guest room. Between her taking care of me, my mom bringing me every meal, and my brothers dropping in from time to time, I haven't had any time at all to think.

To process the fact that the woman I love is living clear

across the country from me, and I haven't even had the chance to tell her exactly how I feel. It's wild that I faced down death—literally—yet I'm terrified of saying three little words.

"Here we are." She stops in front of a door.

"Wait—" I look down the hall, then back at the stairs. "This isn't your place."

"What do you mean?"

"Your apartment is there," I point to the next door over. "This is too close to the stairs."

Lani rolls her eyes and slides the key into the lock. "You need a hobby." She shoves open the door then steps away to mess with her purse. "Can you hit the lights for me?"

"I know this isn't your apartment, Lani. What—" I flip on the lights and lose my breath.

Alice is standing just inside, wearing an off-white summer dress, her dark hair curled and loose around her face. She smiles. "Hey there, MadCode."

"I— What are you doing here?" I step into the apartment. It's empty of all the furniture with only a suitcase and her purse in the center of it.

Her expression falters just a bit, and I realize what I said sounded a whole lot like I'm not happy for her to be here.

I smile, letting all the joy I feel show in my expression. "You're here."

"They offered me the director job at Web Safe, which got me thinking." She takes a step closer.

"Oh?"

"Should I take what would have been my dream job or follow where my soul is pulling me? Where I feel God guiding me."

"Which brought you here."

"To you." Alice takes another step closer. "I don't know what the future holds for us, Tucker Hunt, but I know that I really don't want to do it without you."

I'm speechless. Am I even breathing?

"Say something, you idiot," Lani urges from behind me.

"When I was lying on that floor, not sure I would live, my greatest regret was not telling you how I felt." I close the distance between us and cup her face with my hand. "You're everything I've been waiting for—everything that I was too afraid to want because of my own guilt. I love you, Alice Sterling. I think I might have loved you from the first moment I saw you staring up at me from that basement."

Alice's eyes fill, and she smiles. "Thank God for that because it would have been really awkward if I'd moved here and you hadn't—"

I slam my mouth onto hers, cutting her off and putting all of the love I feel into the kiss. Her hands wind around my neck, and she pulls me closer as I snake one hand up and bury it in her hair.

My entire future is right here. The happiness I was so afraid to want because I didn't think I deserved it. The peace I've been seeking.

The joy.

And I have God to thank for it because He brought this woman to me in her darkest hour, then stayed by our sides as we fought to survive everything this world threw at us.

He, and He alone, brought us through the storm.

And He blessed me with the chance to love this woman with everything that I am.

EPILOGUE

"That's the last box," Tucker says as he sets it down on top of the rest of them.

I finish putting my favorite coffee cups in the cabinet then turn just in time to have him capture me in his arms and kiss me until my blood is buzzing with love and desire.

"You're moved in, wife."

"I am." I kiss him again then bury my hands in his hair. Everything about this man fits perfectly with me. We're two of a kind. A pair of souls who have found our perfect fit in one another.

"Hey now, wait until the parents are gone," my dad jokes as he and Tommy Hunt bring in a tray of cookies.

"To be fair, we didn't know you were here," I reply with a smile.

My dad sets the cookies down. "A gift from your mother," he says. "She and Ruth are planning a feast tonight. A celebration of your return from your honeymoon and what she calls the official start of your lives together."

I turn away from Tucker, though I press my back into his chest as he wraps both arms around my waist.

"If today is the start, then what were the past two weeks?" I ask with a laugh.

"That's what I told her," my dad replies. "Anyway, we promised we'd bring these here, but Tommy is going to help me hang the TV in our living room, then we'll be over for dinner." My parents closed on a house in town just a few days ago and are selling their place out in California.

It's their fresh start too.

I pull away from Tucker and cross the living room to hug my dad. "Thanks, Dad. I'm so glad you and Mom are here now."

"Us too, Ali. Us too." He steps back and looks at Tucker. "Good to see you, son. We'll see you tonight."

"See you tonight." Tucker waves, and they close the door behind them as they leave. "Now, where were we?" he asks, pulling me back in.

I encircle his neck with my arms and lean into the kiss.

"Want to dance?"

"Dance?" I laugh. "There's no music."

Tucker begins to hum, and I throw my head back in a laugh as he twirls me around the living room while Tango watches curiously from his bed, tongue hanging out.

If my life ended right now, I could say that I'd lived it well. Not just because of the things I've done but because of the love I found. The love I wasn't too afraid to embrace. Tucker is everything to me.

And I think, on some level, I always knew he would be.

"I will never get enough of this. Of you," he whispers as he slows down, swaying me to the music in his head. "You completely consume me, Alice Hunt."

"I feel the same way about you," I reply, then lose myself in him as he kisses me again.

THANK you so much for reading Tucker and Alice's story! I hope you loved it as much as I do! Keep reading for a bonus chapter, PLUS the first five chapters of Dylan's book, Delta!

Happy reading!

BONUS CHAPTER: EMMA

"I think that'll do," I say with a happy smile as I stand back and study both floral wreaths I designed and hung on the church's front doors—soft white sprigs of baby's breath combined with crystal blue hydrangeas, their stems in foam I soaked to ensure they'd remain alive through the Easter celebration we're having tomorrow.

An Easter egg hunt followed by a potluck and some live music. It's going to be a great day, and there's only one thing that would make it better.

"You did a lovely job, Emma, as usual." Pastor Ford says with a smile. "You sure you want to go into teaching? I think you would be great at floral design."

I laugh. "A fallback plan, for sure."

He chuckles. "You won't need one. You're going to be a fantastic teacher."

"Thanks." I bend down and lift the bag of supplies I

brought just in case I needed to tweak anything once we actually got them hung on the doors. "Is there anything else I can help with?"

"Just the centerpieces, you've got those covered?"

"Arranged and in the refrigerator at Karry's shop." I've been working part-time at Karry's Flowers for the last few years to pay my way through college. It's been a gift from God, and I thank Him every day for the opportunity, though I am excited for the next chapter.

Even if the one person I wish I could share it with still isn't home.

"Great. We'll see you tomorrow, then."

"Yes. First thing!" I call out as I head down the steps. It's such a beautiful day that I opted to walk the two blocks to the church. Fresh air wraps around me, and I take a deep breath, enjoying the way the light breeze dances with the strands of my hair that slipped free from my bun.

"Hey, Emma!" Talia Matthews, the diner owner, calls as she places their daily specials board out in front of the diner.

"Hey! French dip today?" I ask, reading her board.

"Yes."

"Then you know I'll be seeing you later," I reply with a laugh as I move past the diner and into the floral shop two doors down.

Once inside, I set the bag down and check on the centerpieces again, just to make sure everything is in its place. Karry is at home on maternity leave, so it's all me. I don't mind it in the least, but the quiet does give me way too much time to think.

And miss him.

The bell overhead dings. "Hey, welcome, what can I do for—" I trail off when I turn to see Tucker standing in the doorway, his expression broken.

My heart falls.

My stomach turns into a pit.

And pain, unlike anything I've ever experienced, guts me. "No."

"I'm so sorry, Emma. They say that—"

"No. Don't you dare say it, Tucker Hunt." Tears fill my eyes, and my throat constricts. I shake my head and back up until I'm pressed against the cooler, as though distance will change what he's trying to tell me.

That the man I love more than life itself—

The man I want to spend the rest of my life with is dead.

"I'm trying to find out what happened, but they say he's gone." Tucker's voice breaks, and he sinks to his knees, unable to stand any longer.

They say he's gone.

He can't be gone.

I just opened a letter from him last month.

I'm not even sure how I manage to walk, but I close the distance between us and sink to my knees. As I wrap my arms around my love's twin brother, I lose the fight against the pain that's ripping me open and pouring acid into the wounds.

God, please, no. Why would You do this to me? Why would You take him?

"They said there's no body," Tucker cries. "I'm going to find him. Even if he really is gone, I can't just leave him out there alone. In the cold. He needs to come home."

I hold on to Tucker, barely hearing what he's saying.

Dylan can't be gone.

God, please don't let him be gone.

Keep reading for the first five chapters of Dylan's book, Delta!

DELTA CHAPTER 1: DYLAN

The steady *drip, drip, drip* is slowly driving me mad.

Or maybe it's the fact that I haven't eaten in—I don't know how long.

Or dehydration.

Or the putrid stench of the bodies decomposing on the floor of my prison. Even now it sears the insides of my lungs, burning me up from the inside. At least I can't see them or stare into their dead eyes. This pitch-black hole we were thrown into ensures that.

No, I can't see them.

But I can *feel* them.

The death surrounding me.

They used to moan in agony. Used to plead with God for mercy.

Until, one by one, they fell silent. Leaving only the *drip, drip, drip.*

How long until I join them, too? Why haven't I already?

I've begged for my life to be taken. Pleaded.

Yet, here I remain. Wrists chained in front of me, trapped in a cell of death, ready for whatever nightmare they have planned for me next. The upside to all the pain? Anything new they do is just background noise.

As they torment me, I let my mind drift back to home.

Back to her.

Blonde hair. Sun-kissed freckled face. Eyes so blue they make me want to swim in them forever.

My love.

My Emma.

Would she even recognize me if she were to see me now? Would she see past the animal I've become to the man I used to be?

I've been bound so long, I don't even know what it feels like to be unchained. I'm a creature in a cage. A shackled monster. That's what they've made me.

Light assaults me when the lid covering my prison is opened. It burns my eyes, so I close them tightly, listening only to the sound of the yelling above, in a language I can't understand.

Slowly, I try to open my eyes, but the moment I do, tears fill them. The light is so beautiful. Is this it? Am I dead?

But before the thought can fully form in my mind, the

light is momentarily blocked by two bodies rushing down the stairs toward me.

I grip the hilt of the blade I'd found when I'd felt around the cell for something to fight with. I'd pulled it off of one of the dead—then promised to use it to get justice for us all.

Even if it's the last thing I do.

"Get up," a man orders in a thick accent. I don't know his name, but I know he loves to play with fire. I have the burns to prove it.

I don't listen. *Get closer.*

"I said get up!" He raises a rifle at me.

Does he not know that I don't fear death? It would be sweet relief for me to leave this world. Doesn't he realize just how dangerous that makes me? After all, a man with nothing to lose is hardly a man at all.

The buttstock of his rifle slams into my cheek. I barely feel the pain, though I taste the blood. Instead of letting him intimidate me, I tilt my face up.

And smile.

His dark eyes narrow on me. "You do not hold the power here, American," he growls. "Or have you forgotten?"

"We don't have time for this." The second man—one I don't recognize—rushes over and grips my arm to rip me up to my feet. With all the weight I've lost, it's not a struggle for him to do so.

Together, they drag me out of the hole and throw me to the ground. All around, chaos reigns. Alarms are screeching, armed men are running around shouting orders.

Drip. Drip. Drip.

I can still hear it.

Why can I still hear it?

"Let's go," the second man orders as he tugs me the rest of the way out of the hole.

"No!" With a feral yell, I slice out with the blade.

The man yells when it catches his arm.

"Idiot!" the butt of a rifle is slammed into my gut, and I fall forward, gasping for breath, but I don't remain down long.

Someone yells, but my gaze is focused only on killing the man in front of me.

On killing him just as he killed my friends.

On killing *them all.*

The man raises his rifle and fires.

Two bullets.

One.

Two.

They tear through me and I fall backward—down, down, down—into the hole. The knife stabs into my waist, but as soon as I catch my breath, I roll to the side and tug it free, the pain nothing more than a pinch compared to everything else my body has been through.

I can't feel much of anything anymore…except this

thirst for vengeance. This desire to watch my enemies *burn*. Not even bullets can stop me now. Not after what they've done to me.

Two men descend into the hole again. Shadows that momentarily block out the sunlight once more.

I can't see their faces, but it doesn't matter because they're *all* the same. Monsters masquerading as men. Threats to be eliminated. The world will be safer without them here. Isn't that why I went through all of this? Why my men were cut down? Because we were sent here to stop these monsters from committing genocide?

I remain still, waiting for my chance as one moves to my cuffs. *Bad move, Enemy.* They think I'm dead. They probably want the cuffs for another member of the living. But they won't get that chance. I won't let them do to someone else what they did to me.

The cuffs fall off of my wrists, clattering to the ground. Summoning what little strength I have left, I lunge to my feet and slash out with the rusted blade.

"Dylan!" someone yells, but I don't recognize the voice. "Stop!"

I can't stop. Don't they see that? They've turned me into exactly what I was always afraid of becoming: a killer. I slash out again and large hands grip my arms. I'm slammed to the ground, face-first, a knee between my shoulder blades.

"Let me go!" I spit. "I'm going to kill all of you!" I

thrash beneath them, but within seconds all the energy leaves my body and I fall still. Breathing is a struggle; it has been since well before this moment.

Honestly, I've been struggling to draw breath since I left home.

Since I left *her*.

"We need to get him out of here," a man says.

"I'll cover you," another replies.

Their tones are strained, tense. But they don't have the accents my abductors have. Does that make them different? Or are they merely here to take away what's left of me?

I'm flipped, then lifted and draped across a shoulder. The man carries me toward the steps, and I don't fight it. Instead, I close my eyes and let my thoughts drift back to the small shred of humanity left in me.

Golden hair.

Soft brown eyes.

Freckle-dusted skin.

Maybe this will finally be the end for me. Maybe I'll finally find peace—if that even exists. I'm beginning to believe it was all a lie. But as I drift away, letting myself come to terms with what will likely be my last moments, I picture her face.

And in my imagination, I get the chance to say goodbye.

DELTA CHAPTER 2: EMMA

The fall sun kisses my face as I make my way down Main Street. A light breeze toys with the strands of hair that escaped from the braid I put it in this morning, and over-head, birds soar through the cloudless sky.

Man, it's so beautiful outside today. Such an absolutely lovely day to be alive. Reaching up, I gently touch the cross around my neck. *Thank You, Lord, for this day.* It truly is a gift.

Smiling, I let my hand drop as I head up the walk and toward the diner. Lunch is *calling* me. Has been for hours since I skipped breakfast. But I had a goal—and now that goal is met. My reward? Food.

Delicious food.

The door is propped open, so I can smell the scent of fresh apple pie before I've even fully entered. I don't know that I've ever been more grateful that I already got my run in this morning. Because that means *two* slices of Talia's delicious pie for me today. One for after lunch, the other for dinner.

"Good morning, Emma," Talia greets as I step inside. Her slightly greying hair is pulled back in a high ponytail, just as it always is whenever she's working. "I'll be right with you."

"No rush at all." I beam at her, then take a seat on one of the orange barstools at the counter before pulling out my list and marking off the last errand I finished. *Check on bounce houses. Check!* It's only just now lunch time, and I've already made an impressive dent in today's To Do list.

It's been a great day.

"What can I get for you today, lovely?" Talia asks as she sets some wrapped silverware in front of me.

"Chai tea and a grilled chicken salad, please, ma'am. And two slices of apple pie to go."

"You got it. We still on for your birthday dinner tomorrow night?"

"Of course." I grin. "My mouth is already watering."

"Good." With a smile, Talia heads into the kitchen, leaving me to glance around the diner and see who is currently grabbing lunch. Sheriff Gibson is in a booth with his mother, both of them laughing happily as they enjoy their lunch. I offer him a wave when he glances in my direction.

Then there's Kennedy Hunt's parents, who both offer

me kind smiles as they make their way up to the counter to pay their tab, alongside Alice Hunt's parents. They're relatively new to town, their daughters having married two of the five Hunt brothers. According to Lani, they bonded shortly after Alice's parents located here last year.

I've lived in Pine Creek my entire life—well, almost my entire life. I was born in Massachusetts but was put up for adoption when I was only a few days old. The couple that adopted me relocated back here, where they both grew up.

I was nine months old when we came back, so for all intents and purposes, this place has been my home for my entire life. I know everyone and they know me. We all support each other, which I was certainly grateful for after my parents' accident thirteen years ago. I'd barely been eighteen when I lost them. But I had a town to rally around me. An entire family of people who made sure I didn't lose myself, too.

That familiar knot of grief wells up inside of me and I have to actively fight it back down. It was a season of grief and pain. One thing after another for three years after I lost them. God is the only reason I survived, and I believe wholeheartedly He guided the town to close in around me so I didn't feel so alone.

"Here you go, honey." Talia sets a mug down in front of me, the hot water already turning a pale brown thanks to the bag of fresh spices steeping inside. "Food'll be up in a moment."

"Great. Thanks." As she steps away, I slide my list back into my purse, then withdraw my latest read. A swoony romance about two people who survive a plane crash and end up marooned on an island. Rivals to romance—my favorite kind.

There's just something about that moment when they finally realize that *everything* they've been fighting against is everything they need.

If only things worked like that in real life. An all-too-familiar face swims into the front of my memory, but I bat it down.

No. There is no time for shattered dreams and broken hearts right now.

This has been a good day, and it will continue to be a good day.

As I focus on the words printed across the pages, I completely tune out the world around me, letting myself be fully engulfed in the story, the characters, the everything. Here, I can block out all of my own problems and watch as the characters solve theirs. Here, things are easy. A safe formula I can count on.

Girl meets boy.

Chaos ensues.

Boy chooses girl over everything.

There is no life after the "happily ever after" where things can still fall apart.

"Hey there, bookworm."

I jolt a bit, then turn and smile at Riley Hunt as he slides onto the stool beside me. The third oldest, Riley has always been a bit more laid back then the rest of his brothers.

His dark hair is a mess of loose waves, and he's wearing his ranch clothes which means he's been out working rather than running errands. Not surprising. The Hunts are hard workers and the first to lend a hand if things go sideways.

"Hey, yourself, Mr. Hunt. No Romeo?" I ask, noting that his adorable German Shepherd service dog is nowhere to be seen.

"Nah, he's with Jules today. She's going to meet with one of her charges and they love dogs. She's hoping he'll help the girl open up a bit, and I know he'll keep my wife safe. Win, win, all the way around."

After suffering trauma no one should have to go through, Jules turned her pain into strength and now spends quite a bit of time in Dallas, at the headquarters for Find Me, a company that rescues trafficking victims from all over the world.

Frank Loyotta, who runs Find Me, occasionally calls in outside help for particularly hard cases. All five of the Hunt brothers have been recruited on more than one occasion to aid in rescue missions since they run their own search and rescue company. And now, Jules is the one who helps these victims transition back into whatever normalcy they can find. Because she's been through it, too.

"It's so great she's doing that."

"She loves it." I can see the pride all over his face.

"I'm glad." I beam at him, then look at the book he set on the counter in front of him. "What did you bring today?"

"A thriller. You?"

"Romance." I hold mine up. "You know me."

He laughs. "That, I do."

I practically grew up alongside the Hunt family. First, it started out with me being friends with the youngest of the Hunts—Lani. We bonded over both being adopted and became friends despite the one year age gap between us.

Then I met Dylan. And my entire world shifted. *If only it would shift back.*

"Riley. What can I get for you?" Talia asks, her friendly smile always warm and inviting.

"A burger and fries for me, a club sandwich with extra crispy bacon and a bag of potato chips for my dad, and another burger with no mayo and a side of onion rings to go, please." He doesn't say who the last burger is for, and he doesn't have to. I know that Dylan prefers onion rings to fries, and he hates mayonnaise. The Independence Day parade picnic cemented that when the potato salad got left out too long and he got sick to his stomach.

"You got it." After making a note on her pad, she heads back into the kitchen.

"How are things going out at the ranch?" I ask, hoping he doesn't know what I'm *really* asking. *How's Dylan? Has he decided he misses me as much as I miss him yet?*

"Not too bad. Dad's truck is on the fritz and since Elliot is out of town on mission, I'm on mechanic duty until he gets back."

"I'm assuming Dylan is helping?" When he doesn't answer right away, I dramatically roll my eyes. "His name isn't a bad word, Riley. Since I happen to know he's the only one of you who can't stomach mayonnaise, I know he's helping you."

Riley shrugs. "Sorry, not sure where you stand."

"Nowhere," I reply. "We don't stand anywhere and that's just fine by me."

"Yeah, he's helping. If by helping you mean humming every time he thinks I'm doing something wrong."

Humming. Dylan has an excellent voice. One of the best out of all the brothers. There was a time when we thought he was going to go into music. Then he'd chosen the military and everything went sideways.

"Well, he does like to make you crazy."

"Yeah. We get blips where he's himself, and even as annoyed as I used to get, I'm just glad to see a bit of him shine through."

My heart aches. What I'd give to see that side of him again, too. "Good. I'm glad to hear it."

Because I genuinely can't discuss Dylan anymore without completely losing it, I go back to reading, or at least pretending to read, and a few seconds later, Riley opens his book, too.

Lani and I have been friends for forever, and books are something Riley and I bonded over a long time ago. But my real connection to the family lies with Dylan—the youngest of the brothers.

A man I've loved for as long as I can remember.

Pain blossoms in my heart, grief that just won't go away no matter how many years pass. No matter how many times he treats me like I mean nothing, I can't let go of what we *were*.

I suppose that's my burden to carry.

I pray constantly for God to take it away, to remove my feelings for Dylan, but so far that particular prayer hasn't been answered. Someday, maybe, but not today.

"Here you go." Talia slides the chicken salad in front of me, so I close my book and set it aside.

"Thank you."

"You're welcome. Shout if you need anything else."

"Will do." I bow my head. "Lord, I ask that you bless this food. Let it nourish my body. Thank You for the wonderous blessings you bestow upon me. I pray this in Jesus' name, Amen."

"Amen," Riley says beside me.

I pour the dressing over the top of my salad and mix it in, then take my first bite. It's the first time I've eaten today, since breakfast consisted of a protein shake after my run, then a mad dash out the front door so I wouldn't be late to the Saturday staff meeting at the school where I teach Kindergarten.

"Any big plans today?" Riley asks.

I finish chewing and swallowing my current bite. "Just preparations for the school's fall festival. Then I'm headed over to Charlene's place for a bit."

"How is she doing?"

"Not great," I reply sadly. Charlene Thomas lost her husband of nearly sixty years last month. She's been struggling with depression, on top of the Alzheimer's that's been slowly pulling her further and further away from us. Most of the time, she forgets to do basic tasks, so even though she has a full-time nurse, I still head over at least once a day to sit with her and help wherever I can.

"I'm so sorry to hear that. Is there anything I can do?"

"Actually, if you have time, her back porch has a couple of loose railings. She likes to take tea out there every afternoon, and I'm honestly worried that she's going to fall through one of these days."

"Consider it done." He smiles.

"Thanks so much." I open my notepad and check off the line that says *Get Charlene's Porch Fixed.* Because if one of the Hunts says they'll do something, it's as good as done.

"You had that on your to-do list?" he asks, amused.

"I did. It's been on there for the last couple of days. I've fallen a bit behind. It's actually happenstance I ran into you because I was going to call Bradyn this afternoon."

"You and those lists," he says with a laugh.

"Don't mock. They keep me organized."

"I bet you still add 'make a list' to your lists."

I glare at him, though a smile turns up the corners of my lips. "That happened *one* time. Dylan never let me live it down." His name used to roll so easily off my lips. Now, it's like a boulder falling on my toe. My happiness dies just a bit, so I turn my attention back to my salad.

"You okay?" Riley questions.

"Fine." I say it a bit sharper than I meant to, so I offer him a smile. "I'm completely okay," I add.

"Okay. Well, you know I'm here if you need me. We all are."

"Thanks, Riley." Even though Dylan is their brother, they all supported me during the months when Dylan was rehabilitating. After the initial hospital visit ended horribly, I waited the whole year for the day Dylan would call and want to see me again, but it's a call that never came.

"No problem." He offers me a smile, then returns to his book, so I finish eating in silence, all while my mind constantly replays the moments I had with Dylan before everything fell apart.

DELTA CHAPTER 3: DYLAN

The heavy bag swings, creaking the chain as I drive my fist into the side of it.

Again.

Again.

Every muscle in my body is warmed up, my skin slick with sweat, but I'm nowhere near tired despite being out here for nearing four hours. It's not unusual, though. Sleep eludes me more often than not.

I step back, then spin and kick, slamming my foot into the bag and sending it swinging wildly on its chain. The ache in my chest isn't unfamiliar; honestly, I'd be worried if I woke up one day and it was gone, but that doesn't mean it's easy to deal with. And ever since I saw Emma standing in the sunlight, her pretty dress flowing softly in the early fall breeze, it's felt like an anvil on my chest.

If only it would crush me already and get it over with. This slow, torturous pain is killing me.

"I thought I saw a light on." Tucker, my twin brother, steps through the open door of the gym. His dog, Tango, rushes to greet my dog, Delta, and the two of them almost immediately start wrestling.

"Wanted a quick workout in before bed."

"Didn't you work out earlier today, too?" Tucker questions, leaning back against the refrigerator holding all of our cold pre- and post-workout drinks.

"Yeah. So?"

"So, is everything okay?"

"It's fine." I slam my fist into the bag, wishing this conversation was already over. But, Tucker being Tucker, he only pries more.

"You haven't been coming around as often, so I just want to make sure you're good."

"You just got married a few months ago," I remind him. "So, no, I haven't been around a whole lot. Seems to me you'd want some time to be alone with your wife." I undo the cap of my water, not bothering to remove the wraps from my hands because I'm nowhere near tired enough for sleep yet.

"Fair enough, but you know we like having you around." He crosses his arms.

I hate that he still feels like he has to take care of me.

And I hate it even more that I really do miss my brothers. Even if I am happy for all of them and their newfound romances, love just isn't in the cards for me. Not now. Not ever. Which means this is the new normal. They'll be starting families and living their happily ever after while I grow old alone, waiting for the day I no longer have to live with cement caked around my ankles.

I set my water down and turn toward him. "Look, I did some work out at Charlene Thomas' place earlier, and now I'm trying to get one final workout in today since I have to be up early to paint over there and likely won't get one in tomorrow morning, okay?"

Tucker doesn't look at all like he believes me. "You saw Emma over there, didn't you?"

I drop my head into my hands and let out a frustrated breath. "She's an off-limits topic, and you know that."

"Do I?" Tucker crosses his arms. "Did she say something that upset you?"

"Emma?" I ask. "Of course not. She never says anything mean to anyone ever." She's pure light. Always has been. Which is why I can't be anywhere close to her. The darkness in me will devour her light.

And this world *needs* her light.

It already has enough darkness.

"Tomorrow is her birthday."

"I'm aware," I growl.

"Just making sure." Tucker uncrosses his arms and

pushes off the refrigerator. "Want me to hold the bag? Might be easier to beat it up if it's not going anywhere."

"No, thanks." I unwrap my hands. "It's late. I'll probably just call it a night."

"You sure?"

"Yeah." I hang my wraps up then grab my bottle of water on my way out the door. "*Hier,* Delta," I call my dog, using the German commands they were all trained with as puppies. Easier to control your dog when few others can interfere.

He hops up from where he was laying, and trots over toward me.

Tucker whistles for Tango, who also joins us as we step out into the evening air. It's nearly eleven in the evening, and the moon is high overhead, casting a silver glow over the ranch that has been my home for my entire life.

If only it still felt that way.

Truth is I haven't felt at home anywhere in a long, long time.

I doubt I ever will again.

"You sure you're good? I can come hang for a bit. Alice is wrapping up some work stuff."

"Nah, I'm good. Thanks, though."

Tucker offers me a nod before he turns away.

"Hey, Tuck?"

He turns back toward me. "Yeah?"

"I'm really happy for you and Alice. I hope you know that."

Tucker smiles. "I know, bro. Love you."

"You, too."

Delta and I climb into the utility vehicle I drove over here earlier, then wait until Tucker has pulled his truck out of the way so I can head home. As soon as he's out of the way, I make the five-minute drive over toward the acre of land my parents gave me to build my house on.

We each have an acre—including our youngest sister, Lani, though she's still living in an apartment in town and hasn't started building anything on her land just yet. Personally, I think she's waiting until she finds her happily ever after, too, though she will never admit as much.

My home comes into view—a simple, single-story, three-bedroom cabin that has been my home since I built it a couple of years after returning home from my last deployment. It's a good house. Sturdy. But that's all it is to me—a structure built to protect me from the elements.

I thought time would make it feel more like home, but the truth is, no matter how many days pass—it's still just a house. And I'm still a man barely alive.

Used to the routine, I don't have to call Delta as I climb out. He simply falls into a trot beside me while we climb the porch steps. I unlock the door, and he trots inside, so I follow, hanging the UTV keys up near the door and retrieving my truck keys and wallet from the counter.

With them in hand, I grab the glass vase I'd picked up earlier, add some water, then head out and lock up behind me. The wildflowers I planted in front of my house are the only part of this place that brings me any spark of joy.

Because they remind me of *her*.

Colorful, chaotic yet organized, beautiful—they're Emma.

It's a sweet kind of torture to see them and see her, but it's the closest I can get without dimming the light burning bright within her soul. So, I take what I can, though it's never enough to satisfy the starvation I've suffered since losing her.

Tucker knocks on the doorjamb but doesn't pause before coming into the hospital room. I can't bring myself to look at him. Even though we're not identical, my twin is a painful reminder of who I was before hell descended upon me.

"Hey, brother. Look who's here?"

I don't even have to look to know it's her. I can sense her like an animal can sense a storm headed their way. That's what she is to me: a storm sent to sweep me away and carry me into a past that no longer exists and a future that will never come to pass.

"Hey, Dylan." Emma's gorgeous face comes into view

as she steps in front of me. Her blonde hair has been swept out of her face and braided down over her shoulder. The light dusting of freckles on her face are apparent even in the dim hospital light.

I don't respond. What can I say? I'm not who she's looking for. Not anymore.

She steps up beside the bed and reaches down to touch my hand. The moment her skin touches mine, I jolt away. My breathing turns ragged, and I clench both hands into fists as I close my eyes tightly.

I'm not in danger.

I'm not in danger.

But no matter how many times I repeat the mantra over and over again, I'm still unable to put a leash around the panic clawing through me.

Fight. I need to fight. They'll kill me if I don't.

I'm not in danger.

They're going to take what little is left of me.

I'm not in danger.

"Brother, breathe."

"Get away from me!" I roar, shooting up off of the bed. Everything around me is gone, and all I see is red. My hand closes around skin, and I hold on.

A woman screams.

Hands grip my shoulders and shove me back down. But I will not be kept down. Not again. Never again.

"Stay down!" a man yells.

He'd like that. They all would. But I won't give up without a fight.

"Dylan, it's me!" That woman screams again. Her voice is familiar, but they'd want it to be, right? A trick to keep me from fighting.

"You're hurting her, Dylan!"

"Dylan, you're safe," that woman whispers to me.

The red begins to dissipate, and my surroundings return. I'm not in the pit—I'm in a hospital room.

I'm not alone—I'm with— Oh no. I release the hold I have on Emma's arm, giving Riley the ability to rip her away from me. Tucker's hands release me, and he steps back.

They're all staring at me like the monster that I am.

"Get her out of here!" I yell. "Now!"

"Dylan, it's—" Emma starts.

Hot tears sting my eyes. "Get out! I don't want to see you!"

Breathing is nearly impossible with the vise around my lungs, but I do what I can to draw in ragged breath after ragged breath while Riley ushers Emma out. Tucker remains where he is, but I barely see him as I curl onto my side, one hand gripping the hospital railing with such force my knuckles turn white.

I could have killed her.

I could have killed her.

I would have killed her.

Why couldn't they have killed me first?

DELTA CHAPTER 4: EMMA

"Happy birthday to you, our dearest Emmaline!" Mom leans into the camera lens and smiles. Her green eyes are so full of life, so bright and happy. Who would have known, less than two months later, they would be forever closed?

"We love you so much, baby!" Dad calls out from behind the camera. He turns it to face him and waves; then the video ends.

"Love you guys, thank you." Tears stream down my cheeks, but I let them fall, soaking in the grief from losing them as well as the happiness they gave me for the first eighteen years of my life.

Every year on my birthday, I watch that video right after waking. That way, I can spend my morning with them and get all my crying done before I head out into the world. Since church is this morning, I imagine I'll get a whole mountain full of happy birthdays, and I want to embrace them with a smile, rather than with the gnawing grief that sinks in when I remember that I won't get to eat my mom's chocolate cake with peanut butter frosting or enjoy the steak dinner Dad always made every year.

I stand and disconnect the USB connecting the camcorder to my television then place it gently in the cabinet where it will wait to be used again next year. Then, I head into the kitchen for the tea I left steeping.

As I make my way down the counter, my grey tabby, Ash, comes trotting out of my bedroom. "Oh, hey there, bud. Finally decide it was time to wake up?" I ask as I squat down to run my hand over his back. He arches beneath me, already purring. "I know what you want. Breakfast, right?"

At the mention of food, he shifts his bright blue gaze up to me for a moment, then heads for the laundry room where I keep his food.

Chuckling, I top his bowl off then return to my tea while he eats.

After adding some honey and a splash of milk, I carry my mug out onto the back porch. The sun is just beginning to climb over the horizon, sending rays of gold, purple, and orange out over the world.

My backyard is a beautiful array of color, thanks to the Knock-Out roses I planted at the beginning of the season. With a smile on my face and my feet bare, I step out onto the soft grass. The breeze toys with my hair, and I close my eyes, taking a deep breath.

"Thank You, O' Lord, for this day," I say aloud, then turn to head back in so I can get dressed for church. As I do, a vase overflowing with colorful wildflowers catches my eye.

It's sitting on the railing of my porch, closest to the gate that leads out to the front. Sunlight makes sparkles in the glass glitter wildly, but they blur completely as tears fill my eyes.

Every year.

He does this *every* year.

Yet, he can't say more than three words to me.

Anger hits me out of nowhere. Whether it's due to the lack of sleep I got last night or Charlene's confusion yesterday, I'm not sure. But I know that I need to let him go. That I need to stop waiting for some miracle to happen and just move on with my life.

So, I stomp over to the gorgeous flowers and carry them inside. Unlike years before, though, I don't display them on my kitchen island. Instead, I shove them into the same brown box I'd used to carry in the crockpot I ordered online then get beneath the counter and grab the other vases left for me over the years.

Ten of them.

By the time church service is over at noon, my anger has dissipated, and the box full of vases in my car makes me feel a bit ridiculous.

I'd had every intention of driving to the Hunt Family Ranch this morning but changed my mind the second I got behind the wheel. Why should I give him the satisfaction of knowing just how deeply he cuts me?

What's worse is I know that's not what he means to do.

The vases are Dylan's way of showing me that he still cares. Even if it can't be what I want, he's trying to be kind.

But I'm so far past his gestures of kindness. I want him to just leave me be.

Desperately.

"Happy birthday, honey!" Talia greets me as she wraps her arms around me in the aisle between pews.

"Thank you."

"Are you coming in for dinner tonight?"

"Have I missed a year?" I ask.

"Good." She and my mother ran in the same circle growing up, so after my parents died, she and her husband kind of took me under their wings. Since they couldn't have children of their own, and I was a bit of an orphan, it worked out.

We spend holidays together—birthdays—whenever the mood strikes.

She looks past me and waves. "Oh, I'll see you tonight, okay? I need to catch Ursula before she leaves."

"Sounds good. See you tonight."

I retrieve my purse from the pew then start out, right as Kennedy Hunt—Bradyn Hunt's wife—steps into my path and wraps her arms around me.

"Happy birthday, Emma!"

"Thanks," I reply with a smile as she releases me.

"Happy birthday, Ems," Bradyn says, a warm smile on his face. The eldest of the Hunt's, he was always a surrogate big brother to me. Truthfully, they all were.

Everyone but Dylan.

I never saw him as a brother. He was always—I trail off when he moves into my eyeline. It's distant as he's standing beside his parents while they talk to Pastor Ford, but he's there. And when he looks up at me, hazel gaze locking with mine, I momentarily forget that Kennedy has started talking to me.

We've always been this way—drawn to each other. Or, at least, I have.

"So, what do you think?"

"Huh? Sorry, I didn't sleep well last night."

Kennedy smiles knowingly. "I know you have plans with Talia and Connor tonight, but are you up for a girls' night tomorrow to celebrate? Nova is still out of town and won't be back until next month, but Jules, Alice, Lani, and I are ready and available. Sound good?"

"Yeah." I smile. "That actually sounds great."

"Perfect. Then it's a date." She hugs me again. "See you tomorrow!"

"See you."

Kennedy and Bradyn walk out hand in hand. I hate the jealousy that sneaks into my thoughts. Jealousy that I'm not wrapped around Dylan's arm right now. That he's only across the room but might as well be a million miles away.

I need to get out of here.

I'm headed to Charlene's next, so I wave to Ursula and Talia as I step out onto the front steps of the church. Manners dictate that I should go to Dylan and thank him for the flowers. However, the first couple of years I did that, he acted like he had no idea what I was talking about.

He'd completely brushed it off, despite me knowing without a doubt it's him leaving them. So, ever since that third year, I've just pretended that I didn't find the most beautiful assortment of flowers on my porch.

I won't ever forget that first year, though. How happy I was, thinking he was reaching out, only to find out that he had no intention of ever moving past the brokenness that formed between us ever since he got home.

I'm just reaching for the handle of my car when Ruth Hunt calls my name.

With a forced smile, I turn to face Dylan's mother. She's one of the sweetest humans I've ever met, and I absolutely adore her, but if she's there, then Dylan's not far. He always rides with his parents on Sunday mornings.

Ruth rushes forward and embraces me, her floral perfume familiar and welcoming as she wraps both arms around me. "Girl, you are aging backward."

I laugh, appreciating the compliment while also grateful that Dylan seems to not have followed her out here. Maybe he's inside with his dad. "I appreciate that, Mrs. Hunt, but it is so not true."

"It is absolutely true." She smiles at me. Growing up, I'd spent so much time with the Hunts that Ruth practically became a second mom to me. Between hanging out with Lani and my relationship with Dylan, the Hunt Ranch was my home away from home.

Ever since Dylan came home, though, it might as well be a foreign country.

"Well, thank you."

"You're welcome. Any big plans?" she asks.

"Dinner with Talia and Connor."

"That's so wonderful." She smiles then eyes the box of vases in the backseat of my car. *Oh no. Does she know?* "Those are lovely."

"Thanks. They were a gift."

"Well, I hope you have a great day, sweetheart. Please, don't be a stranger. I miss seeing you."

"You, too."

"Emmaline Franklin?"

I turn at the mention of my name, the voice unfamiliar, and see a handsome, dark-haired man lingering off to the right.

"I'll leave you to it, honey. Happy birthday." Ruth gives me one final hug then heads back toward the church. But the smile on her face as she surveys the man, then me, doesn't quite reach her eyes.

"Yes. That's me. Sorry. Do I know you?"

He smiles, and a dimple appears near the right side of his mouth. "No, you don't know me. Not yet, anyway." He outwardly cringes. "That was—wow—sorry, I just—I don't know how to do this."

"Do what?"

He laughs. "Can we go somewhere to talk?"

I open my mouth to tell him that I have somewhere else to be, but then I notice Dylan lingering near the porch steps, staring intently at me. Both hands are curled into fists at his sides, but he makes no move to close the distance between us.

Is that jealousy?

Good. Which, of course, I know isn't a kind way to think about it, but right now, I'm struggling with who I should strive to be, and the pettiness of knowing he'll suffer not knowing why I'm talking to this man.

"Sure. We can walk over toward the diner if that works? It's right there." I point toward the diner, and he turns to follow my gesture.

"That works. Thanks." He waits for me to start walking before following along, and I'm so struck by Dylan's gaze fixed on us that I don't even realize I haven't asked this man his name until we're crossing the street together.

"I'm sorry, I didn't ask you your name."

"And I'm sorry that I completely forgot to tell you." He reaches for the door and pulls it open. I move inside, and he follows.

"Hey, honey," Talia greets. Her gaze shifts curiously to the stranger. "Table for two?"

"Yes, please. Thanks."

"Of course. Sit anywhere you like."

The man leads us toward a booth near the back then slides into the side that places his back near a wall. It's a move I only recognize from the time I've been out with the Hunts. None of them want their backs to a door.

I sit across from him. "Your name?" I press again.

"Mattheus Karver," he replies with a smile.

"Karver, I don't recognize that name. Are you from around here?"

He chuckles. "No, regrettably, I grew up on the other side of the country."

"What can I get you two?" Talia asks as she sets two wrapped sets of silverware in front of us.

"Uh, just chai tea for me, please," I ask.

"Sweet tea," Mattheus says. "Thanks so much."

"You got it." Talia leaves the table.

"So, you know me but didn't grow up around here. Care to explain?"

He smiles and runs a hand through his dark hair. "It's actually a long story."

"I have time." *Not really, but I'm here.*

"Happy birthday, by the way. I was so shocked to see you standing there that I completely forgot to say it."

"Thanks. But, you were shocked to see me standing in the place where you came to find me? Since I haven't ever seen you at church before, and you're not from here, I'm assuming you were there because of me." I realize after I say it just how presumptuous it sounds, though, and my cheeks heat.

"I was. Um—I did not think this through." He reaches into his pocket and withdraws a folded-up photograph, then slides it across the table at me.

Lifting it, I stare down at the old photo of a blonde woman wearing blue scrubs and cradling a baby in her arms. "Who is this?"

"Your mother," he replies. "Birth mother, that is."

The blood drains from my face. "Excuse me?"

"Here you go." Talia sets a mug of tea down, alongside his sweet tea. "Aww, who is that?" she asks as she looks at the photograph.

"My birth mother," I whisper.

"What?" Talia's tone is shocked. "Seriously?"

Mattheus clears his throat. "Yes. Her name is—"

"Wait." I put my hand up. I decided a long time ago that I didn't want to know the name of the woman who decided

—before she ever really knew me—that she didn't want to keep me. As far as I'm concerned, Patricia and Emmit Franklin are my parents.

Mattheus reaches out and gently touches the hand that I have resting on the table. "I know you probably have a lot of questions, and I can answer all of them. Well, most of them." He smiles at me then glances up at Talia, who rests a hand on my shoulder and squeezes lightly.

"You know where I am if you need me."

"Thanks."

"Anytime, sweetie. You two holler if you need anything else."

As she walks away, I keep staring down at the photograph. The woman is looking down at the infant as though it's the single most important person in her life. So, if this really is my mother and me, then why didn't she keep me?

"You said you can answer my questions?"

He withdraws his hand. "Anything. And if I don't know, we can find out together."

Slowly, I set the photograph down and level my gaze on his. "Why didn't she keep me?"

"Oh, Emma," Mattheus says softly. "Your parents were told you died right after birth."

Horror mixes with my sadness, and I gape at him. "What?"

He nods, expression turning somber. "A nurse stole you

from the hospital. We're not sure what happened after that, but at some point, you were placed up for adoption."

"They stole me?"

He nods. "Your adoptive parents wouldn't even have known. When they couldn't find your family, they did the next best thing and put you into the best home they could find. All the while, your parents had no idea you were still alive. There was a funeral and everything." He reaches into his pocket and withdraws a cell phone then taps the screen a few times. "Here."

Mattheus offers me his cell phone, so I take it. A marble headstone gleams beneath bright sunlight.

GWENDOLYN VICTORIA KARVER.

Born October 2nd, 1989. Died October 2nd 1989.

Gone but never forgotten.

"Karver." I look up at him. "That's your last name."

He smiles and nods. "I'm your older brother. Older by two years." His dark eyes glisten beneath the lights overhead.

"Brother?" I somehow manage the single word despite the lump in my throat. "I have a brother?"

"Yes. I've been trying to find you for the last six months, ever since we learned that you were alive."

"How did you find out?"

"We were contacted by a woman who knew the nurse

that kidnapped you. She wouldn't give us a name but told us that you were alive and had been placed in a home nine months after you were kidnapped from the hospital. She said she couldn't live with herself anymore then hung up without giving us anything else. Mom and Dad are—they're beside themselves."

"Mom and Dad. They're both alive?" Is it possible that I still have family out there? That what Mattheus is saying is true, and I'm not really all alone?

"Yes." His gaze softens. "I read about what happened to your adoptive parents. And I'm so sorry for your loss. Were they good people?"

"The best," I reply then wipe tears from my eyes.

"You had a good life, then?"

"So good." I smile then pick the photograph up again after sliding his phone back over to him. "Why didn't they come?"

"They don't even know I'm here. Neither of them wanted to disturb your life. But I needed to meet you. I mean, a sister! I have a sister. That was a cool revelation at the age of thirty-seven."

"Tell me about it." I look back down at the photograph. She has the same color hair as I do. Are her eyes the same, too? Does she have freckles? "How long are you in town for?"

"Just until tomorrow night," he replies. "I need to get home, but I'm—" He trails off. "I'm hoping you'll come, too. Even if it's just to meet them. They would love to know you."

"I don't know." The truth is, I would love to go and meet them. But I'm scared.

What if they don't like me?

What if they don't want a relationship with me?

"Just think about it, okay?" He reaches into his pocket and puts some bills on the table.

"You're leaving?"

"I want to give you some time. But don't worry, sis, I'll see you soon, okay?"

I smile up at him. "Okay." I offer him the picture back, but he shakes his head.

"Keep it." He sets a piece of paper holding a phone number onto the table between us. "This is my cell. Call me when you've made up your mind, okay? No pressure, though. It was enough to just get to meet you." With one final smile, he turns and leaves.

The second the door closes and he's on the street, Talia slides into the booth. "Okay, girl, spill. Who was that?"

I stare down at the photo, then smile. "My brother. He's my older brother."

DELTA CHAPTER 5: DYLAN

Forty-five minutes.

That's how long I've stood in this church parking lot, waiting for Emma to leave the diner. Riley joked that it's because I'm jealous, but it's not. Not entirely, anyway. I'd noticed the man who approached her as he lingered in the back of the church during service.

He wasn't there for the Gospel, but rather the entire time, his gaze had been trained on Emma. At first, I brushed it off. She's gorgeous, so the fact that she captured his attention doesn't surprise me.

But when he'd beelined for her after service, something felt wrong.

Off.

So, here I wait. Watching. Making sure she leaves.

The stranger left a few minutes ago, and I snapped a

couple of cell phone pictures for Tucker to run through facial ID. I know the man doesn't live here, which makes him a potential threat—at least in my opinion.

Unknowns are unpredictable.

I like my life to be predictable.

She steps out onto the street like a ray of sunshine in her yellow and white striped church dress. After waving goodbye to Talia inside, Emma makes her way across the street, a smile on her face. But as she gets closer, I note the red-rimming her gorgeous eyes.

Eyes that are currently narrowed on me.

"What did he do to you?" I demand, already prepared to hunt him down and make him pay for causing her pain.

"Nothing." Emma crosses her arms. "What do you want, Dylan?"

What am I supposed to say? That I was worried and wanted to make sure she was safe? Or that the idea of her sharing a meal with someone else makes my skin crawl? "I didn't recognize him, and I wanted to make sure you were okay."

Emma's glare turned molten. It's something about her that always fascinated me. Emma is the happiest person I've ever met, but her temper—slow to come by—is a force to be reckoned with. "You don't care whether or not I'm okay, Dylan. So stop pretending otherwise." She tries to walk past me to her car, but I remain where I am.

"I do care."

"Why? Because you bring me anonymous flowers every year? You think that earns you the right to ask me about my life?"

How do I explain to her that I'm doing everything I can? That those flowers are the only way I can safely show her how much she means to me?

"I can't keep doing this anymore, Dylan."

"Doing what?"

"This." She gestures between us. "Whatever this is, I'm done with it."

"Nothing." The moment the word leaves my lips, I wish I could take them back. "We're just—"

"Just what?" she demands, tears filling her eyes. "Go ahead, I would *love* to hear what you have to say about it. What are we? What am I to you?"

I swallow hard. *You're the only piece of joy I have left in my life, and I'm so afraid to taint it that I can only watch from a distance.*

"Who is he?"

She gapes up at me, her broken-heart right there for the world to see. *I* did that. I'm more of a risk to her than anyone else, so why did I do this? Why did I linger around when I bring nothing but pain.

"He's none of your business."

"Emma."

"No." She glares up at me, standing closer than she's been since I got back ten years ago. So close that I can see each and every color variation in her gorgeous eyes. "You don't get to care anymore, Dylan. You threw that away when you decided I wasn't allowed to be a part of your new life." She shoves past me and unlocks her car then shoves her purse inside before whirling on me again. "You are going to leave me alone. Do you hear me? No more sneak flowers on my birthday, no more showing up when I'm working late. You don't want to be in my life? Then *don't* be in my life!" She's yelling furiously now, so loud that people who are walking by the church pause to look.

The edges of my vision begin to cloud. "You're making a scene." I need her to stop yelling. I need to regain control of myself. Of my racing heart.

She seizes up, her already furious gaze darkening like the sky before a storm. "Oh, I'm making a scene? Fine." Emma rips the backdoor of her car open and pulls out a box containing what are now wilted flowers—and all ten vases I've brought for her over the years. "Here's your scene." Furiously, she shoves them into my hands. "Take these back. And don't even think about pretending like they aren't yours." Angry tears stream furiously down her cheeks. "How dare you ruin this for me, Dylan Hunt. How *dare* you act like you care when we both know I'm nothing but a guilt project for you."

I toss the box to the side, not caring that the vases

break, as my own temper flares. "A guilt project? What is that supposed to mean?"

"You know exactly what it means. Poor little Emma had her heart broken. Poor little Emma still needs big, strong Dylan Hunt to look out for her." She rams her finger into my chest, and my heart hammers.

My breathing grows ragged, and tunnel vision takes over.

All while she's still yelling at me.

I can't breathe.

I can't see anything but anger.

Red.

Fury.

"Hey! What is going on here?" *Bradyn.* His voice grounds me, but it's not enough.

Emma is still yelling.

"I don't need or want you around me, Dylan. You got that? Keep your distance, and stay out of my life!" Her door slams.

"Dylan."

"I can't—I can't breathe." I try to suck in a breath, but it's strained as though I'm trying to breathe through the hollow part of a pen.

"Come on."

"Don't touch me. Please. I just need a minute." The voices are loud in my head—the yelling. The *anger.*

"I'm not going to," Bradyn says. "But we need to get you in my truck, okay?"

"Yeah."

Bradyn lifts the box, so I follow him over toward his truck. By the time he's set the box in the bed of his truck, my heart rate has slowed and my breathing has regulated. Something my older brother realizes as we both climb inside.

"What happened?" he asks.

"She poked me." I touch my chest where her finger hit. Even through my shirt, I can feel the puckered scar beneath. A scar that exists because I had a dagger driven into my chest so slowly I could feel it tear through each muscle fiber.

"What was the fight about?"

"Some guy was talking to her," he says. "I waited around to make sure she was okay. She's right, though. I lost the right to care a long time ago."

"You didn't lose the right to care," Bradyn corrects. "But you did lose your ability to be a part of her life when you closed the door on her."

None of my brothers pull punches. I don't, either. It's just not how we were raised. But right now, I wish that Braydn would let me have this one. At least, until my breathing regulates.

"What's with the box?"

"Gifts."

"From you?"

I nod. "I'd leave flowers on her porch every year for her birthday."

"Awww, so that was you. Riley owes me fifty bucks."

I glare at him as he puts his truck into Drive. "You bet on me?"

"Yeah. Riley overheard her, quite a few years ago, thanking you, and you denying it. So, we made a wager."

"On whether or not I was taking her flowers."

"Yeah. None of us could catch you in the act. So, kudos there, brother."

As we hit Main Street, we fall into silence. All I can see is her furious expression. Pink cheeks, wide eyes—she'd been hurt. Was that really all because of me?

I can't keep living in this messed-up nightmare of what my life used to be. But I don't know how to make it stop.

How do I get off this twisted rollercoaster?

"Why were you back in town?"

"Mom said you asked to linger behind. I figured you'd need a ride home, so I came into town looking for you."

"Yeah, I guess that was good foresight."

"I thought so. Call it brotherly intuition."

"It's good you got there when you did. There's no telling—" I trail off, not even wanting to think about what could have happened had he not shown up. Would I have completely lost myself to the past? Would I have fought back? Hurt her?

"You wouldn't have done anything to Emma, Dylan."

"In those moments, I'm not me anymore."

"You wouldn't have hurt her," he repeats. "When I got there, you were doing everything you could to put distance between the two of you. Which means you were rational enough—even in the panic—that you knew who she was."

"It was on the way out," I tell him.

He's quiet for a moment.

"I need to keep Delta with me. I got comfortable and left him at home." He can sense when I start to lose myself, and so far, he's one of the only things that grounds me in the present. Even my brothers struggle to bring me back from the brink.

More than once, I've attacked them in the middle of an episode.

Which is something Emma will never understand. It's not that I don't want to be a part of her life. Honestly, it's the exact opposite.

Emma is *everything* to me. Whatever tattered remnants of my heart remain will belong to her until they put me six feet under. Maybe even after that.

She's the air that I breathe.

The sun in my sky.

But that time in captivity changed me.

It made me a monster.

Someone unworthy of even breathing the same air she does.

No matter how badly it hurts, I know that she deserves a lot better than half a man.

Thank you for reading the sneak peek! Get your copy of Delta and continue the Hunt Brothers Series today!

A second chance at love sparks a fight for redemption.

Dylan "Delta" Hunt thought he left his past behind when he returned from war. Haunted by all he's seen, he's built walls around his heart, convinced that peace and love are beyond his reach.

Emma has never stopped loving Dylan, even after the man she knew came back a broken stranger. She's spent years trying to reach him but has failed every time. Now, an unexpected revelation about her estranged family pulls her into a dangerous mystery, and Dylan might be the only one who can help.

When Emma vanishes without a trace, Dylan is forced to confront the feelings he buried long ago. But the real question is, does he have enough light inside to bring them both home? Or will rescuing her cost him what little peace he clings to?

Dive into a gripping story of lost love, redemption, and courage in this Christian Romantic Suspense.

Get your copy of Delta today!

Scan the code below with your phone's camera to find all the places Delta is available!

ABOUT THE AUTHOR

Jessica Ashley started her career in 2016 writing romance novels for the secular world, before feeling the Lord pulling her in a different direction.

She is now a three-time award winning author of Christian romance, and has published nearly twenty novels and novellas since 2024.

She is an Army veteran, who resides in New Hampshire with her husband and their three children.

You can find out more about her and her books by joining her newsletter via her website: https://jessicaashley books.com/ or by joining her Facebook group, Romance, Redemption, & Rescue: Jessica Ashley Books.

Member of the ACFW.

Awards won:

- *First-place in the Romantic Suspense category of the Firebird Q1 2025 Book Awards. (Pages of Promise)*
- *Readers' Favorite Gold Medal Winner for excellence in writing. (Bravo)*
- *Literary Titan Gold Book Award Winner. (Echo)*

ALSO BY JESSICA ASHLEY

<u>Coastal Hope Series</u>

Pages of Promise: Lance Knight

Searching for Peace: Elijah Pierce

Second Chance Serenity: Michael Anderson

Tactical Revival: Jaxson Payne

Perilous Healing: Silas Williamson

<u>Coastal Hope Short Novels</u> (*Website Exclusives*)

Badge of Hope: Alaric Simmons

<u>Coastal Hope Novellas</u> (*Website Exclusives*)

Pictures of Hope (*Coastal Hope Prequel Novella*): Alex & Lilly

A Coastal Holiday Short: Caleb & Carmen

A Coastal Valentines: Lance & Eliza

A Coastal St. Patrick's Day: Elijah & Andie

A Coastal Easter: Michael & Reyna

A Coastal Thanksgiving: Jaxson & Margot

A Coastal Christmas: Silas & Bianca

The Hunt Brothers Search & Rescue

Bravo: Bradyn Hunt

Echo: Elliot Hunt

Romeo: Riley Hunt

Tango: Tucker Hunt

Delta: Dylan Hunt

Hunt Brothers Short Novels *(Website Exclusives)*

Lima: Lani Hunt

Hunt Brothers Holiday Novellas *(Website Exclusives)*

A Hunt Brothers Valentines: Bradyn & Kennedy

A Hunt Brothers St. Patrick's Day: Elliot & Nova

A Hunt Brothers Easter: Riley & Jules

A Hunt Brothers Thanksgiving: Tucker & Alice

A Hunt Brothers Christmas: Dylan & Emma

Iron Tide Brotherhood

SEAL of Honor: Zane Knox

SEAL of Bravery: Garrison Holt

<u>**Other Standalone Novels**</u>

Critical Velocity: Beckett Wallace